MONSTER GIRL DOCTOR

3

BY YOSHINO ORIGUCHI
ILLUSTRATED BY Z-ton

Arahnia Taranterra
Arachnida
Lately, I've even felt strange to myself.
Arahnia, you're definitely sick.

Saphentite
Neikes

Tisalia Scythia

To try and capture
Dr. Glenn's attention...?
Miss Arahnia, you still
haven't given up on
him, have you?

CONTENTS

MONSTER GIRL
DOCTOR

VOLUME
3

STORY BY
Yoshino Origuchi

Seven Seas Entertainment

MONSTER MUSUME NO OISHASAN VOLUME 3

© 2017 by Yoshino Origuchi
Illustrations by Z-ton
All rights reserved.

First published in Japan in 2017 by SHUEISHA Inc., Tokyo.
English translation rights arranged by SHUEISHA Inc.
through TOHAN CORPORATION, Tokyo.

Seven Seas books may be purchased in bulk for promotional,
educational, or business use. Please contact your local
bookseller or the Macmillan Corporate and Premium Sales
Department at 1-800-221-7945, extension 5442, or by
e-mail at MacmillanSpecialMarkets@macmillan.com.

Follow Seven Seas Entertainment online at
sevenseasentertainment.com.

TRANSLATION: David Musto
ADAPTATION: Ben Sloan
COVER DESIGN: Nicky Lim
INTERIOR LAYOUT & DESIGN: Clay Gardner
PROOFREADER: Jade Gardner, Stephanie Cohen
LIGHT NOVEL EDITOR: Nibedita Sen
PRODUCTION ASSISTANT: CK Russell
PRODUCTION MANAGER: Lissa Pattillo
EDITOR-IN-CHIEF: Adam Arnold
PUBLISHER: Jason DeAngelis

ISBN: 978-1-626928-67-1
Printed in Canada
First Printing: August 2018
10 9 8 7 6 5 4 3 2 1

PROLOGUE 1:
A Winter Scene

THE WINTERS IN LINDWORM were long. The region had always been cold, and the town of the dragon, nestled at the foot of the Vivre Mountains, saw snow piled high every year. As winter continued amidst this unending snow, the hustle and bustle of the city grew quiet.

The multitudes of monsters inside the city each spent the winter in their own ways. Those confident in their own strength—the giants and centaurs, for example—shoveled the city streets and with it earned their daily wage. Reptilian species like the lamia and lizardfolk hated the cold, and stopped going outside almost entirely. Similarly, many of the aquatic species spent their time underwater, where the change in temperature was less severe.

This year, the winter brought with it an infectious disease. Fortunately, it wasn't anything too severe—nothing more than a rather bad cold. The symptoms mainly included coughing, fatigue, and fever, but while it wasn't a life-threatening illness, it was spreading like wildfire throughout the city. Even the Litbeit Clinic had become swamped by combating the epidemic.

The clinic's doctor of monster medicine, Glenn Litbeit, was kept busy examining patients. The pharmacologist, Saphentite Neikes, made and prescribed medicine. The two spent all their time and energy on the clinic. They had hardly gone outside the whole season. But, perhaps partly because of their fervor, the winter came and went without anyone dying from the disease.

However, there was one small incident near the end of winter.

Saphentite got sick.

✖ ✖ ✖ ✖ ✖

"How are you feeling, Sapphee?" Glenn said through the door to Sapphee's bedroom.

Sapphee didn't answer him. She looked languid as she lay in her bed, her long lower body soaking in a large basin filled with hot water.

"I decided to make eggnog and brought some for you," Glenn continued. "Also, I boiled some water. I'll leave it all here, okay?"

"............"

There came no reply. Thinking it strange, Glenn entered.

"The clinic's perfectly fine right now, so get lots of rest, okay?"

"............"

Again, Sapphee didn't respond, but gave a slight nod of her head. Glenn wondered if she was too sluggish to even talk.

While they had been swamped with treating the cold epidemic, Sapphee had ended up catching it herself.

"Khoff! Khak!" Sapphee coughed repeatedly.

Anyone could come down with a cold, but a lamia's was naturally caused by different germs and had different symptoms and different treatment methods from a human cold. It was said that a lamia's symptoms often appeared in their respiratory organs, such as the lungs, throat, and nose.

Glenn put his finger in the basin where Sapphee's lower body was soaking and checked the water temperature.

"It's cooled down a little. I'm going to add more water, okay?"

Sapphee nodded her head again. Glenn didn't know why, but it seemed she was doing everything she could to avoid talking. He even wondered if he had done something to upset her—but there was nothing that came to mind. Ignoring it for the time being, Glenn poured the water from the kettle into the basin.

If Sapphee were human, an effective way to combat the cold would be to warm up and sleep. Pulling a blanket over her head, her body temperature would rise and she would sweat. Once she started sweating, she would just have to keep herself hydrated due to the loss of water in her body.

Lamia, however, were a cold-blooded race of monsters. Their bodies didn't give off any heat, so they couldn't maintain their body temperature with only bedding and blankets. For them, it was said the most effective method was a warm bath, the most suitable temperature being approximately eighty-six degrees Fahrenheit.

By submerging their lower bodies in moderately warm water, lamia could then use the heat from the water to warm up. If their body temperature became warm enough, then using blankets and a fireplace to retain heat became effective. If they could maintain a high body temperature, then their immune system would work better to help fight off the cold, but—

"Hey Sapphee, you aren't hiding anything are you?" Glenn asked the pharmacologist, who was persistent in maintaining her conspicuous silence.

"............" Sapphee only shook her head.

As the doctor caring for her, Glenn proceeded to examine Sapphee. He was sure her flushed face was due to the warm bath. On the other hand, her heavy breathing was caused by her stuffy nose, which forced her to rely entirely on her mouth for respiration. When this happened, the inside of the mouth inevitably dried out.

"Sapphee. Let me see inside your mouth for a second."

"N-nuh fwhay," Sapphee replied.

"Look! Your words got caught! Something's happened to your mouth, hasn't it?" Just when he thought she was finally going to speak to him, he noticed the pronunciation of her words was off.

Due to the cold, her immune system was weakened. The inside of her mouth was dried out. These conditions could end up causing several other conditions. For example, she could have a cavity or a mouth ulcer. Stomatitis in particular presented itself at times when a patient was feeling unwell or undernourished.

Glenn wondered if she had been neglecting her meals due to her large amount of pharmacology work.

"Come on, show me. Show me where it is," Glenn said.

"D-Doctwor Gwenn. You know, I can handle a little stomatitis on my own... I can make some very effective medicine for it," Sapphee replied.

Glenn found Sapphee's stomatitis-induced lisping as she called him "Doctwor Gwenn" rather novel. "What are you talking about—you're a *patient*. Forget it. Just let me treat you for once."

Sapphee seemed to have finally resigned herself to Glenn's insistence and opened her mouth. Glenn placed his hands on Sapphee's cheeks and examined the inside. He tilted her head slightly and turned her toward the light from the window so he could see clearly.

"Fhey, Doctwor. Hlease make dis fwick," Sapphee struggled to say.

"Yeah. I know," Glenn said, nodding to Sapphee and continuing his examination. He assumed it must be embarrassing for her to have his face so close to hers.

"Aaaaaaah..." Sapphee groaned.

Glenn couldn't see anything abnormal. She had a very clean and pretty mouth, without a cavity to be found.

There are some subspecies of lamia that have poison glands inside their teeth, but Sapphee wasn't one of them. He would have probably been more careful if she did have some poison in her body, but Glenn didn't hold back when it came to Sapphee.

And because of this lack of hesitation, Glenn stuck his finger inside of Sapphee's mouth.

"Hnguuugh...?!"

"Oh, sorry," Glenn replied.

"Fwngh, nghfwub!"

Glenn had no idea what Sapphee was saying, but it was clear that she was angry with him.

Unconcerned that his finger was covered in Sapphee's saliva, he felt the inside of her cheeks, then pulled them out from the inside and examined her gums as well.

"Nnnghh..." Sapphee moaned.

"Hmm... Looks like there isn't anything wrong with your gums."

Due to the foreign object that was inserted into her mouth, Sapphee's saliva started to build up. It was a good sign, Glenn thought. He hoped it would keep her mouth from drying out as much as possible.

The inflammation wasn't on her gums or on the inner part of her cheeks. In that case, Glenn thought—

"So your tongue."

"Ahh...Fhaht." Sapphee's glare assured him that he was right. He regretted not asking her from the start.

"All right, then, I'm going to look at your tongue, okay?"

"Aaaaaah..." Sapphee gave a lapping sound, and keeping her mouth open, stuck out her tongue.

The tongue of a lamia was around two times the size of a human's, elastic and flexible. It had nerve cells for sensing smell in addition to taste. Glenn grabbed the tip of Sapphee's and examined it.

"Angghh..."

Looking at the length of her tongue, one might doubt whether Sapphee could fit it all inside her mouth. The secret was that there was muscle inside her throat. A lamia's throat was supported with cartilage, and was constructed to fork left and right. It was more flexible and could extend more than one would expect.

Because of this, even if they swallowed a chicken's egg whole, they wouldn't choke. Normally, their long tongue was stored in the partitioned space within their throat, and only extended when necessary. By putting their tongue out and back in again, lamia were able to sense the taste and smell of everything around them.

"Yup—here it is," Glenn said. Under the middle area of her tongue, there was a portion that had turned white. He was right. It was stomatitis.

The mouths and tongues of the lamia had evolved in a unique way that could sometimes be a weakness. For example, if there was any mouth inflammation caused by a bacterial infection— even nothing more than a small infection—there was risk that the inflammation could suddenly spread further while the tongue was stored inside their throat.

In the worst cases, the inflammation didn't stay on the tongue, and extended to the throat or even the lungs, leading potentially to pneumonia. Due to the throat's structural complexity, it was easy for bacteria to lay dormant inside, and if the inflammation worsened, the body couldn't quite heal it all on its own. This was particularly pronounced during times of cold weather, when the body's immune system was weaker.

It was no more than some inflammation, but Glenn thought that for a lamia, it was best to treat it sooner rather than later.

"And we have...no medicine, it looks like," Glenn said.

"Fwan fwaht I hahn fwaen...!"

Glenn was sure that Sapphee could make the medicine, but he couldn't have his patient make it for him. Sapphee mumbled something while her mouth was open, but Glenn couldn't really understand it.

"Nothing else I can do. I'll have to use a temporary treatment," Glenn said, glancing at the items he had brought in: the ingredients necessary to make eggnog. When it came to colds, eggnog was an absolute must.

It was made by putting egg yolk in brandy, and adding in milk and sugar. Mixing in a small amount of honey and spices could also help make it easier to drink. Glenn had gotten his hands on farm-fresh eggs, so he could make quite a high-quality version of the drink.

Eggnog was fundamentally effective for warm-blooded races. Since cold-blooded species weren't able to generate heat on their own, food and drink that warmed the body didn't have any effect on them. However, considering that proper nutrition helped to speed up recovery, drinking eggnog was an effective remedy even for lamia.

Glenn borrowed a cotton swab from Sapphee's room and lathered it with honey.

"The honey will help the inflammation."

"Fwan hwaff ahfhy...Hanh." Sapphee mumbled, jumping a little.

Once the cotton swab sucked up a good amount of honey, Glenn dabbed it on the inflamed area of Sapphee's tongue.

"Hnh! Aaaaahooonnh...!" Sapphee groaned.

"Sorry, just bear with it a little while," Glenn replied. Sapphee's body trembled, as if in pain. Glenn thought it obvious that touching the inflamed area directly would be painful for her.

"Aaahh uhhh...!"

It was impossible to tell what Sapphee was saying, but her face was grimacing in pain.

The inflamed area of her tongue was rather large. Glenn thought it natural that she would be feeling a considerable amount of pain, but he wondered why she hadn't told him about her tongue. Sapphee surely knew for herself how much worse it could get if she left the inflammation alone.

"Ah... Dwefifos..." Sapphee groaned.

"I know, I'm almost done," Glenn replied.

Honey possessed a sterilizing effect. In ancient times, they would wrap honey-lathered bandages around wounds, and it would protect the wound from festering. It wasn't a treatment used much now, but Glenn felt it was sufficient to work as a temporary measure.

"Hoofhwaafuu..."

Glenn's finger was covered in honey and saliva, but he continued to apply the honey to the inflamed area, unfazed. Once he decided that enough had been applied, he ended his treatment.

"Nh... Ph-phew."

"Thanks for bearing with me, Sapphee," Glenn said.

"...Thank you," Sapphee replied with a glaring look that suggested there was more that she wanted to say. "All the same Doctwor, my mouth is all sore now. I'm glad you were thorough, but still..."

"S-sorry. I took too long, huh?"

"I knew this would happen, and that's why I didn't say anything about the sore," Sapphee said as she wiped away the drool dripping from the side of her mouth. "And one more thing."

"Y-yes?" Glenn replied.

"Having your face so close to mine was...embarrassing." Saying this turned Sapphee's face a far deeper shade of flushed pink than Glenn's. Pulling the blanket over her head, she hid under the covers. Glenn thought she shouldn't have said anything if it was just going to make her feel so self-conscious.

His face was also flushed.

Glenn's response and treatment had been the correct course of action, considering the possibility that the inflammation could progress. However, he thought she might have been correct that he didn't show enough care and consideration for Sapphee while treating her. In fact, Glenn thought that his treatment might have ended up becoming a little aggressive and overbearing, due to their almost familial relationship.

"Um... Well, Sapphee, do you want some eggnog?"

It was a blatant attempt at getting back in her good graces, but eggs and alcohol were two of Sapphee's favorite things. While Glenn had prepared the eggnog because it was effective at treating colds, he had also done it because he knew it would make

Sapphee happy while she lay sick in bed.

"...Did you make it yourself, Doctwor?" Sapphee asked.

"Huh? Yes, of course," Glenn replied.

"You're totally clueless about cooking, Doctwor, yet you're so good at making things when it involves treatment of some kind, aren't you?"

She was right, Glenn thought. He left all of the meals in the clinic entirely up to Sapphee. He would have liked to help, but unfortunately he had no understanding of how to cook. Moreover, Sapphee rather seemed to enjoy herself when she was cooking, which made it harder for Glenn to try and get involved.

"Thank you," Sapphee said, taking the glass from Glenn.

A scattering of spices floated on top of the pale yellow eggnog. The drink was also enjoyed as a normal cocktail, so Glenn had tried serving it to her in a glass that was a bit fancier.

Glug, glug, glug.

It was over in an instant. Without a moment's hesitation, Sapphee gulped down the eggnog in one breath. Glenn wondered if it was because she had been thirsty, or some other reason entirely.

"Phew..." Sapphee let out a sigh. "I made sure to finish it all, Doctwor."

"R-right." Glenn replied. It appeared the combination of her two favorite things had been tasty after all, as Sapphee gave a satisfied lick of her lips. It had plenty of nutrition, so Glenn was sure it would immediately start to work toward healing her cold and her inflamed tongue.

"...Dr. Glenn, did you know?" Sapphee asked.

"Know what?" Glenn replied.

"It appears that long tongues are favored by members of the opposite sex... My tongue is long, even compared to other members of my species," Sapphee said, poking her tongue out once again.

Glenn couldn't argue that her tongue was overflowing with sexual charm. He was often enthralled by the way Sapphee's tongue moved when she was licking something—although most of the time, when a lamia was sticking out their tongue, it was to simply smell food.

If that was the case, Glenn thought, then the food she was sniffing for right now must be—

"I-I could also be good at kithing, too, you know?" Sapphee said.

"You've got a cold—don't say things like that! You couldn't even say it properly!" Glenn retorted.

"Hnnnnn, yeah buuuuut!" Sapphee said, diving under the blankets and twisting her body around. She had just said how embarrassing having Glenn's face so close to hers had been, yet here she was, talking about kissing.

"What's gotten into you all of sudden?" Glenn wondered.

"Hmm... Well... I'm a little tipsy, Doctwor," Sapphee said, casting a flirtatious glance toward Glenn.

The amount of alcohol in eggnog was definitely not enough to make her drunk. Glenn figured it was just too embarrassing for her to say without using the alcohol as an excuse. He had to admit it was very much like her to act this way, considering how bad Sapphee was at expressing her feelings.

"Honestly..." Glenn said.

Patients grew listless when stricken with a cold. They became lonely, and anxious to get better. Saphee's mixture of sullenness and a desire to be looked after was characteristic of those who had become sick. Glenn guessed that her using an excuse to cozy up to him was also because of how wretched she felt.

There was only one thing he could do.

"There's still some time left for lunch today, so I'll stay with you a little while longer, okay?" He said.

"R-really?" Sapphee replied.

"Yup. But there won't be any kisses."

"Nggghhhh, pleeeease just forget about that!" Sapphee cried in an agony of embarrassment. She didn't often allow herself to rely on others, so she wouldn't immediately turn to Glenn for help in moments like this. However, this made her all the more pitiful to Glenn, and he couldn't just leave her alone.

As he added hot water to the basin, Glenn wondered if, perhaps, he wasn't already caught in the trap of a lamia in love.

I truly am no match for Sapphee, he thought in speechless admiration.

PROLOGUE 2:
The Waterways Commemoration Ceremony

AT LONG LAST, around the time Sapphee recovered from her cold, spring came to Lindworm.

Spring was the festival season. In the Waterways, the merfolk held multi-day carnivals, and at the arena, there were the annual promotion trials. Both monster and human alike grew restless for the season of revelry on the horizon.

With the arrival of spring, Sapphee increasingly cast suggestive looks toward Glenn. Even he could guess that she wanted to go sightseeing around the Waterways. He imagined that her aim was to buy some seasonal merchandise only available at that time.

But just when Glenn had decided to make time and go with her, a single letter fell out of the sky, almost as if it had chosen that exact moment to arrive.

✖ ✖ ✖ ✖ ✖

"Hellooo!"

The window of the clinic was thrown forcibly open with a bang. The sudden intruder barged into the clinic, oblivious to the patients waiting to be examined. Both Glenn and Sapphee looked at the scene with exasperation.

"Illy. How many times do we have to tell you to come in through the door?" Sapphee said, her eyebrows twitching in anger.

"It's an express delivery to the clinic! Look, see, it's from the Central City Council!" Illy replied.

"Listen to people when they're talking!" Sapphee ordered.

The young girl's habit of entering through the clinic's windows was already established. A harpy with brilliantly colored wings, her name was Illy. She had a deep connection to Glenn, who had saved her from a blocked oviduct and diagnosed the molting of her feathers during her growing phase.

"So how is it, Illy?" Glenn asked. "Your job with Scythia Transportation, I mean."

"It's fun! I can fly as much as I want! Miss T. is always complimenting me, and I stand out, too!" Illy replied.

"That's good," Glenn said.

Illy lived in the harpy village, but she'd officially become an employee of the Scythia Company in early spring. Now she worked as an airborne mail deliverer. She had learned the names and faces of the people of Lindworm, and it didn't take her very long to get used to the city. For someone who liked flying more than anything else, one could say she had found her calling in life. Nevertheless, Glenn thought, he definitely wanted her to fix her bad habit of nonchalantly barging into the clinic through the window.

"Okay, here! You have a delivery!" Illy proclaimed.

"Hm. From the council... So from Miss Skadi?" Glenn asked.

"Yes, yes. She *was* the one who gave to me! All right, I've still got a lot of deliveries left!" Illy declared, and promptly flew out the window, just as quickly as she had come.

"She's sure in a hurry, isn't she...?" Glenn mused.

"Well, still, that's just perfect for a girl like her," Sapphee replied.

At Sapphee's words, Glenn gave a strained smile. He thought that it was precisely because of how energetic Illy was that she could enjoy being so busy. It was clear from her animated expression that she was living a fulfilling life as an employee of the Scythia Company.

Glenn immediately checked the letter that Illy had delivered. The wax seal was stamped with a dragon crest, and Glenn could tell that it was a handwritten letter directly from the city council representative herself, Skadi Dragenfelt. He was sure the contents of the letter must be of quite some importance.

"An invitation to the Merrow Waterways Commemoration Ceremony...?" Glenn read. "I see. The reconstruction is over. It's an inauguration ceremony."

The Merrow Waterways had a complex structure. It was a comfortable town for merfolk and many other aquatic monsters to live in, but because the canals had been created by remodeling the existing townscape, there were still unused ruins poking out of the water. These unused ruins had even been used as a hideout by slave traders. Glenn's first meeting with Illy, when she was suffering from her impacted oviduct, had in fact been in such a hideout.

Glenn had heard that the remodeling project had been moving forward during the winter, under the direction of Skadi's personal attendant Kunai Zenow. That those very slave traders were all trained by Kunai and taking part in the remodeling was truly a strange twist of fate in Glenn's eyes.

At any rate, Glenn thought, it appeared the reconstruction had finished without incident. No longer would the Waterways be home to strange gangs of people. He was sure Lulala must have felt safer too, since she called the Waterways her home.

"It says here there is a festival to commemorate the remodeling of the Waterways. It looks like there's going to be a lot of flashy events, parades, choruses, you name it. Oh, it says here that Lulala is going to appear as a songstress, too," Glenn read from the letter.

"Oh, I definitely want to make sure to see that. Perhaps, on the invitation..." Sapphee trailed off.

"Of course you're invited too, Sapphee." Glenn replied. Sapphee's name was clearly written on the invitation as well. Skadi could be quite tactful.

A document containing the details of the ceremony was included in the envelope, and it seemed to Glenn that it was going to be a grand event. Naturally, since they were reopening the Merrow Waterways, he was sure there would be a considerable number of street stalls and booths at the event as well.

More than anything else, Glenn wanted to hear the songs of his merfolk friend Lulala. As the doctor looking after her continued recovery, he was also curious about how her throat was doing.

"We have quite a lot to look forward to, don't we, Doctor?" Sapphee said.

"Sapphee, have you gotten over your cold?" Glenn asked.

"How mean, Doctor. Just how long ago are you talking about? I'm quite fine now," Sapphee said, looking in high spirits as she waved the white tail on her lower body back and forth. She loved the items that were sold in the stalls of the Waterways, so Glenn imagined she was quite happy.

"Together. We'll go around to all the shops together," Sapphee said. Now that Glenn thought about it, it had been a while since they'd both made their way out to the Waterways. During the winter months, they were so swamped with work that they hadn't even been able to get out of the clinic to go shopping.

"I know, I know. But right now, we have work to do," Glenn replied.

"But of course. Thank you for your patience. Next patient, please." Sapphee called out. They had been unabashedly prattling on in the waiting room, but the regular patients there didn't seem upset by it at all. If anything, they appeared to find the sight of the doctor and pharmacologist conversing back and forth to be both pleasant and heartwarming.

The friendly atmosphere was precisely because this was such a small city clinic. No such atmosphere existed at the Central

Lindworm Hospital—a huge facility situated on the main avenue of the city, that worked day and night to fight against disease.

Spring had finally arrived. Having fought the epidemic until the flow of patients dwindled, Glenn surmised that it might be the perfect time for the Litbeit Clinic to relax a little bit.

Etching the date in the letter for the following week into his mind, Glenn once again returned to work.

× × ✖ ✖ ×

On the day of the ceremony, there wasn't a single cloud in the sky. Glenn and Sapphee entered the Waterways on foot. Previously, it had been extremely inconvenient to traverse the canals by land, but now there were new bridges and pathways built above them. Glenn was sure it was more accessible by boat as well.

"Now you can even get this far on foot, huh. They really added a lot of bridges, didn't they...?" said Glenn.

"They were put in place for tourist use. With this, it'll be easy to come and do some shopping," replied Sapphee.

The two of them talked as they looked out at the Waterways, marveling at how it had been developed even further into a tourist destination. There were stalls and street stands on either side of the bridges. The traders didn't necessarily appear to be residents of the Waterways, and whether human or monster, the most enterprising individuals had already set up shop. There were also now food stalls, something quite hard to operate out of a boat.

"It's wonderful, isn't it, Dr. Glenn? I wonder if we'll be able to see all the shops..." Sapphee mused.

"Y-you're not actually going to try and look at them all, are you?" Glenn stammered.

"Well, all of them might be a bit... Oh, but I would like to go to that stall there. And that stand over there, too." Sapphee replied. The two of them had a time limit today. Sapphee immediately began to devise which shops she should visit.

Glenn had enjoyed slowly drifting through the Waterways by gondola, but he couldn't deny the convenience of being able to walk around on his own two feet. Taking a peak under the bridge, he saw gondolas stream unceasingly up and down the canal. Glenn doubted there would be fewer tourists using a boat to make use of the canals. He was sure that going forward, the gondolas would still be essential for tourism.

"First up is the main bridge," Glenn said to Sapphee, who seemed on the verge of being hypnotically drawn toward a stall.

"I-I know," she replied.

The two of them were headed toward the heart of the Merrow Waterways. The biggest and most naturally wide canal of the Waterways had a bridge newly constructed across it, known simply as the main bridge. Glenn had heard there was a parade that occurred every day at the base of the bridge. There were special seats for those who wanted to watch the parade from up close, but naturally, there was always a throng of people who crowded around to try and grab a seat.

Today, however, there was no such crowd. In fact, there wasn't a single normal tourist to be found. It was lavishly decorated with a banner for the inauguration event and flags bearing the symbol of the city council, but the only people standing on the bridge were members of the city council's personal security force.

Glenn continued forward without hesitation. The security guards didn't try to stop him, suggesting that they were aware of his invitation. He spied the form of the person he was looking for on one of the side paths of the Waterways. At the foot of the bridge, there was a staircase that brought one up to the main canal. When Glenn and Sapphee carefully descended the stairs, the woman he was looking for was standing along the water's edge.

"Good day, Miss Skadi, Miss Kunai," Glenn said, greeting the pair.

"Dr. Glenn, you came?" Kunai replied.

"Thank you very much for your generous invitation," Glenn said. Both he and Sapphee bowed their heads in thanks. Their inviter, Skadi Dragenfelt, remained silent and gave a gentle nod. As usual, her face was covered by her veil and there was a mysterious aura surrounding her. While she was both the city council representative and the most influential and powerful figure in the city, her appearance was that of a child. Her voice was also quite soft, and without her attendant Kunai to speak for her, Glenn had no idea what she was saying.

It appeared Skadi had just arrived at the ceremony herself and would soon give an address from atop the main bridge. This explained why the area around the main bridge was only populated by people from the city council, in contrast to the hustle and bustle throughout the Waterways.

Having been personally invited, Glenn imagined they would have a good seat to listen to her address—the question on his mind was simply how much of her words he'd actually be able to hear.

Either way, he thought, he was sure that Kunai would raise her voice and give the address in her stead. Being her loyal retainer, Glenn was sure not a single word of her master's got past her. As a flesh golem, Kunai's ears and eardrums were both stitched together from dead flesh, but where Skadi was concerned, Glenn thought her ears might actually be more powerful than those of the living.

"The Lady Draconess was worried that you would be too busy to come. Is the clinic all right with you here?" Kunai asked.

"Yes, well, we're only closed for the morning." Glenn replied.

"I see. It's a well-earned break, so make sure to take your time and enjoy the ceremony," Kunai said. She had an armband on her right shoulder that indicated she was part of the security team. As was expected of Skadi's attendant, she was also helping to keep the ceremony safe and secure. Glenn didn't have a problem with that, but her armband appeared to be fixed to her upper arm with its pin driven directly into her flesh. Kunai had a tendency to treat her own body roughly, thinking it didn't matter since she was a corpse. Glenn was considering whether to give her a word of warning about it when—

"Oh! Dr. Glenn! You came!"

"Now now, don't move. Stay still."

"Okaaay."

Glenn heard a familiar pair of voices. On the canal, he could see many gondolas and merfolk in the water. Seeing how extravagantly the gondolas were decorated, he assumed they were preparing for the parade. Everyone was moving about in a rush both above and below the water's surface. Glenn was startled when he spied two faces he recognized.

One was Lulala Heine, who had the lower half of her body submerged in the water. She was a mermaid songstress who lived in the Waterways. Glenn assumed she was singing in the parade. She had an elegant dress wrapped around her that reminded Glenn of many flashy species of tropical fish. The dress floated in the water and spread out like a flared skirt.

And there was one other face he recognized.

"Arahnia..." Glenn sighed. It was the arachne dress designer, Arahnia Taranterra Arachnida.

There was no denying that Lulala was a patient of his—he had given her medical treatment and periodically checked in on her to see how she was doing. Arahnia, however, was different. She had feigned illness to trick Glenn and had tried to rape him, all as part of her own agenda.

Yet, as if Arahnia herself had forgotten all about that, she was fixing Lulala's clothes and humming to herself as she swapped out decorations and ornaments on the outfit. Arahnia was dangling upside down from the pier of the bridge by her silk, but she seemed to be consumed by her work. She looked just like a real spider as she hung inches above the water and faced Lulala.

"Why is she here...?" Even her close friend, Sapphee, was surprised to see Arahnia in attendance.

"Madame Arahnia is in charge of designing the costumes for all the merfolk singing at the ceremony today," Kunai replied. "Not just the designs, but everything from taking measurements and sewing to finishing each outfit was all done by her hand. Right now, she's in the middle of her final checks. It's a huge task for sure, but her work ethic is top-notch."

"Oh my, Arahnia is?" Sapphee replied.

"Yeah. Anyway, with how carefully she finished everything, even the merfolk have been complimenting her work. Loose Silk Sewing has quite a skilled young employee on their hands."

"Is that so? To think she'd be praised so highly..." Sapphee said.

Glenn thought that for how big Lindworm appeared, it was actually quite small. His circle of acquaintances interacted in ways that even he wasn't aware of. Given Lulala's and Arahnia's personalities, it didn't seem like they would have any opportunity to meet each other, but when he considered their roles as a songstress and a costume designer, he realized that there did seem to be a connection between the two.

He just hoped that Arahnia wouldn't have any untoward effect on the pure-hearted and innocent Lulala.

"The Lady Draconess is beyond pleased that such a large number of people, arachne and merfolk included, have cooperated to make today what it is. From this spring onward, the Waterways will become even more lively than ever before," said Kunai.

"Yes, yes. There'll be much more shopping to do, won't there?!"

Sapphee said, her love of shopping shining through her smile. It wasn't too much of a stretch to imagine she already had a plan of what shops she wanted to visit.

"............"

"Yes?" Glenn replied. Skadi Dragenfelt had spoken. Glenn would describe her voice as being even quieter than the sound of a mosquito flying through the air. It was truly a rare occurrence for him to catch what she was saying.

"*I'm glad you were able to come. Please enjoy yourselves*—is what my mistress said," the undead bodyguard relayed to Glenn, speaking on Skadi's behalf.

"I-Is that so?" Glenn stammered.

"I've said it many times already, but the Lady Draconess is truly delighted that so many people have come together for the ceremony today. Lindworm has really become splendid. It's proof that humans and monsters are living together in good health... Of course, she is also very satisfied with your efforts, Dr. Glenn, to keep the residents of the city healthy."

"I see," said Glenn. He had never seen Skadi's actual face. He was sure her opinions were just as Kunai described, but without being able to see her face, he couldn't actually feel like she was delighted, even when told so.

Moreover, what had Glenn curious was Skadi's tail. Poking out from the bottom of her robe, it was a thick and sturdy dragon's tail. Covered in scales that sparkled with the color of yellow sand, it drooped like it was being pulled along the Waterway's stone pavement. When Glenn had seen it before, it had been standing up at the base, and he was sure the tip had been swaying back and forth.

"Well, the time's come. We'll be starting soon. Seats have been prepared, so just show your invitation to the security guards. All right, then, Lady Draconess, let us be off," said Kunai.

"............" Skadi gave a nod of her head. Climbing up the stairs, she headed toward the main bridge. Glenn assumed she would give some sort of address for the opening ceremony. From the start, Skadi's power and influence had played many different roles in making the Waterways into what they now were. Just as Kunai had said, Skadi was surely happy to see the Waterways grow even livelier.

That was precisely why Glenn was curious about her tail dangling weakly on the ground.

"Well, then, let's get to our seats, too. It looks like they're offering drinks over there as well..." said Sapphee.

"Yeah..." Glenn replied.

"Doctor? ...Doctor!"

"Huh? Oh... What?"

"Why are you standing there and spacing out for?" Sapphee said, pouting. "I've been trying to get your attention."

"...You figured it out?"

"Of course," Sapphee replied, as though the answer were obvious. Glenn didn't think it was showing on his face that clearly. It was plain to see he couldn't fool a childhood friend that had been with him for as long as she had. "Now, I wonder what in the world you could possibly be so concerned with. Arahnia?

Miss Lulala? Miss Kunai, or Miss Skadi? Hmm which woman could it be, Doctor?"

"I-If you're going to force it out of me, it's Miss Skadi—but hold on a second, Sapphee, you're really close," Glenn replied.

"Even though you're here with me, and even though we're going shopping together after this, you're staring off into space thinking about another woman! Hmph!"

"That's not it."

"Hmph."

Glenn expected her to coil herself around him at this rate and lightly pushed Sapphee away from his face.

"There's just something that's got me curious... But you know, I'm sure it's just my imagination running wild..." said Glenn.

"Ooh?" Sapphee replied with a blank look on her face, as though she had no idea what Glenn was talking about.

Glenn wasn't knowledgeable enough about dragons to make a diagnosis of Skadi just from her tail looking unwell. As a doctor, he was supposed to be well versed in every type of monster, but dragons were different. He thought it would be good if he could get her permission to examine her just a little bit, but that was something that could be saved for another day. He wondered if a being as powerful as a dragon even felt sick or unwell to begin with. He was sure that nothing would happen to Skadi just from giving a small speech, anyway. He asked himself why he was even so worried.

"I understand that because of your job, even the slightest things can concern you, but...make sure to keep me in your thoughts, too," said Sapphee.

"...Okay."

Being spoken to by Sapphee like this made Glenn want to scold himself for getting lost in his own thoughts. He couldn't hold back a strained smile as he looked at Sapphee's embarrassed, innocent expression. Worrying about the smallest of things was a bad habit of his.

Glenn decided that since they were at a celebratory festival, he should try and enjoy it with Sapphee as much as he could.

✗ ✗ ✖ ✗ ✗

The ceremony had begun. Glenn was right—Skadi stood on a stage built on the main bridge and was going to give an address. She looked dignified as she climbed up on the platform precariously built into the bridge's handrail. Everyone was eager to hear what she had to say.

"Since it started last year, the great Waterways reconstruction project has had the support of each and every citizen of Lindworm, and has been able to end safely by this inauguration date. Along with my gratitude to the many individuals involved in this project, I, Skade Dragenfelt, offer a small fire dragon blessing to the newly-reborn Merrow Waterways..."

While Skadi was the person standing on the stage, Kunai was the one relaying her message. Glenn knew that, given the volume of Skadi's voice, her words wouldn't reach the ears of everyone gathered here. This wasn't the first time Kunai had spoken for Skadi, but there were political opponents of Skadi who felt it very suspicious that the city council's representative didn't speak with her own words.

Glenn had also become curious—why was Skadi's voice so quiet?

"They've invited a lot of people besides us, haven't they?" Sapphee whispered in Glenn's ear. They were sitting in seats that had been specially arranged for those with personal invitations. The area they were seated in resembled a sidewalk café and had a good view of the main bridge where Skadi stood. A large number of the other guests surrounded them.

"Really?" Glenn asked.

"Yes. That over there is the representative of the Scythia Company... Miss Tisalia's father. There's also Aluloona from Aluloona Plantation. Even the boss of the Kuklo Workshop. That open seat... Oh, that must be Dr. Cthulhy's seat. Skipping out again, I see."

"Dr. Cthulhy's very busy—that's why," Glenn chimed in.

"Over there is the head of the Lindworm branch of Loose Silk Sewing, it looks like. Oh, and Arahnia's with her, too," Sapphee continued. It seemed that all the representatives of the major businesses and organizations in Lindworm had been invited. Arahnia was the designer at Loose Silk Sewing and must have been attending along with her boss.

All of a sudden, Glenn felt nervous. He worried that a simple town doctor such as himself was out of place at such a ceremony. Unaware of Glenn's unease, Sapphee calmly sipped the tea they had been served. She wasn't the type to get nervous when surrounded by important people of great stature.

"Seven mermaids have graciously accepted my request to be here for today's ceremony. As you all enjoy the beautiful voices of these merfolk, I ask that you enjoy the newly-rebuilt Waterways to your hearts' content." Skadi's words resonated through the Waterways through Kunai's voice.

The entire bridge was astir. Whistles and applause showered Skadi in praise. As the city council representative, she certainly had quite a few political rivals, but she was also very popular with the citizens of Lindworm. Glenn thought perhaps it was because of her frequent trips out into the city, where she walked around with Kunai in tow.

"Finally... This is something extremely, *extremely* personal, but it is also something I would definitely ask for those assembled to hear," Kunai said. Continuing the speech, Skadi reached out her hand to the bridge handrail.

"Ten years ago I gave this former fortress town the name of Lindworm. The name Lindworm means 'sky dragon.' They are a species of dragon that fly through the air. Why did I give it a name like that? Gossipers will claim that since I, Skadi Dragenfelt, am a fire dragon, I gave it the name of a dragon because I intend to rule over this city. However, that it absolutely not the case."

Even among dragons, there were a number of different species. Sky dragons. Fire dragons. Poison dragons. In Glenn's home in the eastern edge of human territory, it was believed there were dragons there completely different from those found in the western monster territory. They were mysterious creatures that had a crocodilian head, a snake-like body, and could fly through the air without any wings.

Glenn wondered why there were so many different species of dragon. One explanation was that dragons were originally beings that existed close to the gods. When the dragons separated themselves from the gods and lived too long on the ground, they were corrupted by the earth, and their bodies greatly deteriorated. It was a satisfactory explanation, but Glenn still wondered.

To some extent, dragons remained mysterious creatures. There was much about them that was impossible to understand with his knowledge of biology.

"This city is...a place for humans and monsters to live. There may be problems. There may be disputes. There may be disasters. I'm sure there may be people from other places that say all sorts of things about our city's way of life. However, I believed that by giving the city the name of a dragon, no matter what happened, the dragon would protect this town. And by dragon, I don't mean myself. I believe in the divine protection of the founder of our species, far up in the heavens."

Skadi wasn't the ruler of Lindworm, despite often being mistaken as such. The administration of Lindworm was decided on by a group of influential members of the city, including Skadi, conferring together on issues. Skadi was their representative, but that didn't mean she had any authority to decide things on her own. Naturally there was a difference between the influence her voice held compared to the other voices in the city council, but that was entirely because of her own competence and ability.

There wasn't anyone who believed she was trying to take over the city for herself.

"Consequently, I... I will soon..."

Everyone waited for Skadi's next words. Everyone imagined that she was about to say something important.

Yet, they didn't come. Glenn wondered if she was unsure of what to say, but it was strange that the speech that had flowed so smoothly up until that moment had suddenly stopped.

Kunai also glanced over at Skadi. The fact that her voice-by-proxy, Kunai, was suspicious meant that Skadi's words had indeed faltered. The audience waited with bated breath for Skadi's next words.

The next moment it happened. Skadi looked as if she were taking a bow.

"Miss Kunai!" Glenn reflexively called out, and stood up. The bridge was a ways off, but he was sure his voice had reached it. Pushing his way through the audience, Glenn began to run.

What had looked like a bow had been Skadi falling forward. Her balance faltering, Skadi was held up by Kunai next to her. Kunai's anguished cry reached Glenn as he ran to the bridge. Glenn wondered—had she fainted? Was it some kind of spasm? Was it just a slight fit of dizziness?

No, he thought, it wasn't that. No matter how many times Kunai called out to Skadi, there was no answer.

Skadi had completely lost consciousness. It was imperative that he give her first aid.

However, the problem was that there were so many people.

To make matters worse, both ends of the bridge were overflowing with audience members trying to hear Skadi's speech. There was a limit to how many people he could push aside with his slender arms. Not only that, there wasn't anyone in the crowd who knew what was going on, and he found himself in the middle of mass chaos.

Glenn was desperate to get through, but at this rate, he thought he might arrive at Skadi's side too late. A delay in the initial response was often fatal when it came to emergency medical treatment.

"Hngh... Miss Skadi!" Glenn yelled as he writhed through the crowd, trying to move forward, when—

"Doctor, this way." Sapphee said, seizing Glenn by the hand. Sapphee slithered her way through the gaps in the crowd in a way Glenn thought was perhaps expected of a lamia like her. Even when it looked like they wouldn't be able to get through at first glance, using her lamia body, she was able to forcibly squeeze herself through. Times like these made Glenn realize just how reliable she was.

"Please hurry," said Sapphee.

"I know," Glenn replied.

Under the lamia's guidance, Glenn was able to slip through the crowd. After getting through the mass of people, he saw Skadi's collapsed figure in front of him. At her side, Kunai held Skadi's arms and desperately called out to her. With her master in a critical state, Kunai's already fair complexion grew even paler.

"Please don't move her. Somebody! Get me a stretcher!" said Glenn, firing off instructions.

"Oh! You came! Thank goodness..." Kunai replied, a look of relief spreading across her face. "She suddenly fell forward. She doesn't respond when I try calling out to her..."

"It could be trouble with her heart or brain. Does Miss Skadi suffer from any chronic diseases?"

"Well..." Kunai looked around, worried. It seemed to Glenn that she happened to know of some chronic disease, but it wasn't like Kunai to be at a loss for an answer. Glenn thought he saw her glance toward the crowd and realized it might be something she couldn't talk about in such a public place.

"I understand. In any event, I'm going to begin emergency first aid," said Glenn, bringing his face close to Skadi's veil. She was breathing. He immediately went to take her pulse. Since she had scales around her wrist, Glenn put his hand through the side of her robe and took her pulse from her neck.

It was then that Glenn realized Skadi wasn't wearing anything else underneath her robe. He was startled, but he knew now wasn't the time to comment on it.

Her pulse was weak, but still there.

"I've confirmed she's breathing and that she still has a pulse. Let's transport her immediately. Miss Skadi's regular doctor is... Dr. Cthulhy, correct?" asked Glenn.

"Y-yeah," Kunai replied.

Glenn had been able to confirm that she was breathing and that her blood was flowing properly, in which case, there wasn't much else he could do on the bridge. He determined that they needed to head for the Lindworm Central Hospital and treat Skadi there, together with Cthulhy. He was sure that even she would be surprised at the circumstances of their long-awaited reunion.

It was well past the time for the ceremony. Just like Kunai, many of the people gathered there watched intently as Glenn examined Skadi.

✳ ✳ ✖ ✳ ✳

The rumor soon ran through all of Lindworm. It quickly took on a life of its own. Embellishments and exaggerations were added to the story until it had become a monster, with little left of the truth.

It morphed into a completely groundless rumor that someone had plotted an assassination attempt on Skadi. Was it the farmer Aluloona, recognized as next in line to become the city council representative? Or was it the branch manager of Loose Silk Sewing, who always enjoyed scheming and plotting something or another? No, maybe it was the hospital director Cthulhy who poisoned her. These and other such irresponsible rumors ran rampant. Ignoring that she had only collapsed, some even jumped to the conclusion that Skadi was already dead, and managed to crowd into the central assembly hall and cause a scene.

That day, the only thing anyone in the town talked about was Skadi. But the disturbance, to look on the positive side, clearly demonstrated just how much she was loved and how important a person she was to the city.

And thus there came an unprecedented treatment, one which would shake the entire town of the dragon to its core. A major dragon surgery was about to begin.

CASE 01:
The Fatigued Scylla

L INDWORM. When one spoke the name of this city, they spoke about a former fortress town. During the previous war, it had been a stronghold, built on the front lines of the human forces. The fortress had barely any facilities that weren't expressively dedicated to combat. However, when Skadi came, she gave the fortress town the name of Lindworm and remade it to be suitable for civilians to live in.

The arena had formerly been a place where prisoners were forced to fight for entertainment. The central city council building had been used for the leading generals to gather and hold war councils. Though these various buildings and facilities were rebuilt and remodeled, their general shape remained as it had been during the war. It had been decided that the buildings were so massive that it was better to use them than destroy them.

The Central Hospital had also been repurposed from one of the military facilities. It had formerly been a military hospital, but was heavily remodeled after the war and changed into one for the citizens of the city. It had been a long and difficult process to court a doctor of monster medicine to come to the hospital, but in the end Cthulhy Squele was named director and the Central Hospital was given its current structure.

As almost a sort of bonus, Glenn also opened up his own clinic, but that wasn't a necessary detail to add.

Cthulhy's shrewdness was plain for anybody to see. There wasn't another hospital on the entire continent that could compete with the Central Hospital when it came to practicing monster medicine. With its state-of-the-art equipment and Cthulhy's brilliant pupils, the hospital had a proven track record of treating and healing monsters with both rare and life-threatening diseases.

It would be appropriate to say that, as a town doctor, Glenn's intended role was completely different. This was the first time in a very long while that Glenn had come to the Central Hospital. For a short period of time before opening his own practice, he had actually been a resident working there.

"We haven't really come here since opening up the clinic, have we?" said Glenn.

"That's because we've been busy. Besides, all the things we've been doing were forced on us by Miss Cthulhy. We haven't asked for any help from the Central Hospital, after all," Sapphee replied, clearly displeased with the unreasonable tasks that occasionally came to them from Cthulhy. The two women had never gotten along to begin with, even when Glenn and Sapphee were in the Academy together.

They continued through the enormous entrance. As to be expected, the monsters there were the first to catch Glenn's eye. At the Central Hospital, there were a large number of beds prepared for patients. Both the patients and those working to treat them were all monsters. It was proof that Glenn was about the only praiseworthy human who had aspired to master monster medicine.

There wasn't another single human to be found, but Glenn was used to such an environment and didn't really pay it any mind. Ever since he enrolled at the Monster Academy, he had grown used to feeling the odd-species-out in a crowded room.

A nurse passing by bowed her head. Glenn remembered that she had been a senior pupil of Cthulhy's when he had been a resident here. They hadn't been particularly close, but she waved toward Sapphee with a smile on her face. If anything, the nurse had been better friends with Sapphee.

"I guess since everyone knows our faces, we don't even need to go through reception," Sapphee said with a carefree tone to her voice. Normally, it would be difficult just to meet with the hospital director, but as Cthulhy's personal pupils, no one questioned Glenn and Sapphee.

"Will Miss Skadi be okay?" Sapphee asked.

"I'm worried, but I'm sure she'll be fine... I hope," Glenn replied.

The ceremony had been at noon that day. Skadi had collapsed and was carried to the Central Hospital that afternoon. Glenn had given her emergency first aid, but all the follow-up treatments had been under the Central Hospital's jurisdiction, and he hadn't been allowed to participate. This was because Skadi's regular doctor was her old friend—Cthulhy Squele.

Once the sun went down, Glenn and Sapphee made their way toward the Central Hospital once again. Although Skadi's primary doctor was their teacher, Glenn was the one who had happened to be present when Skadi collapsed. It was natural for him to be worried about her condition.

Glenn also wanted to see the teacher who had taught him medicine, and who he hadn't seen in close to a year. Of course, as the patient, Skadi was the top priority, but Glenn thought it was okay to take the opportunity to enjoy a reunion with his teacher. Despite living in the same city, they were both so busy that they had almost no opportunity to see one another.

"Dr. Glenn, I'm just going to say this now, but..." Sapphee said with a grim look on her face. She had been in a foul mood ever since they arrived at the hospital. "Don't get carried away just because you're reuniting with Dr. Cthulhy. Got it?"

"I'm telling you, it's fine, Sapphee. Dr. Cthulhy isn't interested in me anymore, and besides, she's worried about Skadi right now. We're not going to be able to have a nice long chat or anything," replied Glenn.

"I certainly hope that's the case."

The hospital director's room was at the end of a corridor. Glenn hadn't seen any patients in a while, so he assumed this area had been portioned off for the clerical and administrative functions of the hospital. The number of employees at the hospital dwarfed their small clinic, managed by just the two of them.

From the hallway, they had a good view of the courtyard. It was well maintained, and even equipped with a fountain. It was smaller than the fountain in the central plaza where Lulala sang, but Glenn thought it must have been built to try and improve the atmosphere inside the hospital's walls.

Not only that, he thought, the water was essential. Even for Cthulhy.

"Are you in, Doctor? It's Glenn… Saphentite is here with me as well," Glenn said, knocking on the hospital director's office door. It was high quality, made from oak.

"Please, come in," said a voice from beyond the door.

"Thank you," Glenn replied. He was seeing his mentor for the first time in a long while. With a mixture of nervousness and excitement, he opened the heavy wooden door.

The first thing he saw was tentacles.

"Oh my, it's been so long, Glenn…!"

The tentacles stuck themselves to Glenn's face. They were unmistakably the arms of an octopus, but these sprouted from the scylla's lower body, and as such it was more accurate to call the long, sucker-equipped tentacles legs rather than arms.

Whether they were referred to as arms or legs, the long tentacles tightly stuck themselves to Glenn's arms and face. The suckers began sticking themselves all over him, starting with his shoulders, then feeling his neck and face. Despite his best efforts to get used to the sensation of the suckers squeezing up against his skin, he had never quite managed to do so.

He thought she must have just been in the water, as her tentacles were slightly damp. The suction power of the suckers was extraordinary—enough to leave red marks on his skin even when Cthulhy made sure to restrain herself. Although he could say the affectionate physicality was nostalgic, Glenn still felt it was a little much.

"Dr. Cthulhy...!" Sapphee shouted. "You're such a terrible teacher... Knock it off and stop coiling yourself around Dr. Glenn this instant!"

"Oh, Saphentite, you're here too? You can just leave now. I've got something to say to my brilliant pupil here," Cthulhy replied.

"Absolutely not!" said Sapphee. With a look of anger, she tried to rip off the tentacles that had stuck themselves to Glenn. However, Glenn himself knew very well how frivolous it was to try. The tentacles that grew out of the scyllas' lower bodies were a mass of pure muscle, and very powerful. Once the suckers were stuck to something, they didn't remove themselves very easily. It was something he had come to understand very well during his time as Cthulhy's pupil, when she would stroke him with her tentacles without mercy.

"Glenn," said Cthulhy.

"Yes?" Glenn replied.

"You've gotten kind of old," Cthulhy declared in a somewhat appalled tone of voice, as her tentacles separated themselves from Glenn with a pop. Still only seventeen, Glenn would never have expected to be told he had grown old. But then again, that was the kind of person his mentor was.

Cthulhy Squele, the authority on monster medicine. She was without rivals at the Academy, but one could say that she had a little problem—or rather, a big problem—with her personality, her attitude, and her behavior.

"It's been some time, my cute and *darling* little pupils," said Cthulhy.

"It's been...quite a long time, Doctor," Glenn replied.

Cthulhy was still a very beautiful woman. Molting species of monsters never showed any aging in their skin in the first place. Perched on her intelligent-looking visage was a high quality pair of glasses. Paired with her white coat, she had the appearance of a genuinely brilliant woman doctor. The truth was that she was indeed quite a clever woman.

Then there were the eight tentacles that poked out from under her short skirt. Her tentacles had a striking resemblance to those of an octopus and wriggled at will to help Cthulhy's movement, working both as arms and legs. Those that had just released Glenn slapped and stuck to the floor as if to make sure it would support her, carrying Cthulhy's body along.

The tentacles were the scyllas' most distinctive characteristic. The scylla were a combination of a human-like vertebrate with the distinctive characteristics of the invertebrate octopus, something rarely seen even among the many species of monsters. There were many mysteries surrounding how their bodies were constructed and no complete explanation for how they came to be. Because of this, they were often the subject of ridicule and said to be descendants of a malevolent god.

While Glenn wouldn't say that she was the descendant of a malevolent god, Cthulhy herself *did* have a malicious side to her.

"Yes, yes, allow me to give you a proper greeting as well," said Sapphee. "It has truly been quite some time, Dr. Cthulhy. It appears you have your sights on Glenn just like always... You're a middle-aged woman and you still haven't fixed your bad habit of trying to seduce young boys? Don't you think it's about time you get that checked out? That cradle-robbing sickness of yours, I mean."

"Oh, be quiet. Don't go nitpicking at other people's propensities. I can see that *you* still haven't fixed that crafty, overly-jealous personality of yours either, have you?" Cthulhy replied.

"If *someone* didn't make passes at him, I wouldn't have to be so jealous."

"Oh my, please do forgive me. I just want to cherish my cute little pupils, you see."

"I'm pretty sure that *I'm* one of your cute little pupils too, you know."

The two of them were smiling, but their relationship was the absolute worst. Glenn believed they had had a normal student-teacher relationship when they were at the Academy, but once Glenn arrived at the school, things grew oddly complicated between them. Glenn was an old friend of Sapphee's, and Cthulhy had had her eyes set on the young fourteen-year-old, so he imagined it would have been more unusual if they *had* gotten along.

Despite all of this, Cthulhy had effectively taught them medicine, and Sapphee had inherited Cthulhy's knowledge of pharmacology. They may have had a complicated relationship, but there was no question that Sapphee respected Cthulhy as a doctor.

One would have never known it from the attitude she took toward Cthulhy, however. Even now, Sapphee's snake tail and Cthulhy's octopus legs seemed on the verge of coming to blows with one another. They'd always gotten into quarrels with each other during their time at the academy.

"Even so, you were so cute back then, Glenn, and now you're all grown up, aren't you?" Cthulhy remarked.

"It's been three years since I first entered the Academy, after all," replied Glenn. Although still young, he was an adult. For someone of Cthulhy's disposition, this was something to lament, but Glenn realized that Cthulhy was just the type of woman to mourn his maturation at their long-awaited reunion.

"Well, I'll still welcome you in, at least. How is the clinic?" Cthulhy asked.

"Not so bad, we're getting by somehow... The two of us," replied Glenn.

"I'm going to remind you that I didn't give you that clinic just for you two to enjoy some lover's tryst, you know. If the two of you neglect your duty to treat your monster patients and carry on with one another, then I'll ask you to leave," said Cthulhy.

"As if we even had the time for that..." said Glenn. Just that winter they'd been frantic in trying to deal with the cold epidemic. Though Sapphee and Glenn had been able to get through the busy season, to be perfectly honest, they hadn't had the time to get involved in anything that wasn't related to their primary jobs.

Perhaps Glenn had wanted Cthulhy's praise at their long-awaited reunion—to hear her say that they had done well or that they had really worked hard. But his strict mentor only cast a sharp, penetrating glare from behind the lenses of her glasses.

Even now, it made Glenn feel like he was back in class and taking one of her pop quizzes.

"Dr. Cthulhy, as for why we're here..." Sapphee said, moving the conversation forward.

"I know. You're here about Skadi, right? I wasn't able to attend the ceremony, but it was lucky that the two of you happened to be there. She was carried here immediately," said Cthulhy.

"You couldn't make it? I'm sure you just thought it was a pain to go," Sapphee responded.

"Well, after all, the ceremony's got nothing to do with me, does it?" sighed the honest Cthulhy. Her tentacles squirmed, making a sort of shoulder-shrugging motion.

"Miss Skadi... What kind of illness is it?" Glenn asked.

"A very serious one," replied Cthulhy.

"Can you give me any more detailed information?"

"I'm sorry, Glenn. As Skadi's primary physician, it's not something I can talk about lightly. However, it is an extremely rare case, and there isn't anything else like it. Yes, rather than serious, perhaps I should say it's...strange," said Cthulhy.

She was the leading, most prominent authority when it came to monster medicine. Originally, she'd researched the evolution of monsters, to try and clear the stigma associated with her species—that the scylla were the descendents of a malevolent god. Through that process, she ended up conducting research on each species' stages of evolution and how their bodies were constructed. The scylla were a species that were covetous of knowledge to begin with, enough to be known as the "sages of the deep ocean."

Now that Glenn thought about it, she had researched dragons as well. Glenn thought that dragons might possess the most primitive bodies of all monsterkind. In any event, although there were many things about the origins of monsterkind that weren't clear, Cthulhy's duty was that of a researcher—a scholar.

She had become a doctor because she gained extraordinary knowledge of medicine and biology through her research, but despite medicine not being her actual specialty, that she had been able to become the director of the hospital proved just how capable of a woman she was.

And yet, this disease was rare enough to make a woman like her say she'd never seen anything like it.

"I heard Skadi collapsed in the middle of the ceremony. Is that right?" Cthulhy asked.

"Y-yes," replied Glenn.

"Her disease is already eating into her entire body. The biggest danger is her heart. This time, she just fainted from low blood pressure, but...there's a high possibility that next time, the drop in blood pressure could induce heart failure. No, if anything I'd say it's a miracle she hadn't collapsed in front of anyone before this."

"Heart failure?! So it is some disease of the heart, then?" Glenn asked.

"That's right," Cthulhy replied. "She's had it for years. Dragons are troublesome creatures. Even if they come down with illnesses that would kill a normal species, their bodies are so strong that the disease can't quite kill them. Conversely, that only serves to make the time they spend suffering even longer."

Up until just recently, Skadi had been quite active in her work as the council's representative. Glenn wondered how it was possible for her to do everything she had done while her heart had such a disease. Even if she was a dragon, she shouldn't have been able to be so reckless—but no, Glenn thought, it was precisely *because* she was a dragon that it was possible.

Be that as it may, Glenn was sure it had been tough for her. Just as Cthulhy had said, she must have been in considerable pain.

"Ah, Miss Cthulhy?"

"What is it, Saphentite?" Cthulhy replied.

"Could it be that the reason Miss Skadi is covering her face... is because she doesn't want those around her to become aware of her illness?"

Cthulhy gave no answer. Her silence only confirmed that Sapphee was right on the mark. Cthulhy scowled and began chewing on the end of a tentacle. It was something she would do when she was irritated. Just like humans chewed their nails, scylla chewed on their arms.

"It's nothing that I can talk about." There was a tone of refusal in Cthulhy's words. "It's not an illness that is easily cured. Furthermore, a rare dragon disease is beyond even my ability to treat. For the time being, she'll manage, as long as she drinks plenty of nutrients and gets a good amount of rest. She should be waking up soon. But in order to cure her completely, I need to strike at the source."

"Are you saying...you don't know what the cause of her disease is?" Glenn asked.

"Not at all—the cause is clear to see. After all, that's—" Cthulhy started and covered her mouth with a tentacle. A clear signal she was about to carelessly let a secret slip out. She heaved a big sigh and straightened her glasses. "Whoops—that was close. My cute students have gotten me saying too much."

"Dr. Cthulhy, we want to know more about Skadi's condition... We came because we thought we might be of some help."

"Just forget about it and return to your clinic. Listen, the real problem isn't the disease. That's why there just isn't anything I can do about it. As long as that stubborn Skadi doesn't change her thoughts on the matter, there isn't any sort of treatment you or I could give her," Cthulhy said, her tentacles smacking and sticking themselves to the floor as they carried her body further into the room to her director's desk. Piled on the desk was a mountain of documents. Becoming the director of a major hospital meant her job had become enormous and encompassed many different things. There was an octopus pot installed in the corner of the room. Cthulhy didn't even have time to go home and was sleeping here in her office.

Glenn wasn't the only one who was busy. He should have known her absence at the ceremony wasn't simply because of laziness.

"Listen, this much I'll tell you. So after I say this, I want you to leave." There was an affectionate tone to Cthulhy's voice. "The biggest problem is that Skadi has absolutely no intention of trying to treat her illness," she declared as she locked eyes with Glenn. While she may have appeared to be a strict, very hands-off mentor, in her heart Cthulhy thought very tenderly of her pupils. She couldn't neglect her students and was a very caring teacher.

Glenn looked Sapphee in the eyes. She silently shook her head. There wasn't anything the two of them could do. Skadi had no intentions of getting better—Glenn wanted to ask what Cthulhy had meant by that, but it didn't look like she intended to talk about the subject anymore. He concluded that it was meaningless to try and press the issue.

"Thank you for your time, Dr. Cthulhy. I'm very glad I was able to see you," said Glenn.

"Work hard at the clinic, you two," Cthulhy replied, waving a tentacle at them while continuing to sign documents.

Sapphee immediately left the office, as if she had finished all of her business there. Glenn followed right after her but couldn't clear his mind of gloomy thoughts about the rare disorder of Skadi Dragenfelt, and the meaning behind Cthulhy's telling them that Skadi herself had no intention of trying to get better.

As they left the Central Hospital behind them, Glenn grabbed the nurse they had passed by earlier and asked if they could visit Skadi, but sure enough, visitors weren't allowed to see her.

"Even Dr. Cthulhy is grasping at straws, it seems." Sapphee's quiet words as they left the hospital were telling. "With all those tentacles of hers, you'd think she'd be able to grasp at a lot more of them, too."

"That's not the point," Glenn retorted. Sapphee's sarcastic reply was very like her, but he knew it didn't mean she was okay with this situation. To be a doctor, and yet unable to plunge into treating a patient, was bound to be a painful, bitter pill to swallow. When Glenn thought about being in Cthulhy's shoes, his heart ached.

Suppressing his desire to see more of his mentor, Glenn continued down the road to return to the clinic. Sapphee was just as reticent as she walked beside him.

Glenn unconsciously bit his lip as he thought about how, despite being a doctor, he was powerless to help. His frustrations hung over him, heavy as lead.

✖ ✖ ✖ ✖ ✖

A few days had passed since the ceremony. Glenn's days were filled with work at the clinic as usual, but even without going outside, he knew about the uproar in the city. Skadi's collapse at the inauguration was in the city paper that Illy delivered to him. They wrote that although her condition looked serious, no one had a grasp on the actual situation.

To make matters worse, Cthulhy was keeping silent about Skadi's current condition and declining any interviews. This appeared to have soured the reporters' opinions of Cthulhy, and they mixed abusive remarks about her into article after article, writing that she was negligent as Skadi's primary doctor and that she had a duty to explain the city council representative's current condition.

"Sorry for always coming to you like this, Dr. Glenn," Kunai said as Glenn sewed her wrist back together.

"No need for an apology, Miss Kunai. If anything, I should thank you for coming by when you're so busy."

"The city council is in such an uproar, I managed to use my medical care as an excuse to get away," Kunai Zenow replied with a dry laugh. The flesh golem had happened to come by the clinic a little after noon, saying that the stitches on her wrist had come loose and needed to be sutured back together. She appeared as calm as ever, even when carrying her right hand completely detached from her body, but Glenn had become used to such grotesque spectacles.

Glenn was convinced that Kunai had been using her body recklessly again. Yet, he found the appearance of her detached wrist to be a little strange. It looked almost like Kunai had used all her strength to tear off her own wrist. He thought it might be that Kunai's reason for coming had just been an excuse to escape from the Central Council Hall.

"So the city council is in turmoil, after all?" Glenn asked.

"That goes without saying. At the end of the day, the council's representative collapsed, and although she's been discharged, she's still recovering. The next candidate to become the representative, Miss Aluloona, is doing her best to settle things, but the Lady Draconess's political rivals are trying to use this as their chance to take over leadership of the council. Both sides are throwing words back and forth at each other," Kunai replied.

"Miss Aluloona is it…? There were some rumors that she was the one behind Miss Skadi's collapse."

"Ridiculous. Her illness brought on the collapse, and Miss Aluloona is very close to the Lady Draconess to begin with. There isn't a kernel of truth to the story."

Aluloona was the head of the Aluloona Plantation. For a monster with a plant body, such as her, it really was a rumor without a "kernel" of truth, Glenn thought.

"Is it all right for you to be away from Miss Skadi's side, Miss Kunai?" Glenn asked.

"I made sure to ask that of the Lady Draconess myself, but she told me that staying by her side while my wrist was detached from my arm was depressing to look at, and ordered me to come here. There wasn't anything I could do but follow her wishes," replied Kunai. Glenn thought the combination of being unable to stay at her master's side and not belonging in the city council was what had really brought her to be treated.

"...However, all of that is actually just a front," continued Kunai.

"A front?"

"That's right—well—I wasn't lying about my hand being separated, but besides that... I wanted to talk to you."

In a corner of the clinic, Sapphee's tail trembled with a jolt. She hadn't paid much attention to Kunai when she entered the clinic, but her hands had stopped grinding down medicinal herbs, and it seemed to Glenn that she was listening closely to their conversation.

"By 'wanted to talk to me,' you mean..." Glenn began.

"Of course, it's about the Lady Draconess." Kunai nodded solemnly. Sapphee returned to making her medicine. Glenn wasn't sure what she'd misunderstood, but he wondered if something had stirred up her jealousy again. "Have you heard anything about the Lady Draconess's illness or treatment? You are Dr. Cthulhy's disciple, after all."

"My mentor didn't seem to want to discuss it at all," Glenn said. "I don't know anything specific either."

"I had thought as much," Kunai continued. Glenn's hands never stopped their sewing, all the while. He wondered exactly how many times he had sewed Kunai's body together now. He had become completely accustomed to it.

"The Lady Draconess has a serious disease. I'm sure you understand that much?" Kunai asked.

"Yes, of course," Glenn replied.

"Yet, the Lady Draconess shows no interest in being cured and says that she doesn't need to treat it. Dr. Cthulhy agrees as well... Or rather, I should say, she's simply respecting her patient's wishes. As such, there aren't any plans for the Lady Draconess to be admitted again or to go to the hospital for regular treatment," Kunai said, biting her lip, sure of the fact that things shouldn't be left as they were.

"The paper is reporting whatever it wants," Glenn said. "Saying that my mentor is negligent, that she has no passion for medicine, that she's ignoring the disease and isn't explaining anything to the people of the city."

"Of course," Kunai replied, "I don't take everything that comes out in the newspapers to be true. It is the Lady Draconess's will that she not receive treatment, after all."

Now that Glenn thought about it, something similar had happened before. The centaur Tisalia's shoeing. Cthulhy was aware of the fact that Tisalia hadn't been shod, but she didn't suggest it or treat Tisalia herself. Cthulhy didn't approve of becoming excessively involved with one's own patients. Glenn was sure that this case with Skadi was no different.

"I must say that it's likely that my mentor will not go against Skadi's wishes and treat her. That's her way of practicing medicine," said Glenn.

"...Despite you two being teacher and student, your way of doing this is quite different, isn't it?" replied Kunai.

"All that I was taught was medicinal techniques and knowledge. My mentor's true calling is to be a scholar. I've heard it was Skadi's strong urging that caused her to become the hospital director here in Lindworm."

"Those two *are* very old friends," replied Kunai. Glenn thought that there was probably something shared between the two of them that none of them would ever understand.

"However!" Kunai exclaimed, tightly clenching her fist as soon as Glenn finished stitching. Practically hearing the strained sound of the threads, he was afraid that the hand he had just reconnected would immediately come undone again.

"Even if that *is* the case, I can't just stand helplessly by and watch this life-threatening illness get worse! The Lady Draconess showed me kindness in picking me to be at her side. I can't sit by silently as she suffers. Even if it meant, for example, that I was going against her wishes!"

"I thought you'd say something like that, Miss Kunai," replied Glenn. He knew there was no way that Skadi's bodyguard wouldn't do anything in the face of her master's illness. And Glenn had a similar line of thinking. Setting aside the fact that Cthulhy had been his teacher—Glenn was a nosy and meddlesome doctor.

"So that's the real reason you've come to our clinic today, then?" Glenn asked.

"I'm glad you're so quick to catch on. I wanted to ask you to treat the Lady Draconess, Dr. Glenn. I can pay whatever you ask," answered Kunai.

Quite the rich offering, Glenn thought to himself. He wondered if being a bodyguard was really so lucrative. But Kunai was in a high enough position to have people working under her. It was only natural her pay would be different from that of a normal guard.

Glenn had heard that since Kunai was a corpse, she didn't even need food. As such, he imagined the money she spent on daily expenses was probably inconsequential and that her personal wealth must reflect that.

"I assume you know why I am asking you to treat her. Although you might end up infringing on Dr. Cthulhy's work..." continued Kunai.

"She isn't the type to fuss over that stuff," Glenn replied. Cthulhy was absolutely not lazy. However, she didn't spread her tentacles any wider than she had to. She had absolutely no initiative. Glenn thought that if anything, she would thank him for taking on her work for her. "Now, then... First, I'll need to examine her."

"Of course. That being said, it will be impossible to have the Lady Draconess visit here. She has no intention of receiving any medical examination. Thus, I'm going to have to ask you to go to her, Dr. Glenn."

"That won't be an issue," Glenn replied. This wouldn't be the first time he saw a patient that had no interest in his examination. It took a long time to convince Illy to let him see her when he visited the harpy village.

"At any rate, I've mapped out a plan," Kunai said. "You could just visit the Lady Draconess's chambers at the Council Hall." At these words, there arose a clatter of something being dropped.

"D-did you say...her *chambers?!*" cried Sapphee. She appeared to have dropped the mortar she was using for her work. In an instant, she stretched up nearly to the ceiling, poised like a cobra ready to strike. The sense of intimidation she gave off from this position was extraordinary. "Hold on just a second! Dr. Glenn sneaking into a lady's room, you said...?!"

"If they went somewhere else, they'd risk being seen," Kunai replied. "If the convalescent Lady Draconess and the town doctor are discovered meeting, there will be more groundless gossip in the papers. Her chambers are the best place to avoid any prying eyes."

"Th-that may be so, but..." Sapphee stuttered. Glenn wondered exactly what in the world the flustered Sapphee was imagining.

"On top of that," Kunai added, "it would be better for the examination if the Lady Draconess was lightly dressed, correct?

Anywhere else and she would have a hard time taking off her usual robe and veil."

"So Glenn's going to stealthily sneak into Skadi's chambers and have her strip all the clothes off her youthful body?! N-no— it's just an examination... It's just an examination, right? Right, Doctor?!" Sapphee said, frantic for reasons unknown to Glenn. But the way she put it, he had to admit it did sound indecent.

"You don't have to worry—it's just work," Glenn replied. "I've made plenty of house calls for other patients before, right?"

"R-right. An examination... This is just an examination..." said Sapphee.

It was just a simple house call—or at least that was what Glenn had assumed. But, as Sapphee had said, sneaking off in the middle of the night to give an examination was scandalous in itself.

"I'll say this up front. I want you to be prepared," Kunai said with a serious expression, apparently not having paid any attention to Sapphee's panic. "I'm sure you'll be looking at the Lady Draconess's heart, but that thing is beyond my imagination. It's hard to explain... No, I *can* give an explanation, but I have no idea how it happened."

For Kunai, a flesh golem created from piecing together different corpses, to say all of that—Glenn wondered exactly what kind of disease Skadi suffered from. Judging from the way Kunai spoke, it seemed he would understand as soon as he saw it. This convinced him that the reason Skadi always covered herself with a veil and robe was to hide her illness.

However, there was one thing above all else that lay on Glenn's mind—the way Kunai had said, *"when you see her heart."* The heart was concealed behind the rib cage, not visible from outside the body. Yet, the way Kunai spoke almost seemed to suggest she had cut open Skadi's chest and looked directly at her heart.

Glenn shook his head—he had to be overthinking things.

"Dr. Glenn, please. I'm begging you." The faithful bodyguard bowed her head deeply and pleaded with Glenn. He had absolutely no objections and immediately accepted her request. Afterward, Sapphee mumbled to herself about whether Glenn was actually going to examine her, or whether this was some kind of lover's tryst, but Glenn set all that aside for the time being.

And yet, he wondered if Skadi's disease might be much, much stranger than he could even imagine. He couldn't stop those thoughts from creeping into his head.

He asked himself what he would do if the disease proved too much for him to handle. It was a possibility he needed to consider.

✖ ✖ ✖ ✖ ✖

The night of the house call came quickly. Only a few days had passed when Kunai came to visit Glenn at the clinic after he had finished his work for the day. She took both Glenn and Sapphee outside and headed toward the Council Hall.

The hall naturally only had a few people around it at night, and its small security team consisted entirely of Kunai's colleagues and subordinates. It wasn't difficult to convince them of the situation.

What worried Kunai was the possibility of a scandal involving Skadi. She was cautious of any more half-baked articles being written in the city paper and used by Skadi's political rivals. But being seen a little by the security force at the Council Hall wouldn't cause any problems. None of the security team bore any ill will toward Skadi.

Actually, not only did the stationed security team not reprimand them when they came across them, they all nodded as if to say they were aware of everything, which told Glenn just how thorough Kunai's preparations had been.

He had come to the Council Hall once before. A colossal building built out of stone, it was comparable in scale to the arena, and was one of Lindworm's prominent historical buildings. It looked rough from the outside, and though there were a few statutes and engravings decorating it, it was a facility fundamentally devoted to its practical purposes.

Entering from the front, one immediately saw the large assembly hall, where the council discussed matters of importance to the city every day. This time, however, Glenn and the others entered through the back. That way, they were directly connected to Skadi's chambers, Kunai's room, and the guest room that was used to house dignitaries from outside of Lindworm. Previously, when Sapphee had been attacked by a slave trader's poisoned blade, she had borrowed that room to rest and recover.

The moon was dazzlingly bright. Lindworm was famous for its bright full moons, but tonight's was especially bright. Glenn could clearly see Kunai's face in the corridor of the Council Hall without the help of any illumination. The window had been made large to keep the stone hall well lit, which let them walk through the building without any difficulty.

"Here we are," Kunai whispered. "These are the Lady Draconess's chambers." Glenn thought the whispering must have been out of consideration for Skadi. "Someone might come if it gets too loud, and the Lady Draconess hates to be fussed over. I ask that Dr. Glenn be the only one to go in."

"I-I will go, too," Sapphee declared. "Dr. Glenn doesn't show enough consideration when examining female patients, so another female should be there!" She had absolutely no trust in Glenn. But given how many times he had made a mistake when examining his female patients, there wasn't anything Glenn could say to defend himself.

"Sorry," Kunai replied, "but please bear with it. A whole crowd running in would put an unnecessary burden on the Lady Draconess."

"B-but... I guess that's how it has to be..." Sapphee replied.

Glenn thought there hadn't been any need for Sapphee to tag along on a house visit to begin with—but it seemed that no matter what she was told, Sapphee was worried that something beyond the examination was going to happen.

"Now, of course..." Kunai began, a flash appearing in her eye. Glenn was sure her eyeballs had also been taken from a corpse, but he felt the insight housed in those dead eyes was several times stronger than those of the living. "I don't believe that there is even the *slightest* chance of this being an issue, but if I think that anything has happened to the Lady Draconess, I'm going to rush in there. Don't think about trying to do anything audacious, Doctor."

In the end, it appeared that Kunai had been thinking something similar to Sapphee.

"I'm not thinking about that stuff at all... Why are you being so cautious?" Glenn replied.

"Oh? Did you forget about what happened when you stitched up my leg?" said Kunai.

"Ah," Glenn replied, in realization.

"O-of course, I'm fully aware that in my case, it was just part of my treatment, but... Well, um, while that may be true, it'll be a problem if you do the same to the Lady Draconess as you did back then... How should I say it... Hmph, well, she is a dignitary, so give her the appropriate amount of consideration, that's all," stammered Kunai.

"U-understood. I'll be careful," replied Glenn.

"I-I'm counting on you," said Kunai.

Glenn thought the care he had once given to Kunai must have been humiliating for her. At long last, he was able to understand the cause of her anxiety on the matter. Having not been there at the time, Sapphee looked puzzled, wondering what the two were talking about.

"Okay then, please head inside," said Kunai.

"Pardon me," Glenn said. As soon as he went inside, the door shut behind him, but he could still feel the presence of Sapphee holding her breath and Kunai with her ears at attention. It seemed the two of them were still worried after all.

The inside of the room was so bright that it was hard to think that it was still nighttime, thanks to the moonlight streaming into the room from the large window. Due to the especially bright moon that night, Glenn was able to see the canopy bed in the middle of the room, as well as the design on the lace curtains surrounding it.

"Miss Skadi," said Glenn.

"............"

In the middle of the moonlight there stood a young girl. Wrapped in her nightclothes, the dragon woman truly had the appearance of a young girl no more than ten years old. Glenn thought this was probably his first time seeing Skadi without her robe on. The slender dragon looked in danger of collapsing in a stiff breeze—so much so that it was impossible to imagine she was a being of such colossal power. Except for her horns reaching up to the heavens and the tail extending behind her—these two traits conveyed that this immature child did indeed conceal within herself the power of a dragon.

Skadi's nightclothes were so thin they were almost transparent. They were well made, and Glenn thought perhaps they were the product of Loose Silk Sewing, where Arahnia worked. It had a flowing design similar to her robe that made Glenn think that loose clothing was a preference of hers.

Standing next to the window and staring up at the moonlight, Skadi slowly turned toward Glenn.

"............" She said something, but Glenn couldn't hear her.

It was the first time he had seen Skadi's face. She had turquoise hair. There were many different species of monster, but Glenn had never seen one with naturally blue hair. There were scales around the corners of her eyes, and from the blue sheen that they also possessed, Glenn assumed the color was one of Skadi's unique characteristics.

He found it mysterious how the tone of her scales changed slightly as they were bathed in moonlight. Glenn concluded that they were minerals. Some component similar to minerals or gems must be mixed into her body in large amounts. He gathered that dragons weren't beings he could make conjectures about with just his own practical biological knowledge.

Her frame, neck, and limbs were all slender. With her blue coloring, she gave off a somewhat lonely impression.

"............" Skadi's lips were moving. Glenn knew she was saying something, but he still couldn't hear. Then, Skadi beckoned to him.

"*Huh?* Oh, come over, is that it?" Glenn replied.

Skadi nodded without saying anything. As Glenn approached, Skadi continued to beckon him, implying that he still wasn't close enough. He took a few more steps forward, and Skadi beckoned him closer again. Glenn ended up half-crouching down and brought his body close to Skadi's. The two of them were close enough to feel each other's breaths on their faces.

"Why are you here?"

It was the first time Glenn had clearly heard Skadi's voice. It was like the tinkling of a bell. This reaffirmed his idea that the reason she was unable to speak normally was her illness.

Glenn returned her whisper and explained the circumstances of his visit.

Skadi nodded after listening to Glenn's explanation. "I see. So Kunai brought you." For now, Glenn was relieved that they were able to understand each other normally. Up until now, he had only ever been able to speak to her through Kunai. Skadi's voice was so quiet the slightest noise would drown her out. Even at point-blank range, Glenn felt he would miss her words if he didn't concentrate fully on her voice. If he hadn't come on a quiet night like tonight, it would probably have been impossible for them to talk to one another.

Well, Glenn thought, all the more reason it was strange that Kunai could have normal conversations with Skadi. He wondered if the flesh golem's hearing really was that keen.

"I've troubled... *worried* Kunai. There's always so little I can do for the ones at my side," said Skadi.

"Miss Skadi?" Glenn replied.

"Oh, no, it's nothing... Dr. Glenn." The tone of her voice suitably matched her authority as the city council representative. "I'll overlook you sneaking into my room without permission. I'll let Kunai off with just a scolding. Seeing how far you've come for my sake, I must make sure I can oblige."

"In that case..." Glenn began.

"Yes, I will allow you to examine me. I doubt you intend to leave empty-handed. Of course... I'm sure it's not something you'll be able to cure, Dr. Glenn," replied Skadi.

It was resignation, Glenn thought. Or, maybe, there was some other emotion mixed in with her words. Either way, it appeared she held no hope in him.

That was natural. It was a disease that even his mentor Cthulhy had deemed to be rare. There was no way her pupil Glenn would be able to cure it easily. However, Glenn had a feeling that Skadi's surrender came from some other place inside of her. Put simply, it was the fact that she had no intention of getting better to begin with. Without that expectation, it didn't make any difference to Skadi whether she was examined or not.

"Okay then, please forgive me, but I'll need you to take off your clothes," said Glenn.

"Mhm," Skadi replied. There wasn't any hesitation. Skadi opened up the thin negligee at her breast. She didn't show any sort of shame or embarrassment. Glenn at long last understood why Kunai had been so bent on clearing everyone out of the room for the examination. Glenn wondered what people would think if he were seen in this situation. The figure of a man in a young girl's bed chambers, making her strip, with his face close enough to hers to feel her breath on his face.

If it wasn't for him being a doctor and her being his patient, it was a scene that would clearly end with him in the care of the Council Hall security force. Glenn made up his mind to be all the more devoted to the duty at hand.

"Now you can see it clearly, can't you?" said Skadi.

Her chest exposed from the opening of her night clothes, Glenn's eyes were drawn to her white skin. Even when taking her childlike appearance into account, she was very thin. Although she had a nominal amount of bulge on her slender chest, she had almost no womanly curves to her.

However, more than any of that, Glenn's eyes were drawn to the middle of her chest. In the middle of what he could only describe as her modest bosom, was some kind of pulsating thing.

"What..." Glenn was amazed. Despite the considerable amount of experience he had gained through his career, he couldn't keep himself quiet when faced with what was in front of him. "What...is this?"

If asked what it was, he could give an answer—it was a heart. It was about the size of Skadi's fist. Considering her figure, Glenn determined that it was a relatively normal-sized heart. But he couldn't believe that it was possible to see a heart—normally protected by the rib cage—so close to the surface of someone's skin. The heart pulsated with a beat, and it glowed turquoise blue on the inside.

Glenn assumed that the blue light was the color of Skadi's blood. If the inside of Skadi's body was mixed with a large number of minerals as Glenn had estimated, then it would stand to reason that her heart would be a blue similar to her scales.

The problem was that the heart that had formed on top of her rib cage looked almost like a tumor.

"...May I touch it?" asked Glenn.

"Hng. Fine," said Skadi.

Glenn timidly touched the heart. It was hot. It wasn't too hot to touch, but it had a heat to it. Glenn tried to measure the pulsing beats, but sure enough, it beat like a normal heart. Fortunately, there was skin surrounding it, but the heart was pushing up through Skadi's skin and making it transparent, as though it were a bulb that had been planted on top of her rib cage.

"Cthulhy says—hng—that it's a malignant tumor," said Skadi through her pain.

"A tumor? Just as I thought. So it only *looks* like a heart," Glenn replied.

"Apparently. However, ever since this tumor formed on top of my chest, it has gradually hijacked the blood vessels in my body. It's trying to spread its 'roots,' penetrate my blood vessels, and alter the structure of my body's circulation... In other words, it means I have two hearts now."

Glenn was dumbfounded. In her current state, Skadi could suffer arrhythmia or heart failure at any moment. The heart was an organ that was directly linked to keeping one alive and possessed considerable strength to continue beating as long as its host remained alive. Glenn posited that if the functions of this tumor were indeed similar to those of the heart, then the burden that having *two* hearts put on Skadi was unfathomable. It was a miracle that her collapse was all that had happened.

If she were a human, she would have long been dead. Glenn was sure that Skadi's disease had been progressing for several years now, just as Cthulhy had said. He was stunned that Skadi was performing her duties as city council representative and working for the sake of the city in this condition.

Glenn could only be astonished at the vitality of dragons and be amazed at the mysterious tumor that could gnaw at the body of such a tenacious being.

"There's nothing that can be done. This is my destiny, after all," said Skadi.

Glenn couldn't remember ever seeing a case similar to this. He couldn't identify the cause of the tumor, but he thought there was a possibility of removing it surgically. If they underwent surgery to remove the heart, Glenn was sure they could treat the symptoms it was causing. He knew, however, that it wouldn't be that easy.

Even just from looking at it, he could tell that this heart was receiving blood and beating properly. As long as blood was pumping through it, just the act of removing the tumor itself would cause massive bleeding. It was imperative that he analyze the disease and draw up a precise surgery plan.

"The dragons weren't ground-treading creatures in the first place," Skadi continued. "A long, long time ago, our ancestors came down to the earth from their place close to the realm of the gods. However, they were influenced by the miasma on the ground, and their forms changed. Some lost their limbs and became the wyrms. Others lost their front legs, becoming wyverns. I've heard that in the east there are dragons whose appearance changed even more drastically. And some, like me, changed into a form similar to humans."

Stroking the heart, Glenn continued to think. He couldn't deny that he would be unable treat this disease himself. Inside Skadi's slender chest, this heart tormented her. Her breathing had gradually become more labored. He had been right, he thought, and the second heart was causing her quite a bit of pain.

"I became close to humans. I can no longer return to my previous fire dragon form. Blood was spilled all across this continent because of the great war. That impurity and corruption built up—hng, ha-ah—I'm sure this disease is because of it," continued Skadi.

"I'm sorry, just a bit more," Glenn replied.

"Um... Uh... Dr. Glenn...?"

Glenn hadn't listened to most of what Skadi was saying—rather, he had been concentrating on his examination. He didn't believe her half-fairy tale story about the corruption of the earth or the realm of the gods had anything to do with her disease.

That dragons had come down from the skies, and their appearances changed over the course of their long lives—Glenn found that fact intriguing. He knew that coming from Skadi meant it must be true and that it involved a world Glenn couldn't even imagine. The Giant God Dionne that lived in the Vivre Mountains had also lived since ancient times, and was a species beyond his imagination.

But those facts and this disease were two different things. Tumors weren't created by miasma. They were a phenomenon that occurred when for some reason or another, an organ became swollen and grew in size. If that was the case, Glenn could use his knowledge to identify the cause of the tumor—or at least, he thought he could. At the very least, he *believed* he would be able to as he continued his examination.

"Um... Dr. Glenn... So you get it? I don't have any plans of treating this..." Skadi stammered.

"I'm going to continue my examination. How are your scales, I wonder...?" Glenn replied.

"Ah! Hng... Um..."

Dragons had scales in various places. They weren't smooth like Sapphee's, but bristled slightly with sharp, sword-like points. It appeared Glenn could cut himself on them if he touched them the wrong way. Being careful not to slice his fingers, Glenn stroked the dragon's scales ever so lightly, observing them.

"Hyah! Ah! Th-that tickles!" protested Skadi.

He checked the scales around her neck, on her back, and around her waist. All of them had a color closely resembling the blue heart that could be seen through her transparent skin. He needed to consider that her second heart and her blood vessels were made of a texture similar to her scales. Glenn imagined that a normal surgical needle wouldn't even pierce through them.

"Pardon me, but please allow me to examine here, too," said Glenn.

"Hng?!" Skadi jumped and let out a surprised yelp. Glenn had continued on to her tail.

"Uh, that's, um... a little..." said Skadi.

"The color here is different, it looks like," Glenn replied.

Skadi's tail color was gold or—he thought—possibly ocher. It wasn't sharp to the touch and was smooth like a snake's tail. Thick and strong, it gave Glenn the impression that he would be knocked out cold if he were hit with it. Judging from the difference in its color and touch, it was completely different from the other parts of her body. Glenn's curiosity was unending.

"During the ceremony, your tail was sagging. So you were straining yourself after all, then?"

"U-um my tail, gathers, um, nutrients. That's why, um, when I'm feeling under the weather it becomes thinner and hangs down... Ah, hng! H-how much longer...?" Skadi pleaded.

"I'm sorry, just a bit more."

There was a species of lizard native to harsh environments that stored nutrients in its tail in preparation for times of scarcity. Glenn wondered if Skadi's tail was similar. He thought it might be possible to measure a dragon's health by looking at the condition of their tail.

"U-umm... My tail's...sensitive, so... Ah!" protested Skadi.

"Hm? But I was sure I saw you fight with it before," Glenn replied.

"Th-the base is, s-sensitive... Hnnnn!"

So that's what it was, Glenn thought. Yet, his examination wasn't yet over. This time, his eyes moved toward the area around her back. Dragons were supposed to have wings similar to a bat, but there wasn't anything on Skadi's back. Once he lowered his gaze, however, he was immediately able to find them.

"Gyaaaah?!" Skadi exclaimed.

"Are these your wings...?" asked Glenn.

"Ah—Ah! Hng"

Growing from the small of her back was a pair of bat-like wings. Glenn thought them extremely small, even considering that they were folded up together. Fully extended, he imagined they wouldn't match the length of his arm span. It seemed extremely unlikely she would be able to fly with them, even if she flapped with all her might.

They gave the impression of only the atrophied remains of wings she once had. Glenn tried touching them. As soon as he did, Skadi's whole body jumped as if an ice cube had been placed against her back.

"Ah...Hng! S-stop, um, my wings, they're really..." Skadi said, struggling.

"I'm sorry, but since the disease is affecting your heart, I have to see if there are any other abnormalities elsewhere," said Glenn.

"Hnnnnngh! Th-the remains of my wings, it's too muuuuuch!" Skadi let out a voice Glenn had never heard before. "I-I'm telling you, it's too much...! Ahn, Dr. Glenn... Are you, listening to me...?"

Glenn was definitely listening. However, the examination took priority over Skadi's objections. Even if she was somewhat ticklish, all he could do was ask her to endure it for now. Fortunately, he didn't see anything irregular on her back. It seemed that Skadi's problems were limited to just the formation of the second heart in her chest, after all.

"Unh... Augh, ngh." All of Skadi's dignity as the Lindworm city council representative was long gone. Glenn had intended to do his best to be careful, but he couldn't help but become engrossed by his first experience giving a dragon a medical exam.

"Auuuugh..."

Focused completely on the disease, Glenn hadn't turned his eyes toward the most vital part of the exam—the patient herself.

Skadi was half-crying, yet trying hard to endure the tears, and to look at her, anyone would think she was just a normal child. Though, of course, she had aspects that were very different. She had many of the characteristics of a cold-blooded species. Glenn wondered if a "dragon" was an organism that mixed the characteristics of a snake and a lizard—but now wasn't the time to think about that.

"What's going on?" The door opened and Kunai rushed into the room. "I could hear the Lady Draconess crying! What exactly...is...going...?"

That's right, Glenn thought. There was no way a faithful servant like Kunai would let her master's cries pass her ears without response. And now that she had taken a step into the room, he could imagine the scene it presented would lead to even more of a misunderstanding.

No, Glenn assured himself. There was no way Kunai could misconstrue the situation. Even if she looked toward Glenn as he appeared to be forcing a young girl to take off her negligee and driving her to tears, when he remembered that Kunai had been the one to lead them there, he was positive she would understand that it was all part of the examination.

Or at least Glenn thought that she *should have* understood.

"............!" Sapphee didn't say a single word, even when she entered the room and saw the scene before her. But from the twitching of her eyes and the way her tail was up and shaking like a rattle, she was definitely ready to explode in anger, if still, for the moment, putting up with it. The fact that she was bearing with it meant that Sapphee understood that Glenn hadn't done anything indecent to Skadi to make her cry.

"Dr. Glenn," Kunai said, darting forward without hesitation. She tore Skadi away from him, adjusted her nightclothes, and fixed Glenn with a sharp glare.

"No—um—Miss Kunai? I believe you understand, but this is part of the examination," stammered Glenn.

"Of course. I understand very, very well, Dr. Glenn," Kunai replied. "You've mended my own body many times after all. You're often much more devoted to your examinations than you are willing to enjoy the body of a woman—oh yes, I am very well aware of your stranger personality quirks, Dr. Glenn."

That in itself was a misunderstanding, Glenn thought. He wasn't completely without any thoughts about the bodies of the monsters he examined, but as a doctor, it would be rude for these thoughts to show on his face or in his attitude, so he simply had to be careful. Naturally, the real problem lay in how much he was able to put that theory into practice.

"Nevertheless," Kunai said, yanking out her short sword. Glenn wondered in shock where she had been hiding it. It was hard to imagine there could have been a sword concealed on the lightly-dressed golem. "Yes, despite that, I will need you to apologize for making the Lady Draconess cry. As my sole mercy to you, I will try to make it painless and slice through your neck in one blow."

"W-wait just a second! That's a bit much, isn't it?!" replied Glenn.

"Of course, I won't let you die alone. I'll immediately cut open my own stomach. I'm the one who arranged for this to happen. I will take responsibility and go with you to the grave."

"What point is there in *you* committing suicide?!" asked Glenn. Considering she was made out of a collection of corpses, he couldn't believe what the flesh golem was saying.

But he understood. Kunai had gone mad. She had probably lost control at the unfamiliar sight of her master's tears. However, even if that were the case, Glenn wasn't sure he could stop her. Kunai Zenow was a seasoned warrior and had reached the top rank in the Lindworm Arena.

"Heh heh heh! I beg your apologies, my Lady Draconess—I will make this matter right this very moment..."

"Don't start parading out those eastern customs!" Glenn said. He couldn't even laugh at the idea of committing double suicide with the undead.

"W-wait just a minute, Kunai. It's okay, it's okay. I'm fine." Clinging to Kunai, Skadi was able to hold her down.

"Understood," Kunai replied. Skadi's pleading seemed to be the trigger. Kunai finally appeared to get a hold of herself. The usual calm shine returned to her eyes. "M-my Lady Draconess. Has any harm come to you?"

"I'm okay. Calm down a little," Skadi replied.

"I am always calm," Kunai declared nonchalantly. She probably tried to remain calm at all times, but because of how serious she was, it had truly looked like she was going to mete out justice against Glenn.

Anyway, Glenn thought, he had gotten out of trouble for now.

"That's enough, right? The exam is over. I'm... I'm going to rest a bit more," Skadi said, rubbing the leftover tears from her eyes.

"Certainly—forgive me for interrupting you during your rest," Glenn replied.

Skadi separated herself a little from Glenn. She seemed to be saying something, but with even just the small distance between them, Glenn could no longer pick up her voice.

That second heart—it was putting a burden on Skadi's original heart. Glenn thought that her inability to speak louder could also be due to the pressure that the second heart was putting on her chest. That second heart had laid roots inside Skadi far, far deeper than what Glenn had been able to see from the surface.

"...I wonder if dying would fix that adulterous habit of his," Sapphee muttered to herself, watching the exchange. Glenn was sure that Sapphee didn't intend for him to hear, but for some reason those words came to his ears much more clearly than normal.

From Glenn's perspective, this casual murmuring of Sapphee's was many times more frightening than Kunai brandishing her sword at him. He swore to himself that he would no longer give any easily-misconstrued examinations.

✖ ✖ ✖ ✖ ✖

It was still dark when Glenn and Sapphee left the Council Hall. Since it had grown quite late, Glenn and Sapphee both prepared for bed as soon as they got back to the clinic, but Glenn lay awake the rest of the night, thinking. How could they get rid of that second heart? Could he even heal such a rare disease?

The tumor had resembled a blue jewel. He wondered if the light was peculiar to the tumor, or if, perhaps, all dragons' hearts were accompanied by that metallic luster.

They had to get rid of the tumor. If they didn't, Skadi's life was truly in danger. Glenn wondered if he would be able to remove it using the surgical methods he was familiar with. Throughout the night, the thoughts swirled around his head.

✳ ✖ ✖ ✖ ✳

"...And?"

Glenn went into action the next day. After finishing the day's appointments, he headed straight for the director's office at the Central Hospital. His expression was so grim that he looked as though he were a soldier marching into enemy lines. Following behind him, Sapphee had a rare look of worry. She hadn't thought he would be doing something so direct right on the heels of what had happened last night.

In the director's office, Cthulhy was grappling with the innumerable documents on her desk. Behind her glasses, her pupils bore the same languid luster they always had.

"What are you asking of me?"

Glenn hadn't kept anything back from Cthulhy. He told her everything about the selfish examination he had given Skadi— and the second heart he had found out about as a result, as well as the fact that Skadi would die if the cause of her disease wasn't surgically removed.

And in addition to that, Glenn told her how it was impossible for him to treat her by himself.

"I'd like to ask for your assistance, Dr. Cthulhy," Glenn replied.

"Can't you just work together with Sapphee? You can't keep relying on your teacher forever, you know," said Cthulhy, curtly.

She was right. Sapphee *was* his partner. If Glenn sincerely asked her, she would lend him her aid. But he knew that wouldn't be enough this time. Of course, he knew that Sapphee's assistance would be necessary, but that didn't change his mind.

"That second heart of hers has already connected itself to the major blood vessels in her body. The fact that it's beating steadily is proof of this," Glenn began.

The fake heart had already become a part of Skadi's body. If they simply excised it, the blood flowing into it would hemorrhage. With that, there was no doubt the blood loss would prove fatal.

"To excise the tumor, it will be necessary to sever the blood vessels in the tumor and immediately connect them back to their original blood vessels. In order to connect the blood vessels without placing too much stress on the patient and to avoid hemorrhaging, it will be important to have speed and a lot of hands on deck," he continued.

He wondered if blood transfusion research was still being done at the academy. When Glenn had been there, blood transfusion as a treatment still wasn't ready for clinical practice. He remembered that there hadn't been anything more than a few successful animal trials.

If transfusion treatments were more established, they would be able to supplement the blood Skadi would lose in the surgery. However, when Glenn thought about it longer, he realized there was no way for them to procure dragon blood in a hurry anyway.

"That's why, with all your hands, I wanted to ask for your help, Dr. Cthulhy," Glenn said.

If they just had Cthulhy, she could use the eight legs of her lower body and the two arms on her upper body to effectively perform the surgery. It would be possible to perform multiple operations simultaneously—linking blood vessels back together as they excised the tumor. With her cooperation, Glenn was sure they could manage the surgery with twice, or even three times the speed.

Cthulhy listened in silence, not looking up to face Glenn.

"If you performed Skadi's surgery with me—"

"Thirty points," Cthulhy said, cutting Glenn off.

Glenn had been graded, just like when he was in the academy. He felt a twinge of nostalgia, but it was gone in an instant. His time studying under Cthulhy had long since passed.

"Glenn, you're talking about surgery, but did you get the patient's permission? Skadi doesn't want to be treated. That's, well, her own egotistical decision to find herself a good place to lie down and die, but... No matter what, you can't administer treatment so long as you don't have the patient's consent," Cthulhy continued.

"For that, well... I'll convince her."

"Come back to me when you have," Cthulhy replied.

Her argument was sound. Glenn, however, had no plans to acquiesce quietly. He had faith in his own convictions.

"In that case, suppose I'm able to convince her—will you lend us your help, Doctor?"

"Um, Dr. Glenn. You shouldn't be too unreasonable. I'm sure Dr. Cthulhy has her own ideas," said Sapphee. She looked worriedly between Glenn and Cthulhy. It appeared to Glenn that she couldn't side with either of them. He continued on, unconcerned by Sapphee's objections.

He wasn't convinced. Cthulhy was supposed to be Skadi's close friend. Despite that, Skadi remained without treatment and didn't even try to turn to Cthulhy for help. Cthulhy, for her part, had named herself as Skadi's primary doctor, yet hadn't forced anything on Skadi and was neglecting her.

Glenn couldn't understand it. He wondered who would be left with the most regrets if Skadi actually died. It was obvious, of course —Cthulhy would. If she acquiesced to Skadi's wishes, Cthulhy was the one who would regret it most of all. Glenn had no idea how the two had formed their deep friendship, but what he did know was that when Skadi had become apprehensive about the lack of capable doctors in Lindworm, it was Cthulhy she had hired as the hospital director.

Skadi was sick, so all she had to do was rely on Cthulhy. If she did, then Glenn was sure Cthulhy would respond. If the two of them had had a proper doctor-patient relationship, he was sure that he wouldn't even have had to be involved to begin with.

"I will convince her," he said. "I will change Miss Skadi's way of thinking."

"..............."

"So please lend us a hand. Let's save Miss Skadi together. You know you'll regret it... So please don't even think about saying those sad things about not saving her, Dr. Cthulhy."

She was thought of as a lazy woman. She would immediately give Glenn any annoying job she had, and Glenn had heard that even at the hospital she only dealt with a small fraction of the patients. "Bothersome" was declared to be her favorite word, so she was often misunderstood. Even at the academy, she was said to often leave her students to their own devices.

But Glenn knew—it wasn't laziness. No matter who she was dealing with, Cthulhy would draw the line somewhere. She didn't venture past doing only what was necessary because she, herself, didn't like it when people pushed her. But what his mentor hated most of all was when someone bluntly interfered with her own ideas and shouted unnecessary things at her—exactly like Glenn was doing now.

"You're just an amateur. You sure make it sound simple, don't you?" Cthulhy replied, glaring at Glenn as though a tempest raged inside of her. Her tentacles wiggled back and forth like they were a flame expressing her anger. If something sparked her ire, her tentacles had enough force to tighten themselves around Glenn in an instant.

"Glenn. You're talking about excising the tumor, but you're being presumptuous in thinking the three of us can even do that.

Do you even understand how deeply that heart clinging to Skadi has taken root inside her body? That isn't just a tumor. It altered her blood circulation on its own, and is continuing to beat and take all of Skadi's blood for itself. It isn't even accurate to call it a tumor. That thing is like a heart-shaped parasite."

A parasite. Glenn understood at last. That heart wasn't something that grew from within Skadi—it was caused by some external factor. The heart itself might just be the parasite. Although—he had never heard of a parasite mimicking a heart.

"That thing is almost like a mollusk, slowly spreading its limbs little by little. Day after day, it pulls in her blood vessels and eats away at Skadi's arteries. Finally, it will replace Skadi's heart. That fake heart has already stretched its limbs into close to a hundred of her blood vessels. Listen, Glenn, do you think you can deal with all of those blood vessels with just those two arms of yours?" Cthulhy continued.

"That's why, with your help, Doctor—" Glenn replied.

"If it were something that could be done with my eight legs, I would have done it a long time ago!" yelled Cthulhy.

Glenn nodded. She had finally spoken her mind. Without a doubt, he knew Cthulhy's sorrowful voice had said what she was truly feeling. Glenn's blunt, impudent words had finally gotten Cthulhy to open up to him.

His mentor was quite the handful.

However, Glenn himself was quite the handful of a student. Thus, it was only natural that Glenn took great pains when dealing with his mentor, just as much as she had taken pains when dealing with him. Fortunately, while they were both a handful, the two of them shared over ten hands between them. That was more than enough, Glenn thought.

"...Hey, Glenn," Cthulhy said. Her octopus legs smoothly spread outward. Glenn instinctively took hold of the tentacles as they wrapped themselves around his arm, but the way they tightened around him was somewhat gentle. There was no pain, and Glenn only felt the sensation of the suckers holding fast to his arm as if they were relying on him for support.

"Yes, Dr. Cthulhy?"

"Can you really...convince her?"

"I'll do everything in my power to," Glenn said. He still didn't clearly understand either the suffering Skadi was enduring or her reason for refusing treatment. He guessed that the reason was something only Skadi knew.

However, he would do everything in his power to treat his patients. If treatment was necessary, then he simply had to convince the patient as well. Of course, with Skadi being the patient, he knew she would be a very tough person to deal with.

"I tried to convince her too, you know. I told her she wouldn't be cured without surgery. Of course that bodyguard... Kunai, was it? I'm sure even she's suggested it every chance she could get. We said all of that, yet the stubborn little dragon girl didn't once even consider changing her mind. You're saying you can do it despite all of that?"

"Yes, I can. I'll try my best," replied Glenn.

"Why are you doing all this? You aren't that close with Skadi, right? You're not like me at all— you aren't her friend or anything like it."

"...That might be true."

"In that case, why?"

The two hadn't known each other for a long time. To Glenn, Skadi wasn't just the city representative, but the relationship they had formed together wasn't one of close friendship, either. Nevertheless, Glenn had any number of reasons for his actions.

"Well, because..." Glenn began. As a doctor, he couldn't overlook Skadi's illness. Nor could he overlook it as a human being. However, the biggest reason was... "You're the one who wants to save Skadi the most, aren't you, Doctor?"

A jolt of surprise ran through Cthulhy's extended tentacles. She looked hard at Glenn. As one would guess from the high-quality glasses on her nose, Cthulhy was extremely near-sighted. As such, her sharp looks weren't because she was in a sour mood, but because she was trying to ascertain what the person she was talking to was thinking.

"What did you say?" asked Cthulhy.

"You've already come up with a surgical plan. You've even been trying to convince Miss Skadi already, correct? Why is that? The answer's obvious, isn't it?" Glenn replied.

"...I suppose so."

"You want to save Skadi more than anyone else does, Dr. Cthulhy. The reason I've come all the way here is because I know that. I feel the same way, Doctor."

Next to Glenn, Sapphee heaved a deep sigh. But while it

was a sigh of exasperation, there wasn't any fatigue or bewilderment mixed with it. It seemed to be defending Glenn's actions, as though she was reassuring him that while things would get tough for them, she would still stay by his side.

He had been able to boldly challenge his mentor precisely because he had Sapphee at his side.

"You two." Cthulhy's tentacles rushed forward. She rose up from her desk and crept toward Glenn and Sapphee. Her spreading tentacles stroked Glenn's face and began sticking themselves to his cheeks with a loud popping sound.

"Huh... Wha—Me too?! Eeek!" Sapphee cried.

The tentacles of the scylla were expandable, and had much more volume than it seemed. They were quite long if they were stretched out to their limit, and with these tentacles, Cthulhy had also been able to apprehend Sapphee.

With the octopus legs and snake tail entangling one another, Glenn couldn't tell what was what, but Cthulhy began sticking herself to Sapphee's scales with her suckers to try and ascertain something.

"You *really* have aged, haven't you?" said Cthulhy.

"I-I am still quite young!" Sapphee protested.

"No, you have aged. You've aged more than I would have ever imagined when I was teaching you at the Academy. You've grown up," Cthulhy said, not giving any heed to Sapphee's rebuttal.

Glenn simply stayed quiet and let the tentacles stuck to his arms and face do as they pleased. He knew from the many times he had been showered in this tentacle baptism before that this was his mentor's way of giving a hug. Despite wanting to show her gratitude, it was too embarrassing for her, and her hugs took on this shape as a result.

"Dr. Cthulhy, if you stick to me that much, I'll... Ah... W-wait a second, where are you touching... Ahn!" Sapphee said, struggling.

This was Cthulhy's awkward expression of affection. Glenn tried as much as possible not to look toward Sapphee as strange noises escaped from her mouth. He had a feeling that if he carelessly looked at Sapphee at the moment, he'd be scolded by her once again. No matter what sort of cries she made, he would do everything he could to avoid paying her any mind.

"W-wait... Ah, Hng...!"

Glenn pretended not to notice. Nothing was happening, he thought.

"Ah, that's my—Hng... Ahn! D-Dr. Glenn... h-help me..."

He kept trying not to pay any attention to what was happening—but it would have been impossible for him, even if his heart were made of steel. He didn't know what in the world she was doing to Sapphee, but the mucus-lathered tentacles had been making some suspiciously sticky sounds for the past several seconds.

"Saphentite. He's given you a lot of trouble, too, hasn't he?" Cthulhy asked.

"Huh... What...?" replied Sapphee.

"Glenn is so young and reckless, it must be hard for you, right?"

"Ah—hng! Um, what are...you talking about?"

"I mean, it's gratitude, it's gratitude from your teacher."

The viscous sound of mucus on scale echoed through the

office. It felt good to be appreciated, but Cthulhy's show of appreciation was far too peculiar, and if anything, it seemed to Glenn like Sapphee was the one exhausted by the whole affair.

"Dr. Cthulhy, um, that's enough, isn't it?" said Glenn.

"You too, Glenn... You're all grown up."

The tentacles went around to the nape of Glenn's neck and the suckers fastened themselves to him. For a moment the tentacle communication continued, with the suckers attaching and detaching from his skin. Just as Glenn felt that the back of his neck was beginning to hurt, the tentacles gave one long final suck, almost like a kiss. Then, finally satisfied, Cthulhy released the pair.

"I'm so happy my pupils are growing up. Pretty soon I'll be able to retire," said Cthulhy.

Cthulhy's wish was to retire and freely devote herself completely to research. She would often comment that she was never cut out to be a teacher or a doctor to begin with.

Sapphee straightened out her clothes and got her breathing back to normal. It seemed that the tentacles had been so unrelenting as to wedge themselves under Sapphee's clothes.

"Still Glenn, even if you're going to perform surgery, there's a whole mountain of problems to deal with," she continued, the face of the exceptional doctor stiffening. "I'll leave convincing Skadi up to you. But even if you get her to agree, we still don't have enough people. Even if you and I work with everything we have, we still won't be fast enough to suture all her blood vessels."

"I-I'll help, too," Sapphee said, putting her hand on her chest, but—

"Saphentite. You're in charge of the anesthesia. It's heart surgery, so we'll need a full-body anesthetic," Cthulhy replied, shaking her head.

"Anesthesia..."

"There isn't any precedent for giving a full-body anesthetic to a dragon. If you fail, then it'll all be over, and there isn't anyone else who would be able to make the anesthetic besides you. You need to make absolutely perfect preparations. During the surgery, it'll be your job to keep track of how the anesthetic is working."

Sapphee made a big gulp. As a pharmacologist, it went without saying that Sapphee was knowledgeable about how to administer anesthesia. She had her own job to do. They couldn't entrust her work to anyone else.

"I want one more person to help us," said Cthulhy. "I want almost no gap in time between when we excise the fake heart and when we stitch together the blood vessels. I want to keep the blood loss as low as possible. If we don't do that, even if we start the surgery, the amount of blood loss could end up becoming fatal."

"...Yes, that is true, but..."

"We still don't have enough people. We just need one more. Someone close to you, Glenn, and Sapphee, too... If there's room to hope, they should be someone close enough to you that you can communicate with just a glance. Despite all that, they have to be a doctor, skilled at delicate work. Especially if they are good at using a needle and thread for suturing," Cthulhy continued.

"Is there someone we could ask here at the hospital...?" Glenn replied.

"Unfortunately, while all I've done here is teach my students to become effective doctors, there isn't one we could rely on that has your level of skill, Glenn."

Cthulhy's words were high praise for him to hear. At the same time, it meant that there wasn't one person in the Central Hospital that could keep up with Glenn and Cthulhy.

Cthulhy had approved of Glenn becoming an independent town doctor, but the key point was that, even now, Glenn was the only one who had received her permission to do so. This was how strict of a mentor Cthulhy was. It was not often that a student of hers could match up to him.

"They don't necessarily need to be a doctor or a nurse. Worst case scenario, they don't even need to know anything about medicine."

Cthulhy's suggestion was completely outrageous, Glenn thought.

"If they're well-versed in using thread and proficient with their fingers, then that's fine," Cthulhy continued. "Someone who can follow my instructions and suture the blood vessels, and someone who can stay in sync with you and Sapphee. At any rate, it has to be someone who can wield a thread and needle as fast as we can…"

"Impossible. There's no way someone that convenient—" Glenn began. *Wait,* Glenn thought, stopping mid-sentence. Right as he began to say that someone that perfect couldn't possibly exist, he suddenly realized something. There was someone like that—just one. They had no medical knowledge, but they were more of an expert with a needle and thread than Glenn was.

What's more—this person was friends with Sapphee. They were probably the most dexterous person in all of Lindworm.

"...Dr. Glenn," said Sapphee, speaking up.

"Yeah."

It seemed that Sapphee had thought the same thing. The two of them exchanged a forceful nod.

"...Do you happen to know someone like that?" asked Cthulhy.

"Yes. Although she can be...a little hard to read," Glenn replied.

"It doesn't matter. Make sure that they can help us perform the surgery."

Glenn wondered if she'd agree to help them. No, he thought, they *had* to have her agree to help. An important step, then, would be to convince her to help, just like with Skadi. It was a problem that he needed to overcome, no matter what, in order to save Skadi's life.

"By the way—what is this person's name?" asked Cthulhy.

"Arahnia Taranterra Arachnida," answered Sapphee. Word for word, it was the exact name that had come to Glenn's mind.

The Self-Deprecating Cyclops

"**N**O THANK YOU." Her answer was immediate. "Such an engagement would be absolutely impossible for one such as myself."

"Please, Miss Arahnia. We came to the conclusion that you were the best possible fit for the job," Glenn said.

"Even if that were true..." said Arahnia, frowning. She seemed to be troubled by Glenn's words. Glenn still believed she was a woman who kept her true intentions difficult to read, but at that moment she did appear to be truly at a loss.

"Miss Arahnia, I've been put in the position of handling all of the preparations for this operation. My master, Cthulhy Squele, will be the one conducting Miss Skadi's surgery."

"Yes, I saw in the papers. How awful, truly."

"Miss Skadi's disease is a rare one without any precedent, so there will be many firsts involved in Cthulhy doing the surgery, as well. That's why I want to gather the best of the best to assist her... Miss Arahnia, that person is you."

"Why, I am thrilled to be held in such high regard. It is an honor to hear that from someone such as yourself, Doctor."

The unequaled expert when it came to a needle and thread, Arahnia Taranterra Arachnida, still had that troubled look on her face after listening to Glenn's wishes. She seemed to be doing needlework of some kind, four of her arms embroidering a piece of cloth faster than Glenn was able to follow with his eyes.

"But I must say..." she continued. "To come while I am working to talk about other employment like this. The branch manager will start keeping tabs on me, you know."

"M-my apologies. Nonetheless," Glenn stammered.

"Just a little joke, Doctor," Arahnia replied, looking as though she was enjoying herself as she took in Glenn's troubled expression. She was just as crafty a woman as ever.

As she had said, she did seem to be in the middle of working. There were a great number of arachne who worked at the Lindworm branch of Loose Silk Sewing. There were women reeling in the silk they produced from their abdomens, women using that silk to sew, and some who were using sewing scissors and foot-pedal sewing machines to make clothes. From silk, to cloth, to clothes, the process required a wide variety of jobs.

Everyone working there was an arachne woman. Of course, Glenn knew that arachne were a women-only race of monsters in the first place. However—

"For a little while now... I've kind of felt like I'm being stared at," said Glenn.

"Well, now, Doctor. That would be because you've brazenly

walked into a business that only employs arachne," Arahnia said with a suggestive laugh. "Arachne are all women, and we have to capture men from other races to have children. It's only natural that the impassioned gazes of these nubile arachne would find their way to you. That's to say nothing of the fact that humans are very popular."

"Humans...are popular?"

"That's right. For you see, human men are small and easy to catch, and they are timid and submissive. With them as partners, we can work them hard for the rest of our lives, and as such, they are quite a bit more popular than men of other monster races. Were you unaware of this?"

This was the first time Glenn had heard about arachne marriage. Hearing this, he could only feel a sense of dread at the ardent gazes boring into him.

While not to the same degree as with dragons, there were still many mysteries surrounding the arachne as well. The fact that they only gave birth to women was strange in the first place. As a basic rule, organisms could only mate with organisms of the same species, but many of the monster races, including centaurs, lamia, and mermaids, were able to mate with humans. But other than the arachne, there were no cases of a species that only gave birth to women.

That they could mate with one another meant that that humans and monsters might actually be quite similar as organisms. Monster-human relationships happened often enough for such a hypothesis to come about. In fact, Lindworm recognized marriages between monster and human, and the centaur Tisalia had repeatedly asked Glenn for a marriage interview.

"............"

Having accompanied Glenn, Sapphee menaced the arachne in the building with a sharp glare. For a while now, her tail had been vibrating back and forth. Her wariness and mistrust was at its peak.

Despite Sapphee's glares, the arachne continued to look toward Glenn ever more, whispering to each other and snickering quietly. It was terrifying that even while they amused themselves in sizing up the man in front of them, their hands didn't stop moving for a single second. Glenn imagined that every one of the arachne women that was gathered there was an absolute expert when it came to clothing.

"Now, now, Sapphee, don't be angry. Everyone here is starved for love and gossip, you know. Why, after all, they spend all day in here working," Arahnia said.

"I'm not angry," Sapphee replied.

"My Sapphee, you truly are precious when you're all full of jealousy like this," Arahnia said, smiling. She was wearing a monocle that appeared to be for her work, but in a strange twist, also had a total of three lenses. Glenn assumed that the differing sizes of lenses had been specially ordered to match up with all six of Arahnia's eyes, but when he considered how expensive regular glasses were, he wondered just how much such a special order would cost. Leave it to a designer, he thought, not to compromise on the quality of her clothing and accessories, no matter the cost.

"Now, if your business is finished, I'll have to ask you to leave quickly. I'll be in quite a pickle if I don't finish this today."

"Please... Can we please work something out? Miss Arahnia. I'm begging you." Glenn bowed his head, but Arahnia simply shook hers.

"I'm a designer. It would be fine if we were talking about clothing, but running a thread and needle through a patient? Why, there's no way I can do that so easily. If I play my part poorly, and the surgery fails... Wouldn't I then have to bear much of the responsibility?"

"I accept all responsibility. So long as you're able to follow our instructions."

"You may *say* that, Doctor, but I wonder what the townspeople would think? If the papers started writing things suggesting the surgery failed entirely because the completely untrained Miss Arahnia had participated, what then?"

"That's, well..."

"They can write whatever they want about me, but the thought of losing the trust of Loose Silk Sewing... Well, I'm sure you can understand, yes?"

Glenn imagined that it was precisely because Arahnia was so obsessive and something of an artist that she became so earnest when it came to her work. That being said, her earnestness was very *unique* and did not necessarily line up with conventional common sense and morality.

"I'm truly very sorry, but I'd ask you to find someone else for this task..." Arahnia began.

"Arahnia," said Sapphee.

Just as Glenn thought that it was going to be impossible to convince her, Arahnia lifted her head at Sapphee's call. He imagined that Arahnia must have picked up on the seriousness in Sapphee's voice. Her hands even stopped their work.

"You're fine with this? Really?" Sapphee said.

"Whether I'm fine with it or not, for me to practice medicine—why, it's just out of the question."

"As long as you agree to work with us, we'll give you constant direction. We'll explain it all to the Loose Silk Sewing branch manager. We'll make you a clinic employee for a little while."

"And?"

"Basically, what I'm saying is," Sapphee said, smiling suddenly, "you'll be able to wear a nurse outfit matching my own."

"I'll do it. No, please, *let* me help you!"

Glenn didn't even get a moment to wonder if Sapphee's persuasion would work. Arahnia even cast aside the fabric she was working on and took Sapphee's hand. Glenn knew that Sapphee's nurse outfit had been specially made by Arahnia herself. Thinking about it further, Arahnia *did* have a strange attachment to her close friend Saphentite

"...*That's* what did it?" Glenn asked.

"What are you saying, Doctor?! Of *course!* Sapphee's outfit is the only one of its kind in the whole world—a miraculous fusion of a strong light-blocking inner layer and a nurse's outfit overflowing with a feeling of cleanliness! Naturally, it would take a considerable amount of adjustment for me to wear it, but a chance to wear *matching* outfits? Why, it's a once in a lifetime opportunity!" Arahnia said.

"Um, couldn't you just wear that normally?"

"Why, as if I would wear a *nurse's outfit* without any reason!"

Glenn couldn't empathize with Arahnia's obsession with clothes at all. Nevertheless, she was finally interested. Despite how she had given every excuse she could think of to turn Glenn down, she had responded with ease to Sapphee's pointed persuasion.

"Now that it's been decided, we have to win over the branch manager immediately! We haven't a moment to lose!" Arahnia continued.

"U-um, Miss Arahnia? Is it really okay?" Glenn replied.

"I'm prepared for the worse! Sapphee and I! The two of us together will make *sure* this is a success! Why, at the end of the day, sewing cloth isn't that much different from sewing blood vessels, right?"

The change in attitude was intense, thought Glenn. With her natural agility, Arahnia rushed off deeper into the building. Left behind, Glenn was stunned by her immediate change in attitude. He wondered if things would actually play out this easily.

"We're close friends, after all," Sapphee said, turning toward Glenn and giving him a wink. "I know her very well. I'm sure Arahnia will be a big help to us."

"Did Miss Arahnia really want to wear a matching outfit *that* badly?" Glenn asked.

"Of course not." Sapphee gave a sarcastic laugh. "I'm sure the reason she was hesitating to accept the offer was because she was waiting for a concession from us. That woman's heart is completely black— she was just pretending that she didn't want any part of it until we proposed a compromise that was convenient for her."

"Is that so..."

So it was all a part of the negotiations, Glenn thought. His failure to notice it meant he was once again relying on Sapphee for everything.

"That's why, with the promise of wearing matching outfits, I pretended to meet her halfway. If she was still unwilling after that, the conversation would be over, so she accepted," explained Sapphee.

"...Wait. If that's the case, does that mean that Miss Arahnia had something *else* in mind in accepting the offer?" Glenn asked.

"Probably. Although I'm sure her desire to wear matching outfits with me wasn't a total lie. I think she'll face the task at hand seriously, but be careful, Doctor."

Glenn had been tricked by Arahnia once before. He knew that he should be cautious around her. Arahnia wasn't at all a bad person, but there were times when she felt that the ends justified her means.

"...Thank you again, Sapphee. I'd be lost without you."

"Of course. You still need a lot more experience, Dr. Glenn."

All Glenn was able to do was once again express his appreciation to his always dependable assistant.

While he had convinced Arahnia—although Glenn questioned if that was the right way to describe it—there was still a mountain of problems to tackle.

First was training Arahnia. Although she was proficient with a needle and thread, suturing a body was not the same as sewing up fabric. They needed to teach her from the ground up about stitching together nerves and blood vessels.

For the time being, Sapphee was put in charge of teaching Arahnia the basics. This was partly because even if Arahnia harbored some other intentions, Sapphee would be able to see through them. Fortunately, it seemed Arahnia was a quick learner, and it was fine to leave her to Sapphee for the time being.

The Lindworm branch manager of Loose Silk Sewing had agreed to let Arahnia visit the clinic under the condition that she would do so until the end of Skadi's surgery, regardless of whether it was a success or not. She said that seeing more of the world and taking part in a different kind of work would refine Arahnia's sensibilities as a designer.

"The branch manager is quite broad-minded, so she doesn't lament when her skilled designer goes off somewhere else." Arahnia laughed as she said this, but Glenn couldn't help but hear Arahnia's cynicism toward the branch manager in her words. Nevertheless, he could tell her cynicism didn't necessarily mean Arahnia had wanted the branch manager to stop her from leaving.

Glenn wanted to help coach Arahnia himself, but he had other things he had to take care of.

First, he had a meeting with Cthulhy to draw up their surgical plan. Since there was no precedent for performing surgery on a dragon, he wanted to properly investigate all points of uncertainty and concern.

Most importantly, he also had to convince Skadi. Glenn had wanted to go through Kunai to set up another opportunity to speak with Skadi, but things weren't going very well. Skadi had already returned to her official business as the city council's representative. It didn't seem at all like she was afflicted with a rare and serious disease. It was almost as if she were throwing the whole rest of her life into her work.

And in order to resolve another problem, Glenn had left the clinic in Sapphee's hands and arrived at a certain place on a corner of the main road.

"All right, then..." Glenn said, wiping sweat from his forehead. He had arrived at the Kuklo Workshop.

The heat was intense. It seemed to come not just from the furnaces themselves, but the fiery passion of the workmen as well. It was a huge workshop, filled with hardworking craftsmen.

It had formerly specialized in blacksmithing, but as the years passed, the workshop had gathered a variety of craftsmen. Now they didn't just specialize in metal, but dealt in all manner of everyday goods, from glassware and pottery to wood processing and brickwork as well. Making textile products would infringe on Loose Silk Sewing's business, so Glenn was sure they had formed some contract with one another, but if he was to put it simply, the Kuklo Workshop handled anything that didn't involve fabric.

Inside the workshop, a number of the giant craftsmen hurried around at their work, while others sat quietly, faces turned down toward their current projects. Glenn could also see a giant machine whirring loudly, although he didn't really know what it was.

A water mill was being used to power the machines. The workshop's production was supported by the stable waters from the Waterways. The canals that ran all over Lindworm weren't just for the mermaids to travel around in, but were also used in many such applications.

Glenn relied on the workshop to supply him with his medical equipment. With the precision that his surgical needles, clamps, and scalpels required, as well as how often he had to throw out his tools for sanitary concerns, he thought that without the aid of the Kuklo Workshop, it might have been impossible for him to be a doctor at all. Indeed, it was the craftsmen of this workshop he had called on previously to make Tisalia's horseshoes. The place had been taking care of him and helping him for a long time.

As Glenn thought these things, he came upon a face he knew among the giants working around him.

"Hey," he called out.

"Eek!" The girl jumped back as soon as Glenn called out to her. "A h-h-human...?!"

"Well, yes, I am human, but it's me, Glenn. Nice to see you, Memé."

"A-ah, it's you, Dr. Glenn... That's all..." The young girl, small compared to those around her, still timidly glanced toward Glenn even after realizing he was a familiar face. "I-it's been a while since

I've seen a member of another race... I still get surprised by people with two eyes."

"Well, I suppose that makes sense. Though I think biologically speaking it's more rare to have only one eye."

"Th-that's true. Only having one eye looks scary anyway..."

Glenn scratched his head. He had called out to a young girl named Memé Redon.

Similar to the arachne of Loose Silk Sewing, the craftsmen of the Kuklo Workshop were entirely cyclops—massive one-eyed giants with strong, muscular bodies. With their large frames, about one size larger than a human being, they were classified as one of the giant monster races. But in contrast to their gigantic bodies, their species was very skilled with their hands.

The young cyclops girl before him—Memé Redon—was no exception. With her craftsmanship earning the trust of the workshop boss, she worked as the only woman apprentice in the whole shop.

Of course, the cyclops's defining feature was their big, round eye. But it seemed that to Memé, her eye was a symbol of her inferiority complex. She hid it by growing out her black bangs, and constantly looked down at the ground. She seemed to have a trace of anthrophobia, and her normal response to just being talked to was always to get frightened and apologize, much as she had done with Glenn.

She often spoke and acted servilely because of her inferiority complex and would make self-deprecating comments at the drop of a hat.

"H-how unusual for you to come to the workshop, Dr. Glenn."

"Yeah, I have a bit of a request to make."

"...Thank you for your patronage, as always," Memé replied, giving Glenn a look that suggested she had something else she wanted to say. The main characteristic of the cyclops—their single eye—projected the feelings and emotions of its owner very clearly. However in Memé's case, her timidity got the better of her, and her eye darted left and right suspiciously. She would rarely look the person she was talking with in the eye.

Glenn himself couldn't forget the shock he was given when he first met a cyclops, but through his work as a doctor of monster medicine, he had simply gotten used to them. But with how shy Memé was, she had become hypersensitive about the looks that other races gave her. As a result, her voice became shrill and panicked when she stood facing another person and talked with them.

"It's been a while since I've been here, but is everyone doing well?"

"I-I suppose. Stiff shoulders and back pain come with the work, so I wouldn't say we're *that* healthy... Heck, even I look pale and have a bag under my eye... I bet I look sick, don't I?"

"Now I never said that, did I?" Glenn replied. It was true that there was a bag under Memé's eye. At first glance she seemed in poor health, but Glenn was sure that it was just a result of poor hygiene and a lack of sleep.

Even humans could form bags under their eyes from the muscles around them growing weak. This was especially true for cyclops because their eyes were so big and heavy, and as such, their orbicularis oculi muscles would tire easily. For cyclops, a bag under the eye was a typical trait of their people and didn't need to be given any extra attention.

"...Is there anything bothering you?" Glenn asked.

"It's fine, it's fine, I'm sure I'm just going to get run into by people and run over by carriages anyway, so nothing's going to change much anyway, even if I say anything," Memé replied.

"...Cyclops do have a hard time with their depth perception, after all. But, if you don't properly watch where you're going, Memé, you'll get in an accident someday."

"A-and look people in the eyes?! I-impossible, totally impossible..."

Glenn sighed. This was how things usually went when he met with Memé. He was worried about whether she would be able to survive in the harsh business inside the workshop, but there were many elderly and middle-aged craftsmen who worked there and treated her tenderly, like she was their daughter or granddaughter. Memé had been accepted by the boss himself and made an apprentice there, so Glenn was sure she had quite the talent as well.

"W-what? You're staring at me..."

"Oh, sorry."

Glenn surmised that she was still around fifteen years old. She had black hair and white skin, and was wearing a thin undershirt and an apron, but it only concealed her chest and stomach, with her shoulders, arms, and back left exposed. Inside the workshop, filled with the hot air of the furnaces, it only made sense to Glenn that she would be wearing such thin clothing.

She wore a style of pants from the east known as "hakama"—

suitable for working in the hot workshop. She had flame-proof sleeves on her arms and with them a pair of leather gloves. Although her clothing was light, she was securely protected from any risk of burning herself.

Cyclops men were large, but cyclops women weren't that much different in size from humans. That said, their hands were a bit on the large side, with thick fingers. Memé gripped a hammer she was using for her work, but it didn't look heavy at all as she wielded it. It gave Glenn a glimpse of why the cyclops were known as a giant race of monsters.

Glenn imagined Memé could probably lift a person around his size. He had been lifted into Tisalia's arms as well—there were many examples of women monsters boasting impressive strength.

Despite how professional and practical she looked, she also paid close attention to her own appearance. The triangular white bandana on her head had become her trademark, and the back of her hair was intricately tied up in a three-part braid. It was quite an elaborate hairstyle. Glenn imagined it took a long time to arrange.

What was even more eye-catching was the earring attached to her left ear. It was a simple piece of metalwork, but something that Memé had made herself. The fact that she could produce such craftsmanship with ease signaled to Glenn that she had a bright future ahead of her.

"What have you been working on lately?" Glenn asked.

"H-huh? U-um, kitchen knives, drawknives... They're having me brush up on the small stuff... I'm still an apprentice, anyway... So I just get all the odd jobs," Memé replied.

"But you've graduated from doing the deliveries, right?"

"I can't *bear* doing any more deliveries... Talking to other people is *terrifying...*"

"Just the same as ever..." said Glenn. Memé laughed in self-deprecation. She had a bit of an eerie look to her as she gazed off in a different direction.

Previously, Memé's job had been to deliver the tools made in the workshop to their respective customers. As such, Memé had always delivered the tools Glenn needed for the clinic. It was sad that even though Sapphee and Glenn were already familiar faces to her, Memé would never look them straight in the eye.

But now, Glenn realized, Memé was being given jobs to work on besides making deliveries. He thought it might not be long before she made a name for herself as the craftswoman of the workshop. Although he imagined for *that* to happen she would have to do something about her timid attitude.

"All right, then. Hey, Memé, is the boss around? I have a difficult job I'd like to talk to him about."

"Oh, yes, hold on..." she replied.

Memé led the way for Glenn, but due to her long bangs and her habit of looking down at the ground, her steps were completely unreliable. Glenn truly wished she would look where she was going as she walked.

There were many dangers within the workshop. The smell of melted iron, the high-pitched ringing of hammers pounding steel, and the heat that made Glenn want to tear off his lab coat. The unique sights and sounds of the Kuklo Workshop had a certain charm to it—slightly different from the tourist appeal of the Merrow Waterways—but if one staggered through the workshop, accidents were bound to happen. In fact, there were many instances every year of a cyclops from the workshop being brought in to his clinic to have their injuries treated.

"Augh!" Memé cried.

Just as Glenn was thinking this, sure enough, Memé collided with a cyclops carrying some materials. Once more, it proved unnecessary to even say—since cyclops had only one eye, they didn't have a proper sense of depth perception.

"Whoops—are you okay?" Glenn said, supporting Memé as she looked on the verge of falling backwards. But that only made things all the worse. Catching her in his arms, Glenn was now peering down at her.

"Augh... G-get awaaay!" Memé shouted.

"Whoa!" This time Glenn was the person being pushed away. Even female cyclops could exhibit a considerable amount of strength in the blink of an eye. But while she pushed him away, Glenn felt that Memé was really the one who was confused. She fell backwards.

"Ow!" Memé exclaimed. The recoil sent the both of them flopping onto the ground. There was a dull sound. The moment Memé fell on her backside, tools of some kind fell out of the front pocket of her apron and scattered about. Glenn wondered if they hadn't been tucked properly into her pocket, or if the force of the impact had just been too great.

"Oh..." said Glenn.

Whatever had happened, Memé had gotten caught by some tool or another. Glenn could hear the sound of tearing fabric. Just as Memé had fallen on her backside, the hakama she was wearing was softly torn in two.

"Aaaaaaaaaaaaaaaugh?!" Memé's cry echoed through the workshop.

With her clothes torn, Glenn could clearly see Memé's underwear from his position on the floor. Everything was in view, from her white thighs to her groin. The slight change of her skin color from her sweat in the heart of the workshop burned themselves into Glenn's vision.

She was wearing a style of loincloth underwear from the east, known as the "fundoshi."

I see, Glenn thought—the fundoshi was both breathable and sweat-absorbent, and overflowing with a type of functional beauty that a craftsman would appreciate.

A few seconds later—Glenn felt that it was only to be expected— in her confusion, Memé slapped his face with all of her strength. With tears streaming from her large eye, Memé left to change her clothes and then returned to showing Glenn through the workshop.

"If you don't properly watch where you're going, you'll fall again," Glenn said.

"No... He saw, he saw everything... Now I'll never be able to get married, though I guess it's not like I was ever going to be able to get married in the first place," Memé mumbled, sniffling. Glenn felt bad that he had seen her underwear, but also really didn't think that she needed to cry so much.

Despite her tears, Memé still guided Glenn along. But between crying and not looking ahead as usual, there was no telling when she would fall down again. Even with all the uproar, it didn't appear that any of the cyclops around them had registered what happened, so Glenn wondered if, in fact, this sort of scene was relatively common with Memé.

Continuing behind Memé on tenterhooks, he arrived in front of a behemoth clad in leather working-clothes.

"B-b-boss..."

"Oh, Memé... And looks like we have a visitor, too," replied the middle-aged cyclops, arms folded. He was the foreman of the workshop. Referred to simply as "boss" by the other workers, he was the greatest craftsman in Lindworm.

Right in front of him was a forge spitting out heat from its gaping mouth. It was the Kuklo Workshop's great forge, and it was said that the fires inside of it burned endlessly throughout the year. No matter the workshop, the fires of the forge were held sacred.

It appeared the boss had just taken some molten iron out from the forge, and a number of cyclops took turns pounding it down with a hammer. It was still impossible for Glenn to tell what they were making, but the forging seemed quite large-scale.

The boss stared intensely at the forging without joining in with the work. Glenn assumed the thing they were making required the boss's direct supervision.

"What on earth has brought you here, young Doctor? We've delivered your tools for the month, haven't we?" asked the boss.

"Oh, no, that's not why I'm here," Glenn replied.

"In that case, is it about payment? You're usually good about paying us properly, so I didn't think there were any problems... Either way, your clinic is a good customer of ours. Waiting a little for payment won't be the end of the world."

"I'll pay you properly. That's not why I'm here, either," Glenn continued. The boss narrowed his one eye and stared hard at Glenn. As one might expect, the gaze of the commanding master craftsman was sharp. His eye was just as effective as his mouth at expressing himself—in fact, sometimes the colossal eye of the cyclops would express something far more eloquently than their speech ever could.

The boss had a feeling that whatever had brought Glenn all the way to the workshop must certainly be trouble if it didn't involve deliveries or payments. It wasn't an unreasonable assumption to make, considering that he was a perceptive foreman.

"Actually, right now I'm making plans for Miss Skadi's surgery," Glenn explained.

"I see. I was there at the ceremony, too. To think the Lady Draconess would collapse like that," the boss replied.

"Yes. Since then, I've gone over it with the director at the Central Hospital, and we think we'd like to operate on her. Therefore, we will need the tools necessary to perform surgery on a dragon."

"Hm. So that's it, is it...?" The boss grumbled, stroking his beard.

Glenn took a piece of parchment from his doctor's bag. It was an order form that listed all the items he wanted made, with the required size and strength laid out in detail. Glenn naturally had Cthulhy's signature on the form as well. Taking the form, the boss quickly ran his eye across the page.

One of the problems weighing on Glenn was the procurement of these tools. He needed the scalpels, for example, to somehow be both sharper than a razor and strong enough to pierce Skadi's dragonscales. He expected the existing needles he used for suturing would break easily, so he required them to be hard enough to not break on a dragon's body.

In short, he needed to have his surgical tools freshly made with dragon surgery in mind. If the Kuklo Workshop was able to prepare the tools with the specifications as outlined on the order form, the probability of success for the surgery would increase dramatically. Glenn thought having the tools would make it somewhat easier to convince Skadi.

The boss scowled at the order form. It seemed as though his single eye would burn a hole through the paper just from staring at it. Memé appeared to be interested as well and took intermittent peeks at the form herself.

"Hmph," snorted the boss.

"Will it be possible?" Glenn replied.

"We'll have to order materials. That'll take time and money. How much can you afford to pay?"

"As far as money's concerned, I am using the Central Hospital's budget for this, so please do not worry. As for the time frame... All I can say is as fast as possible."

"I'm going to need you to decide on a delivery date."

"Then one month, at the very latest."

"Hmmmm," the boss replied, rubbing his hand over his bald head. Glenn thought the boss was most likely over fifty years old, but he had a vigor to him that prevented any signs of weakening from age. He had been a weaponsmith during the great war, and manufactured an abundance of weapons and armor used in battle. The experience he had acquired was different from apprentices like Memé, who knew nothing of war. As a cyclops weaponsmith, he had been lauded as the greatest craftsman among countless others.

That boss now had his head in his hands. Glenn began to understand just how absurd his request was. The cyclops groaned for a few moments, until at last, he looked Glenn in the eyes.

"Alright. We'll do it." His face still wore a scowl, but his sense of responsibility was evident as he spoke.

"R-really?" Glenn replied.

"Yeah. I'll put my cyclops pride on the line. It's gonna be expensive, Doc. We're going to need something upfront to make something like this."

"Please rest assured—you will be paid."

"Hah, I suppose I don't need to worry if the Central Hospital's involved, do I?"

Once a city got as big as Lindworm, the number of monsters that needed treatment naturally grew along with it. That even a small town doctor like Glenn was so busy meant that the number of patients at the Central Hospital were too numerous to even count. It was natural to assume the profit the hospital earned was sizeable. Cthulhy understood how difficult the request was and would spare no expense on the surgery.

"One thing, though," the boss said, cutting off his thought with a small pause. "The needles—that's the only thing I can't contract for."

"The needles?"

"Yeah, to get them down to surgical needle size and make them strong enough to penetrate dragonscale... That will be a little difficult. I'm gonna need to rack my brains about this one. I can't promise for certain that it'll be done by the due date."

"...You're saying you'll make it, though?"

"I can't say for sure, but I'll do what I can."

Glenn thought the request must be quite the tough job for the boss to comment on how difficult it would be. "Understood. So, then, you'll get started on everything besides the needles right away? If the situation with the needles changes, please let me know when I can expect them by."

"Yeah, of course. Give the director my thanks when you see her," the boss replied, smiling as he rubbed his bald head.

Glenn was sure that if the boss said he would do something, he would pull it off at any cost. He knew without a doubt that he could put his trust in the dyed-in-the-wool craftsman temperament characteristic of the cyclops.

On the other hand—assuming that the boss was able to complete the needles, there was a chance they wouldn't be exactly as Glenn had ordered them. He should make sure to let Cthulhy know this information.

"............" The boss cast his massive single eye around him. He appeared to be looking around the workshop. The eye of a cyclops wasn't capable of binocular vision, but their visual acuity and range of vision were far beyond that of a human's. It was an eye with an extremely unique construction to it. Spinning around with ease, it could clearly capture things to the right and left just as it did those in front.

"Memé." At long last, the boss called out to the apprentice who was still glancing now and then at the order form.

"Y-y-yes?!" she replied.

"How about you try making the needles?"

It was an unbelievable nomination. Memé's eye opened perfectly wide and light reflected in her iris, which made it seem that her eye really did emit light of its own.

"It's about time I gave you a job. It's small work, but it's a major task. Try making a needle just as the Doc requested."

"H-h-huh? M-m-me...?"

"You have to start sooner or later. This is a good chance."

"N-n-no way! I can't do it, Boss! I can't make such an important needle!" Memé shook her head so hard it looked like her neck was going to break. A normal apprentice would be in high spirits to be given an assignment by the boss, but Memé didn't seem to think of it that way. "I-I get what your motives are... You're leaving the tools for Miss Skadi's surgery up to a newbie like me and are going to accuse me of being responsible when her surgery fails, is that it?! The surgery will fail because of my needles, and then the town will be in an uproar, and the paper will reveal all my private secrets, and I'll be the laughing stock of the town!"

"You're really a pessimist aren't you? You're the one who's best suited to these kinds of delicate jobs. Stop your whining and get to it!"

"Uuuugghhhh..." Memé looked at Glenn with tears in her eye. He felt like the words "save me" were written across the girl's big single eye.

After thinking for a moment, Glenn smiled at her, saying, "Sounds good to me. Give it a shot, Memé."

"Hnggggggggh..." With all her escape routes cut off, Memé let out an indescribable noise.

Everything within the workshop was managed by the boss. Glenn had a certain position as the customer making the request, but he had no right to speak up about who should be given the work. If the boss said he wanted to try leaving it up to Memé, then Glenn would trust in that decision.

Moreover, while Memé was still an apprentice, Glenn had heard that she was skilled at more delicate work, like metalworking. If anything, she might actually be suited to the work involved in manufacturing the surgical needles.

"I-I-I'll do my best... But don't get your hopes up because... This pressure, this pressure is going to kill me," said Memé.

"What the hell are you saying to the customer? Times like these are when you say you're going to dedicate yourself to getting the job done," the boss chimed in.

"I can't do it, I just can't do it..." She was an awfully pessimistic craftsman, but that was very much like Memé to begin with. The fact that the boss was entrusting it to her meant there was no doubt of her skill—the problem was with her personality.

It appeared to Glenn that the boss had a much higher opinion of Memé than he had thought. At the same time, the boss knew that Memé needed to overcome her pessimistic attitude in order to properly exhibit her skill. He imagined that entrusting Memé with a job so quickly was out of his concern to try and give her more self-confidence.

Glenn hoped it would go well. But seeing Memé staring at the ground, mumbling something under her breath, he thought it didn't seem likely without some trouble along the way.

"Anyway, I ask that you complete this for me. For the success of the surgery," said Glenn.

"I-I-I'll give it everything I've got..." replied Memé.

The cyclops were one-eyed giants. There were times when they used to be misunderstood, due to their appearance, as being crude and barbaric. In actuality, they were a serious species with a keen sense of obligation. They had a stubborn and unaccommodating side to them as well, but they had a strong sense of responsibility and took pride in their creations. Glenn was sure that because they had accepted the order, they would absolutely be able to get the surgical tools together.

Nevertheless, he would be lying if he said that he didn't have his doubts about Memé Redon, who still had her eye cast down to the ground, muttering to herself.

✕ ✕ ✖ ✕ ✕

"What in the world is this...? Hmm, what the...?" Arahnia muttered.

"You're pretty sloppy," Sapphee said. "Dr. Glenn is better at this after all."

"Well of course he is! I'm a total amateur!" Arahnia's cries echoed.

Glenn thought Arahnia's words weren't that unreasonable. She was an expert with a needle and thread, but now she was sewing up blood vessels instead of fabric.

"Hmph. I never thought there was anything more elaborate than lace embroidery. Doctor, are you always doing this sort of work?" Arahnia continued.

"Well, stitches aren't really something we handle everyday... Miss Kunai is obviously the exception," replied Glenn.

"I-I suppose so..."

They were in one of the rooms of the clinic. Arahnia had come to practice suturing again. Although she could use all four of her arms at will and was a quick learner, suturing technique was something that even Glenn had needed a long time under Cthulhy's supervision to master. If anything, he would have been upset if she learned it overnight.

When working in the clinic, Arahnia wore a nurse's outfit that matched Sapphee's. Naturally, it had been modified in various places to fit an arachne.

The hat and red-and-white apron were the same as Sapphee's. The sun-blocking inner liner was fundamentally the same as Sapphee's as well, but it was tailored to match Arahnia's four arms. All of her fake fingernails had been removed for her work, and she had put her hair up in a single ponytail high on her head instead of her two usual pigtails.

When working as a designer, she looked outlandish and fashionable, but now more importance was being put on neatness and practicality in her attire. Putting on the clothes most suitable for the time and place was a personal fixation of the arachne.

"I don't really mind. The chance to sew someone up doesn't come often. You can thank this body of mine." Fortunately for Arahnia, there was someone willing to let her borrow her body to practice suturing.

That was Kunai. The wear on her right arm was severe from overwork and stress, and even if Glenn sutured it back together, it would still come apart easily. This was convenient for Arahnia's practice, and Kunai would visit the clinic every day to offer her right arm up as a practice partner.

"They really are small... How is that, Kunai? Forget the blood vessels, the nerves are what's really hard to see," said Arahnia.

"You can fiddle with them any way you like, I don't mind. Still, to think you're really working here in the clinic, Miss Arahnia. When I first heard, I thought it was a joke," said Kunai.

"I would never joke about something this important... Though I am regretting the choice a little," Arahnia added under her breath. The exhaustion on her face was plain to see.

Glenn imagined it was only natural for Arahnia's exhaustion to be growing worse as she stared day-in and day-out at the nerves and blood vessels in Kunai's right arm. If it weren't for Skadi's surgery, Arahnia and Kunai would never have met like this. As hard-pressed as she was, Arahnia managed to sew Kunai's arm back together.

As a result of the days of continuous training, Arahnia's skill was improving before Glenn's eyes. Just as he had expected, Arahnia's needlework was the real deal. If she kept improving like this, she'd be able to do a reliable job when it came to be time for the surgery.

"Do the very best you can, Arahnia," said Sapphee.

"Sappheeee... I'm so exhausted. I want a drink..." Arahnia pleaded.

"Nope. You *always* drink too much. No drinking for the time being."

"That's just cruel..."

Sapphee was stern with the complaining Arahnia. Glenn even felt a hint of enjoyment in Sapphee's voice as she looked at the worn-out arachne. The two of them had a complicated friendship, and Glenn honestly felt it was a little warped in some respects.

Sapphee had told Glenn that Arahnia was scheming something, but with Arahnia swamped with work in the clinic, he didn't think she had the time to wrap them up in one of her plots. For the sake of her technical improvement, he couldn't afford to ease up now. He planned on strictly looking after her and pushing her to her limits.

"About the Lady Draconess," Kunai said as she was being stitched up. "I keep trying to convince her myself, again and again. She should be receiving some correspondence from Dr. Cthulhy as well, but she is still opposed to performing the surgery. It seems she is hard set in her way."

Glenn wanted to tear his hair out. He couldn't perform surgery without the patient's consent. There wasn't any doubt in Glenn's mind that neglecting her heart disorder was painful for Skadi, and he couldn't understand why she was so opposed to the surgery.

Kunai, sitting in front of him, had once hated doctors, and there had been circumstances where she had refused treatment, but Glenn had never heard about Skadi hating doctors as well. Skadi had a deep, close friendship with Cthulhy to begin with, and had been the one to install her as hospital director.

There didn't seem to be any way to quickly get rid of that heart of hers, besides surgery. If they couldn't perform the operation, then Arahnia's frantic special training and the needles he had requested of Memé would all come to nothing.

"Why exactly is she so against it...?" Glenn pondered.

"It may be a weird thing to hear coming from me, but I think she believes it's her fate," Kunai said with a self-deprecating smile.

Fate. It was true that whether one was human or monster, there would be a time when one's life came to an end. Glenn's job was saving lives, but no matter how many he saved, there was no escaping death when it finally came. Of course, while that was true, there were also undead races, and examples of monsters like

Kunai created by sewing dead tissue together, so this rule might not necessarily apply to them.

"The Lady Draconess loathes the long history of monsters and humans fighting one another, and exerted herself to develop this city where monster and human live together," Kunai said. "To the Lady Draconess, building this city was her mission. And now Lindworm is one of the most prominent cities on the whole continent. It's not often a city grows this populous and has an economy of this size."

"That's true..." Glenn replied.

"The Lady Draconess feels that she has accomplished everything she needed to. Therefore, if she should die from a disease, then she believes it must be fate. She has no regrets. At least, that's what I think her reasoning is."

Though this seemed like it was only a guess, if the bodyguard that was always by Skadi's side saw it that way, Glenn imagined it wasn't far from the truth.

"Now that's tricky, isn't it?" Arahnia said. "I'd just be happy to live as long as I could. Why, I have a *mountain* of things I still want to do."

"The Lady Draconess doesn't think such base thoughts," Kunai replied. "But... That's right—she's never used the word 'death' in front of me before. She says she's going to 'return to the sky.' I wonder if there is some kind of difference."

"Yes. Naturally, I *would* be a rather *base* woman, wouldn't I?" Arahnia replied, pursing her lips in a sulk.

But there wasn't anything wrong with Arahnia's line of

thinking. It was normal for all organisms to want to live well, as long as they were still breathing. Glenn felt that as a dragon, Skadi's philosophy on the matter differed. He also found the way she put it, "returning to the sky," very mysterious.

He wondered if it meant that, to Skadi, the earth wasn't where she belonged. Now that he thought about it, when he was examining her, she had said something similar—that she had come from somewhere close to the realm of the gods.

Glenn wasn't religious, but there were many humans and monsters that held religious beliefs. That she was referencing the gods signaled to Glenn that dragons were indeed the inhabitants of the world spoken of in myth and fairytale.

If he had to choose one way or the other, Glenn shared Arahnia's more base way of thinking about life and death. Nothing came immediately to his mind when he heard talk of the gods and their realm in the heavens. He wondered if gods became sick, if he could give a god a medical exam—these were the only types of questions that came into his head.

"However, we still need to keep trying to convince her. This time, I'll accompany you," said Glenn.

"Right. If we keep it up, the Lady Draconess might change her mind," Kunai replied.

"That's right," Arahnia chimed in. She cut the thread with her surgical scissors. It appeared she had finished suturing up Kunai's arm. Judging from her suture marks, Glenn couldn't quite say she had done it perfectly, but her growth in this short time was remarkable.

Despite this, Kunai gave a disapproving shrug of her shoulders. It seemed clear that the suturing she normally received from Glenn was better, but Kunai had been the one to offer her body as Arahnia's training partner. Glenn felt a twinge of regret, but all Kunai could do was bear with it for now.

"I know I keep saying this, but the young miss representative might just become more stubborn if you do that," Arahnia said.

"Hm..." Kunai replied.

"Thread becomes stronger the more you twist it, but it also becomes stiff and hard to work with. I don't think adding more people will make things better. Sometimes, you have to try pulling back... Well, I will say you don't seem to be very skilled with diplomacy, do you, Miss Kunai?" Arahnia said as she drew out a piece of thread she had pulled from somewhere unknown. Before anyone realized it, she was using her four arms and twining the thread together as though she were playing cat's cradle.

"You see, if you pull too strong, the thread will snap—so discretion is key," Arahnia explained.

"Discretion, you say?" Kunai asked.

"Us monsterfolk aren't so great at discretion, though, are we?" Arahnia said, giggling. Her gaze was pointed toward Sapphee. Sapphee had a somewhat indignant look on her face. Glenn thought that Arahnia was referring to their time in the harpy village, when Sapphee had wrapped herself so tightly around Glenn's neck that he fainted. She had squeezed his neck hard enough to leave marks, but the one who had angered Sapphee enough to go that far was Arahnia.

The two of them really did have quite the complicated relationship. They had something that Glenn couldn't quite figure out between them, but whatever it was might be why they were such good friends.

"In that case, what should we do...?" Glenn asked.

"If a frontal attack doesn't work, then we have to go in from the back. If neither pushing forward nor pulling back works, then dyeing something is the best solution. If a thread is beautiful dyed, then the finished clothing will be just as splendid, won't it?"

"Dyeing...?" said Glenn, puzzled.

Arahnia nimbly wove the thread between her fingers. In doing so, she completed a magnificent spider web between her four arms. The hexagonal geometric pattern looked like a work of art. Glenn once again thought that Arahnia's skill was marvelous, to be able to make such a piece of art in such a short time just by fidgeting with her hands.

"You're skilled at dyeing, are you not, Doctor?" she asked.

"Huh? No, I don't believe so... I don't have any experience with dyeing clothes or anything like it," Glenn replied.

"Why, whatever do you mean? Aren't you always dyeing Sapphee's face red? I wonder exactly what colors you use to get the lovesick Sapphee so bright red?"

"Arahnia!" Sapphee cried.

Glenn realized that what he had thought to be a serious conversation was in fact just a way to tease him and Sapphee. With her face just as red as Arahnia had described, Sapphee went to berate Arahnia, but thanks to her superb ability to run away, the arachne had already escaped the treatment room. Arahnia was just as fast as ever, in contrast to her body's colossal size.

"Looks like she's got you all wrapped up, Dr. Glenn," said Kunai.

"Well, she *is* playing with some thread, right...?" Glenn replied.

"Hahaha. I'm glad to see you're doing well enough to make such jokes," Kunai said. "Don't think about it too much." Kunai seemed to enjoy those types of jokes. Her expression turned gentle.

"This isn't anything to laugh at!" Sapphee said, the only one angry, her face bright red. Glenn felt bad about it, but he found Sapphee endearing when she got angry with someone for pointing out her feelings for him.

Of course, he realized that saying so to Sapphee would only make her angrier, so he kept those thoughts to himself.

✳ ✳ ✖ ✳ ✳

Glenn just kept getting busier and busier. Balancing his daily business of examining patients with making preparations for Skadi's surgery proved to be a difficult task. He had to leave the clinic to Sapphee more and more frequently, always going in and out of the Central Hospital and the Kuklo Workshop. He had also consulted with Kunai and decided on the date he would go to the Council Hall. The day he would speak directly with Skadi was drawing near.

He felt bad about leaving Sapphee to watch the clinic while he was gone. He was entrusting her with work that he was supposed to handle, and he knew it was a burden. Although the helper fairies and Arahnia were there as well, Sapphee was the one who had it worst.

Now that he thought about it, Glenn had been so taken up with things he had to do that he hadn't properly talked to her. Despite sleeping under the same roof, he hadn't shown any concern for her struggles. He realized that while he couldn't relieve the burden he had placed on her, he should at least give her some words of appreciation. He knew that she tended to let her suspicions run wild.

"You're thinking about another woman right now, aren't you Glenn?"

"Eh? Uh, no—" replied Glenn, flustered at being called out for his inner thoughts.

"Believe me, I understand," Cthulhy replied, worming her tentacles across the floor as she walked forward.

Glenn wondered how she had known, and if perhaps his mentor was well versed at reading others' minds. As he thought about it, he *had* heard that Cthulhy could carry on a normal conversation with Skadi. Was that because of their deep friendship or because his mentor could read everything from her expression all the way down into her soul?

Though he thought such an idea ridiculous, Glenn also found himself considering that, given Cthulhy's unfathomable nature, it might not be so far-fetched after all.

"But right now, you need to focus only on your job," Cthulhy continued.

"...Understood," Glenn replied. He was worried about Sapphee, but Cthulhy was right—he couldn't afford to be caught up with her right now.

He had come to visit the Kuklo Workshop again, this time with Cthulhy accompanying him. There was the smell of burning iron and the sound of hammers hitting steel. Through it all was the feeling of intense heat on the skin.

"This place really is hot," Cthulhy said, knitting her eyebrows. Cthulhy was originally an aquatic monster, and fundamentally disliked fire and hot air because of how it dried out the mucus that protected her. Glenn watched her biting down on the tips of her tentacles. It seemed that the workshop was a very uncomfortable place for her to be.

"You should fix that tentacle-biting habit of yours, Doctor," said Glenn.

"It's just like sun-dried squid. Chewing on them relaxes me. You can chew them too, if you want, Glenn," she replied.

"I'll pass..."

Cthulhy had a bad habit of trying to force Glenn to eat her tentacles from time to time. The tentacles of the scylla were a delicacy, but Glenn still didn't have any interest in tasting them. He had heard that in a region far to the west, there was a restaurant where scylla cut off and cooked their own tentacles, but he wondered if that sort of business was even successful. Their tentacles grew back quickly, but nevertheless, Glenn would be distressed to have them offered as food. Not only that, since the chefs were cooking their own bodies, it meant that no one could possibly criticize their cooking, making the situation even more complicated.

"Let's finish this up quickly," said Glenn.

Deep inside the workshop, the boss had taken up a position with his arms crossed. He had on the same frown as usual, and a chieftain-like dignity about him.

"Oh, you came. I wouldn't have expected you to come yourself, Director," said the boss.

"I'll be the one using the tools, so it makes sense that I would want to see them directly, doesn't it?" Cthulhy replied.

The boss pointed to a workbench covered with a high quality piece of cloth, on top of which were the freshly completed, flawless surgical tools.

"Here's what you ordered. Nothing should have been overlooked, but please see them for yourself," he said.

"Hmmm..." Cthulhy said, taking a scalpel in her hand. The blade tip was sharp, and it didn't have any sort of sword-like roughness to it. The edge of the scalpel was smaller than the tip of a finger, but it was keen enough to pierce skin at the slightest touch.

Cthulhy scrutinized the scalpel, and Glenn thought that she had confirmed its integrity when finally—

"Hng."

Cthulhy turned toward one of her tentacles and quickly ran the knife across it. Its sharp edge amputated the octopus-like tentacle with ease. The tip—a piece of flesh about as small as Glenn's pinky—fell to the floor with a plop. The piece of tentacle wove back and forth slightly on the ground before finally falling still.

Glenn was dumbfounded, but Cthulhy wore a nonchalant look on her face.

"It cuts well. I love it," said Cthulhy.

"...Can you *please* not try out blades on your own tentacles?!" Glenn objected.

"Oh, it's fine, we're going to disinfect them anyway."

"It's not just a sanitation problem..." Glenn said, at his wit's end. The regenerative powers of a scylla's tentacles were strong, and a small bit of it being cut off was sure to heal in a few days' time. Nevertheless, whether it was Kunai or Cthulhy, Glenn felt there were far too many people who were rough with their own bodies. He wanted them to treat themselves more carefully—needlessly injuring oneself wasn't something they should be doing.

"There doesn't seem to be any problem with the quality, either. Boss, I'll take them all. However, shouldn't there be more of them here?" asked Cthulhy.

"Yes, thank you for your patronage. The rest are piled up in the back, please take a look," the boss replied.

Surgical instruments were meant to be disposable. Cutting tools quickly lost their sharpness. There wasn't time to sharpen them during surgery, and due to sanitation concerns, they couldn't be used continuously. These conditions necessitated an appropriate number of them be created.

"In that case, can I have you bring all of this to the Central Hospital for me?" Cthulhy asked.

"Yeah. The young guys will bring them later," replied the boss.

The Kuklo Workshop also made deliveries to the Central Hospital. As such, Cthulhy and the boss had been acquaintances for a while. The conversation between the two of them continued smoothly, as if it was all very familiar to them both.

Glenn looked at the numerous tools laid out on the cloth. With just a single glance, it was plain to see how good the craftsmanship was. The boss was speaking with abundant self-confidence, so Glenn thought they probably cut through dragon skin and scale like butter. They had been completed entirely thanks to the workshop's high-heat forges, their highest quality ingredients, and the skill and technique of the cyclops craftsmen.

But among them all, there was one kind that caught Glenn's eye.

It was the surgical needles. Smaller than sewing or fishing needles, a number of them were lined up in the corner. Glenn picked one up, but it was clear that they were of poor quality. They were bent, and none of them were strong enough.

"Oh, those are prototypes," the boss said, looking at the needles. "Memé tried all sorts of things to make some, but... They definitely aren't something that can withstand practical use. She's been stressing over a lot of different things as well."

"I see," replied Glenn. If he were to put it harshly, they were a failure.

However, he knew very well that one couldn't achieve success without failing repeatedly. Glenn and the others were asking for something quite unreasonable in order to make sure the surgery was a success. He imagined Memé's trial and error was all just natural progress.

"Gonna go meet with Memé, Doctor? She's locked herself up in the workshop's prototyping room and won't come out. If you say you want to see her, I can call for her, but…"

"…No, I'll hold off for now," Glenn said, shaking his head after a moment's hesitation. He was sure that Memé's head was filled with thoughts of her first real assignment right now.

Memé was still young, but she was an excellent apprentice that had the boss's favor. This was the first job of a craftswoman with a bright future ahead of her. Right now, Glenn wanted Memé to focus on her own work and not worry about anything unnecessary.

Without saying anything, Glenn had been staring for a while at Cthulhy as she verified the quality of the tools to be delivered. When she noticed Glenn's gaze, she wiggled her tentacles in protest.

"What? Why are you staring at me, Glenn?" she asked.

"Oh no, I just remembered something," he replied.

"Are you just now noticing my beautiful good looks?"

"That's not it… I thought back to my first operation. You summoned me out of the blue, and I had no clue why you were calling me, when all of a sudden, you had me perform my first surgery."

"That *was* how it happened, wasn't it?"

It happened back when Glenn was in the academy. An emergency patient was brought to Cthulhy's research lab who had been unable to be admitted to the nearby hospital. At the time, Glenn had thought for sure that Cthulhy would be the one to perform the surgery, but she designated her then-student Glenn to be her assistant.

Thinking back, Glenn remembered the surgery was to remove a tumor as well.

The patient was a golem. They were a race that formed their bodies by eating mud, but it seemed that the patient had ingested some foreign substance without knowing it, which then became the core of a tumor that formed around it inside them. It had taken everything he had just to operate according to Cthulhy's instructions, and he remembered when he—covered in mud and dirt—finally excised the tumor.

"Ever since then, you've done nothing but ask for the unreasonable, Dr. Cthulhy," said Glenn.

The original reason the patient had been taken in by the academy was because Cthulhy had jumped at the chance for golem-related medical research—although Glenn was sure she hadn't been lying when she said she wanted to save the patient's life.

"What's this? Do you feel bitter that I'm cleverly making good use of you, Glenn?" Cthulhy replied.

"Absolutely not. I'm able to get by now because you were so strict with me, Doctor."

"How stupid," Cthulhy replied, showing Glenn a smile. It had been a long time since he had gotten to see his mentor's smiling face. Cthulhy was rarely one to show her emotions in front of other people. She always seemed languid and lazy, but the truth was that she just wasn't skilled at being sociable. In reality, it was in her nature to hide away deep in the ocean, and living in a city wasn't her forte. In this way, her personality was somewhat similar to Memé's. Of course, that didn't necessarily mean he would be able to get close to Memé.

"I *was* strict? Hearing you use the past tense like that is rather sad. I'm still quite strict," Cthulhy shot back.

"...I'm aware."

"Well then, in that case, can you go and grab me some water?" Cthulhy said, reclining in a makeshift chair she had found. Glenn knew she was asking for water because her tentacles had dried out quite significantly.

The forge at the heart of the workshop contained a red-hot flame today as well. The cutting-edge forge was the pride of Lindworm, and could make extremely high-quality steel. In addition to the main forge, there were other, smaller forges scattered about the workshop with their own fires roaring, inevitably making the workshop hot. This was why the boss and Memé were so lightly dressed.

It was thought that the cyclops' characteristic eye was what led them to specialize in smithing. Unlike the eyes of human forge masters, which were worn down by staring into the high heat of forges without end, those of the cyclops had a unique, almost glass-like membrane covering the surface. Their tear glands were also more active, which kept them protected with plenty of fluid. This meant their eyes could always maintain their moisture, and could avoid any long-term damage even when exposing themselves to intense heat. At least, that was the usual explanation.

The uncertainty about the truth behind their eyes arose from the fact that no one had yet dissected one. Cyclops eyes decayed easily, and immediately disintegrated from a cyclops' remains. The hypothesis that they had a glassy membrane to protect them had been put forth by a scholar who had observed cyclops as they diligently worked at their smithing.

Even if the explanation had come from a scientific dissection, it would have been hard to form any sort of general understanding from observation. The dissection of dead bodies was not viewed favorably. Thus, cyclops research failed to move forward. Their eye was still full of secrets.

Their aptitude for forge work, however, was undeniable, both because of their racial temperament and their bodily characteristics.

"Glenn, what are you doing? *Water*," Cthulhy demanded.

"Yes, yes, Dr. Cthulhy, coming right up," said Glenn.

"That answer only gets forty points. You don't have enough respect for your teacher."

"That's not true. I have nothing but respect for you."

"I don't know about that..." Cthulhy said, looking discontent.

Of course Glenn respected her. In fact, Cthulhy had been the person to try and dissect cyclops remains during his time at the academy. She, too, wanted to know about the structure of their bodies, with their one eye wrapped in mystery. Glenn assumed that in the end, she hadn't been given the necessary permissions.

If they could understand the mystery of the cyclops, then that, too, could prove useful in medical treatment. The secrets of their single eye—found in no other monster race—might save not only the lives of cyclops but other races of monster as well.

Cthulhy may have done as she pleased, but there was no denying she had a doctor's sense of purpose to save lives.

"...I wonder what that information could do," Glenn pondered quietly.

"What?"

"Oh, it's nothing, Dr. Cthulhy."

Glenn poured water into the workshop-made glass cup and handed it to his mentor. Her throat must have been considerably parched, judging by how she gulped down the water.

When it came to technical skill, the cyclops had no equal, and the Kuklo Workshop had put together the most state-of-the-art facilities on the whole continent. Glenn hadn't given up hope that Memé would complete a high-quality, top-class surgical needle for him. Just like when he, Glenn Litbeit, had been a newbie, and completed his first surgical operation.

As he thought about it, even Cthulhy was turning her expectations toward him—both during his time in the academy and now.

Glenn wasn't going to see Memé because that would only put pressure on her. She was a delicate girl, sensitive to the stares of those around her, timid, and had no confidence in herself, but Glenn was positive her delicate nature would create a needle up to the task of suturing a dragon's body.

"What are you grinning about over there, Glenn?" asked Cthulhy.

"I'm just thinking about something that was funny, that's all," he replied.

"What a weird boy... Do you want to eat a tentacle?"

"N-no thank you…" Cthulhy was the last person he would ever want to call him weird.

When they were done, Cthulhy returned to the Central Hospital and Glenn returned to the clinic. He didn't visit the workshop again and didn't see Memé in the end. However, he had no doubts that Memé would bring him her completed needles with a huge smile on her face.

It was a few days later that Glenn came to regret his decision—when he received word at the Litbeit Clinic that Memé had lost consciousness.

✖ ✖ ✖ ✖ ✖

Memé Redon had collapsed at the workshop.

Glenn flew out of the clinic as soon as he heard this. Fortunately, there hadn't been any emergency patients at the clinic, so Sapphee accompanied him. They put up the closed plaque and left the rest up to Arahnia and the helper fairies.

"Memé!" Glenn cried.

Led by the boss, Glenn entered what was referred to as the prototyping room.

"She's here, Dr. Glenn," said the boss.

"Memé, are you okay?" Glenn ran over to where the one-eyed girl was lying down. The cyclops craftsmen all thought of Memé as a daughter and cleared the way for Glenn.

There was no response even as Glenn called out her name. He quickly checked that she was breathing.

"She's breathing," he said.

"Her pulse is weak, but it is there, Doctor," said Sapphee.

"Memé, can you hear me?! Answer me!" Glenn called out to her as he placed his hands on either side of her cheeks. Her big single eye opened a little and there was an ever-so-slight movement in her lips.

Glenn couldn't understand what she was saying, but there had been a response.

"She's conscious. Sapphee, I'm going to get her undressed."

"Yes, Doctor."

Sapphee used her tail to grab a pair of scissors nearby. Glenn took the scissors and began cutting up Memé's outerwear. While her undershirt was thin, it was made of a material that absorbed sweat well. Shearing it open with the big workshop scissors was a simple task.

Her breathing was rough, so Glenn cut her clothes to put less strain on her chest. With her chest exposed, her breasts—big for someone her age—came bouncing out.

"Nh............les," Memé said, but Glenn couldn't catch what it was. Part of it was because Memé's voice was low, but the environment inside the workshop wasn't conducive to picking up her words either. Inside the prototyping room, there were loudly roaring machines Glenn was unfamiliar with. The rumbling noises intruded upon his thoughts.

A colossal machine powered by the Waterways. Glenn surmised that Memé had been in the middle of some sort of work when she collapsed.

"She's still conscious. Let's have her rest somewhere quiet," said Glenn.

"Doc, what's happened to Memé? Is she sick with something...?" the boss asked.

"I don't know. However, I don't believe she has any chronic diseases, so it's hard to believe that it's any sort of life-threatening illness. The workshop is hot, so it might be dehydration."

Glenn put his head against Memé's forehead—her temperature was a little higher than normal. He contemplated whether this was the result of light dehydration or heatstroke. Yet, he knew that a cyclops should be tolerant of the heat. If she truly had gotten heatstroke, then that meant she had been pushing herself beyond her limits for a considerable amount of time.

"Either way, she shouldn't stay here. Let's transport her elsewhere," said Glenn. The inside of the workshop was hot—he was drenched in sweat. Memé was too, but not to a degree Glenn considered abnormal. In which case, he thought, this collapse had been brought on by something else

"You know I told her... I told Memé to make sure she gets plenty of rest," the boss muttered.

"It can't be... You're saying she had been working all day and night?" asked Glenn.

"No—I was sure she wasn't pushing herself so hard that she'd collapse, but... This might my fault. I should have supervised her better."

Working in the workshop was unforgiving. A cyclops's body was sturdy, but every species has their limits. Glenn wondered if Memé had stretched her body to the breaking point. In that case, there was a high possibility that her collapse was the result of overworking.

Cyclops, being so serious and honest, were reliable when it came to their work, but sometimes unintentionally overworked themselves. There were many species of monsters who were serious about their work, but when it came to cyclops, Glenn found their solemnity was a little excessive. Memé might be the perfect example. No matter how weak to pressure she was, she still embraced her nigh-impossible task.

The other craftsmen brought a stretcher over. The clinic wasn't far, and Glenn thought it would be best to have them carry Memé back. Sapphee used her tail to pick up Memé's body and deftly lay it on the stretcher.

Memé's lips moved. The humming of the revolving machine was loud, but for some reason this time Glenn was able to hear her words. He thought her consciousness might be returning.

"Needle..."

Okay, Glenn thought, she was talking about needles.

"Needles...I have to...make them..."

To the last, Memé's words were devoted to her work.

✗ ✗ ✘ ✗ ✗

Memé felt that her giant eye was spinning in circles.

She didn't know where she was looking. Reflecting in her eyes was the figure of her former self.

Again and again the world spun. Around and around in circles.

Memé Redon had heard it a lot ever since she was a child: "But you're a girl."

Even when she was still an infant, Memé was captivated by her father's work. Her cyclops father worked as a craftsman. A cartwright of everything from small wagons to massive carriages, he could make anything that had a set of wheels on it. She had heard that during the war, he even gained experience making chariots.

She had admired the massive, rustic carriages he made, particularly their decorations—the small details like the glass windows and the gold work furnishing the carriages' roofs. One time she had even borrowed her father's tools without permission and fixed some poorly fitted metal fixtures on a carriage's door. Her mom had scolded her by telling her that some tools were very dangerous, but her father only praised her for her efforts.

Traditionally, cyclops craftsmen had always been men. Even now, there were some among the more elderly craftsmen that would scowl if a woman even got near a forge. Memé's father was different. He picked up on her talent immediately and began to train her as a craftsman. It had been several years since Memé was left in the hands of his longtime acquaintance—the boss of Kuklo Workshop—as an apprentice.

There was no arguing that Memé had an interest in glassworking and metalworking. But with her natural timidity and unsociable disposition, she didn't have the confidence necessary to get used to the unknown city of Lindworm. The craftsmen in the workshop were nice, but she was scared of the humans and other monsters. Everyone has two eyes, she would think to herself—it was something she never would have imagined, having come from a village of only one-eyed inhabitants.

As she began learning the skills and techniques needed to become a craftsman, she only managed to make her social skills worse. By holing herself up in the workshop, she never got outside to speak with other people

The boss worried about Memé, and purposely gave her delivery jobs that would lead to lots of opportunities to meet other people, but he didn't see much improvement. On the contrary, he got the feeling that contact with humans and other monsters only made Memé's inferiority complex worse.

There was a reason Memé's hypersensitive mental spirit had withered.

It was the grim realities of the craftsmen's lives.

In the long continuing war, the cyclops were never put on the front lines. They were a mild-mannered race not cut out for battle. However, they were first class craftsmen and served the monsters' side of the war by making weapons. While they previously had made a wide variety of tools, as the long war continued on, crafting weapons became the highest priority. The skills that they maintained only pertained to war. As a cartwright, even Memé's father had participated by producing chariots.

When Memé had come to the Kuklo Workshop, most of the craftsmen were weaponsmiths, including the boss himself. In order to live through the war, the cyclops had had to make weapons.

Before any of them knew it, their skills and techniques had become specialized to creating tools of war.

In fact, the jobs that the Kuklo Workshop got the most often were those that involved making cutting tools. Kitchen knives, normal knives, and hatchets were all necessary for everyday life, but all of them were made by applying methods of weapons production. For the former weaponsmith cyclops, it was very familiar work.

No matter what they created, it had the stench of war on it. Memé picked up on this acutely. She was more sensitive than other people to begin with. She was timid and cowardly. Nevertheless, the work at Kuklo was harsh, and the techniques used to make weapons were applied to the creation of the tools they produced. This fact was too much for Memé's overly gentle heart to endure. The work Memé sought to do involved creating accessories and ornaments—things that had nothing to do with war.

She thought that it would be better if the workshop could just make sculptures and statues instead, and she wasn't the only one. The vestiges of war that Memé felt were also sensed by many of the craftsmen in the Kuklo Workshop. These peace-loving cyclops did not intend to work only with the skills and techniques they fostered during the war.

The craftsmen of the Kuklo Workshop were always thinking—

Give me work. Give us work. No matter how hard the article, we'll definitely be able to make it. We'll make products that've never been seen before. No matter how impossible the conditions are, we'll surpass them. So please, give us work. The war is over. Give us work that doesn't involve weapons. Give us work that won't hurt anyone.

Especially because of Memé's sensitivity to the gazes of others, and her ability to understand the emotions of those around her better than anyone else, she felt like she could hear the silent voices of the senior craftsmen around her. And this was also what Memé wished for herself.

She liked pretty things. She liked glass and metalwork. She liked beautiful ornaments. She also liked clothes dyed with lace and frills, but that was the work of the arachne. It was fine for others to make cutting tools with their uncouth hammers, only concerned with practical beauty, but she wanted to make delicate, colored ornaments with her tools.

That was why she wanted to sweep away the vestiges of war that still remained in the workshop. Of course, a workshop built in a former fortress town was itself one of those vestiges, but that motivated the cyclops even more to seek opportunity in the rebuilding of the city of Lindworm to display their prowess. They watched without saying a word, patient and still. Just as when they made weapons for the war, hiding and waiting was their specialty. Hiding and waiting for what they longed for—an era of peace.

Sure enough, their opportunity to showcase their skill eventually arrived.

Memé distinctly remembered what happened.

"A new director has come to the Central Hospital," Kunai had said. It was a little while after Memé had become an apprentice at the Kuklo Workshop. The city council representative Skadi brought her bodyguard Kunai with her and visited the workshop.

Kunai was raising her voice as Skadi's interpreter, but the words she spoke were unmistakably Skadi's.

"The new hospital director holds progressive ideas and will have this city's hospital provide comprehensive medical care for monsters. What I have written here is a list of the goods she requires. Cthulhy has said she won't accept the position unless, at minimum, this list of items can be prepared."

Every one of the craftsmen in the workshop opened their big eyes wide and looked at Skadi. Even with the gazes of all the cyclops washing over her, Skadi's leader-like posture never broke. At the very least, that was how it seemed to the young Memé. She wasn't good at dealing with others, so whenever someone she didn't know came into the workshop, it was her habit to hide herself in the back and peek out at the visitor.

"Therefore, I would ask all the capable craftsmen in the workshop to complete these items."

The adults all checked the order form and spoke among themselves. The boss scowled. With her skills and technique still unrefined, Memé didn't know exactly what the order form entailed. All she knew was that until this hospital director or whoever came, the workshop would have to work all day and all night.

"It seems that in the past you cyclops gentlemen made weapons." Skadi borrowed her bodyguard's mouth to speak to the wavering boss and his craftsmen. "The items on this list aren't weapons, but medical equipment. I'm sure you will use the same techniques you used to manufacture weapons to make them. However, all of these tools will be used in order to save other people's lives. Let me promise you this—the skill that all of you possess will help someone. You will save lives—far outweighing the blood that was spilled in wartime."

It was the big job that the craftsmen of the Kuklo Workshop had been looking for. Encouraged, they were happy to display their talents to their heart's content.

The work they received from the hospital was especially good for them. For the gentle cyclops, it was using their skills to save others—not for war—that suited them the best. Besides, being the only ones able to do the work, it was only natural for them to take it up with some enthusiasm.

Thus, the Lindworm Central Hospital became a client of the Kuklo Workshop.

Naturally, with the Litbeit Clinic operating independently from the Central Hospital, they also turned to the workshop for their supplies. The Kuklo Workshop became widely known as the biggest in the city and was so busy that even an apprentice like Memé fainted from the amount of work.

With just a small speech, Skadi had inspired the craftsmen. Memé could still remember their excitement back then. She wanted to someday become a craftswoman with skills the world needed, just like the craftsmen had been needed that day. Skadi's words became a major motive behind Memé's goal to become the ideal craftswoman.

Manufacturing tools necessary to save *that* Skadi—there was no way Memé wasn't going to give it her all. Several years had passed since she had first set eyes on Skadi that day. After having said the workshop's skills would help people, Skadi herself was now one of the people who needed their help.

Memé would absolutely follow through on her work.

Her enthusiasm was excellent, but her desperation to accomplish her task shifted into an obsession with the fact that she absolutely couldn't fail. The needles she made would decide the success or failure of the surgery. With this, her hand trembled as she worked. Her face grew pale.

She only ever thought the worst. She knew this negative mindset was probably connected with her habit of looking down at the ground, but she couldn't help it—the eyes of others scared her. They had two eyes. And having two eyes, their gaze was twice as terrifying. Arachne even had *six* eyes. She wondered why they all had so many—one was more than enough, wasn't it? It was incomprehensible to her. She felt like she was going to collapse.

In actuality, she had collapsed. She couldn't even lift her head. The world spun around her—around and around it went. Her desire to complete the surgical needles and her fear of failure combined like coffee and milk into a spiral that seemed to spin about Memé's head.

✘ ✘ ✘ ✘ ✘

Memé's large eye opened wide.

When looking at it up close, the massive eye of a cyclops was truly powerful. Glenn had heard there was a superstitious custom among big farms to employ cyclops women. Their big eyes protected the crops from the birds, and their natural diligence and hard-work was always useful on a farm. It was said the reason they employed women was because all the cyclops men end up becoming craftsmen.

"......Dr. Glenn?" Memé said.

"Oh, you're awake?" Glenn replied.

Memé was in a bed at the clinic. Sapphee, Arahnia, and the helper fairies were all standing by on the other side of the bed curtain. The cyclops stared vacantly for a moment, but before long she gave a surprised gasp. It appeared she finally understood where she was.

"Oh, I-I, have to make the needles..." Memé pushed aside the sheets and went to get out of bed when—

"Bleeeeerg..." She bent over and vomited in agony.

"Now now, slow down. You still need to rest." Glenn calmly caught Memé's vomit in the washbowl he had prepared. Fortunately, it was a light ejection, and only a slight amount of gastric juices collected in the bowl.

Glenn rubbed Memé's exposed back. The combination of her delicate, young girl's frame and the muscularity unique to cyclops gave Glenn a strange feeling as he rubbed.

"Ugh...? I-I feel awful..."

"There, there, you'll be fine, but you can't move quickly like that."

"Nhggg..."

It seemed that Memé didn't realize how bad a condition her body was in. Her pupil seemed to be swirling around in circles.

Of course, that was nothing but an illusion, but the sincerity of emotion displayed in the cyclops's eye seemed to express just how sick she was.

"Dr. Glenn is so kind," Sapphee said.

"Why, he seems even nicer than when he's talking to us, now doesn't he?" Arahnia replied.

"Th-that's not true...!"

"Hardworking girls sure are popular, now, aren't they?" Arahnia added.

"I-I'm a hard worker, too, you know."

"Yes, well, you do drink a lot, Sapphee."

"What's that got to do with anything, Arahnia?!"

The voices on the other side of the curtain were loud and bothersome. Sapphee had become more agitated and flustered ever since Arahnia started coming and going from the clinic. But Glenn still had a feeling that Arahnia's presence wasn't necessarily a bad thing for Sapphee. They had stopped peeking in because it would be harmful to the patient, but Glenn wished that at the very least they'd keep quiet.

"Aaaauuuggh... Why, why do I always get like this..." Memé said. "It's probably just because throwing up suits me... I told myself this time would be different and worked hard... though I obviously wouldn't be able to do it...!"

"Memé, calm down. You're okay," Glenn replied.

"I have no idea what's going on..."

"You collapsed at the workshop."

"Huh? I-I-I did? W-Why?"

"I'm going to examine you now to figure that out."

While it was premature to come to any conclusion, Glenn had already arrived at an approximate cause for Memé's collapse. In order to make the surgical needles, she had neglected her health to a considerable degree.

The symptoms were dizziness and vomiting. Yet, the color in Memé's face now that she was sitting up in bed didn't appear to be all that worrisome. Glenn thought there might be a possibility she was just overworked, but—

"Eeeeeeeek!"

—or at least, he was thinking that up until Memé let out a scream.

"M-my clothes... They're...c-c-cut up..." she stammered.

"Sorry—it was an emergency, so I had to cut them. I'll be sure to compensate you for it," Glenn replied.

"Th-that's not what I mean!" Memé said, desperately hiding her chest.

Memé's shirt was a simple garment that was tied around her neck and only really concealed the front of her. She had nothing on underneath, so just cutting the shirt at her chest left her breasts exposed. She had been immediately transferred to the clinic, so Glenn thought it only natural that she would still be naked.

"Arrrrrrrrrrrgh! I can't take it anymore!" Memé stuck her head under the covers as she screamed. She had always been quick to start crying, but now she seemed truly upset. "Everything's been seen! Everything, everything, everything!"

"...Memé, just calm down a little, okay? I need you to come out," Glenn said with a sigh.

"Bleeeeerrrrg!"

As soon as he spoke, Glenn handed the washbowl to the vomiting Memé, exasperated.

"It's going to be all right, okay?"

"It's not okay at all! No way!"

"Well, can you at least take your head out from under there for me?"

Memé squirmed about under the covers for a moment before finally poking her teary-eyed face out.

"I want to get a good look at you. Can you bear with it for a bit?"

"O-okay..."

"Thank you. Now first, can you show me your eye?"

"Unghhh..." Memé said, giving a sniffing reply.

Glenn peered into Memé's pupil.

In this world, there were researchers who would observe the movements of the heavens and track the paths of the stars in order to discover the truths of the world. Glenn couldn't even imagine such ideas, but it was said that by looking at the far-off stars, one could understand the nature of the world that he lived on.

There was a massive state-of-the-art telescope that these astronomers used for just such a purpose. One time, when Glenn was visiting the Kuklo Workshop, he had seen one of the lenses for that telescope. It had been obvious that the skills of the Kuklo Workshop were indispensable for observing the stars in the far-off skies.

Looking at Memé's eye, Glenn thought of that telescope lens.

"Nhhhg... Don't, look at my eye. It's embarrassing..."

"It's okay—relax your muscles."

"I c-c-can't do it... D-don't look at my face," Memé said, covering her eye and shaking her head.

"Just relax. Take some deep breaths."

"Haaa, fwaaah."

Glenn worried that if she got too flustered she might vomit again and tried to speak to Memé as gently as possible. The girl was the very manifestation of an inferiority complex, and if he didn't deal with it properly, he wouldn't be able to examine her as he would like.

When he examined a monster's body as a doctor, there were times when Glenn felt that the natural beauty of a monster body was much greater than any work of art: a pure, untouched piece of glasswork.

For example, the beautiful construction that allowed centaurs to specialize in running. The elegance produced from a mermaid's curves, befitting their swimming and diving. The patterns and feel of a lamia's scales, sometimes even sensual in their appearance.

"Nhggg..." Memé groaned.

"Bear with me for just a moment," Glenn replied.

"Hng... You're too *close!*"

The eye of the cyclops was a biological peculiarity that possessed this beauty of form and function. Rather than peeking at far-off stars through a telescope, Glenn felt that peering into the deep, abyssal hue of their eyes might actually bring him closer to the cosmos.

There weren't any abnormalities in Memé's eye. Nevertheless, Glenn thought it had something to do with her collapse.

"U-um...? D-Doctor...?" asked Memé

"Oh, forgive me. I sort of spaced out on accident," responded Glenn.

Glenn knew he couldn't tell Memé that he was fascinated by her eye. If he said that to her, the embarrassment of her self-deprecating spirit might cause another collapse.

"It looks like your pupil's movements are a little slow. Is your head a little cloudy?" Glenn asked.

"Hng... I-I've felt dizzy since trying to get up..." Memé replied.

"Look at this for me," Glenn said, taking his pointer finger and holding it up in front of Memé. "Can you follow my finger with your eye for me when I move it?"

Glenn then moved his finger left to right. Memé's eye began following Glenn's finger, but—

"...Ugh-huuurrrrk," Memé once again clasped her hand over her mouth.

"There you go, there you go."

It seemed her nausea still hadn't subsided. When she hunched forward, her cleavage—extremely developed for a girl her age—was exposed by the sheets and stared Glenn directly in the face. He tried as much as possible not to look and rubbed Memé's back.

"Dr. Glenn..."

"Please don't look at me like that. You can go back after you get some rest."

Tears had welled up in Memé's eye from the nausea. The eye of a cyclops was built to easily gather tears, as they protected it from damage. Thus, one of their unique traits was a propensity to quickly become teary-eyed.

"Uh, u-um..."

"Yes, is something wrong?"

"Can I, um...you know...clothes..."

"Oh, yes, right. Sapphee, is there anything that Memé could wear?" Glenn said, calling out beyond the curtain. No matter what happened, he couldn't let Sapphee know that his gaze had been on the breasts of a tender young girl.

Then—

A single layer of cloth came flying in, as if it had been thrown over the top of the curtain. It was a shirt with a plain design. They did have a change of clothes prepared in the clinic just in case, but Glenn couldn't recall this particular shirt.

"Why, please, use that." The voice belonged to Arahnia. "I improvised. Now the size might be a little off, but please do forgive me."

On the other side of the curtain, Glenn caught flashes of her segmented spider legs. He couldn't believe she had been able to complete a piece of clothing in such a short time. It was unexpectedly quick work. But he was thankful that she was such a caring woman.

"Th-thank you... Miss Arahnia," said Memé.

"Please talk to me any time you want to order more of those gothic lolita clothes, okay?" Arahnia replied.

"Th-that's supposed to be a secret!"

"Oh my—I shouldn't have said anything."

It seemed to Glenn that Memé and Arahnia were somehow familiar with one another. Judging by Arahnia's words, she seemed to have something to do with Memé's casual clothes, but even ignoring that fact, they seemed to be close. That was very rare for Memé.

If Glenn had to pinpoint what the two of them seemed to share in common, he'd have to say it was that both of them weren't very sociable. Arahnia was amiable enough, but because of her personality problems, she didn't appear to have many friends. Glenn wondered if that had anything to do with why the two had hit it off so well.

"You too, Doctor!"

"Y-yes!"

Just as he was thinking unpleasant things about her, Arahnia's piercing voice came flying over the bed curtain. "You need to show more consideration after cutting up a young girl's clothes like that! Clothes are a woman's best friend, so I'll ask you to be more careful!"

"F-forgive me," Glenn replied.

Arahnia spoke harshly when the topic turned to clothing. Glenn unconsciously sat up straight at her words.

Memé happily put on her clothes. Despite how embarrassed she had just been, she didn't pay any attention to Glenn's gaze as she put on her clothes—no, he thought, it was probably more that she was so embarrassed that all of her focus was on getting dressed. Thanks to this, Glenn was given a good look at her white back. Even from behind, he could identify her ample breasts in front. Flustered, Glenn quickly averted his eyes.

The shirt Memé put on was plain, but constructed well enough that it was hard to imagine it was made in such a short time frame. He was sure Arahnia had used her own personal silk to make it. Glenn was speechless after being aided by Arahnia's impossible-to-imitate craftsmanship.

Though judging by the short length of the shirt, and the way Memé's lower abdomen peeked out slightly, showing her well-toned abdominal muscles, there were defects that Arahnia couldn't do anything about. Memé herself didn't seem to mind it at all.

"Shall I make some eye droplets, Doctor?" asked Sapphee, but Glenn simply shook his head.

"No, I don't think those will be necessary this time. Memé, does the smell of mint make you feel sick or anything?"

"N-n-no..."

"All right, then. Sapphee, could you bring over a mint potpourri? I think it will make things much easier if we can calm her down with herbal fragrances."

There wasn't anything out of the ordinary with her eye in the first place. Wearing her shirt now, Memé had calmed down. Her face was still a little pale, but her symptoms weren't life-threatening.

"What is wrong with her, then?" asked Arahnia.

"It's simple. She just had a bout of nausea," replied Glenn.

"Nausea? Like a hangover?"

Glenn had heard Arahnia loved to drink. Hearing the word nausea, it seemed she immediately associated it with being hungover.

"I-I didn't drink any alcohol or anything..." replied Memé

"It isn't from being drunk or hung over... It's the same in principle to what we call 'carriage sickness,'" Glenn explained.

"A carriage...?"

In Lindworm, carts were generally pulled by centaurs, but across the rest of the continent the main method of transportation was still horse-drawn carriages. Practice was required to ride horseback, but riding in a carriage didn't require any special skills. As a result, those not used to riding in carriages often got sick.

"B-but Dr. Glenn, I haven't ridden in a carriage or anything either..." Memé protested.

"Yes, I'm sure that's true. But the principle is the same."

"P-principle...?"

"Your semicircular canals. Inside your ears, you've got organs that sense motion and gyration. This is true both of humans and cyclops. Almost all monsters possess these organs."

In lamia, the semicircular canals had developed abnormally. As such, they could move freely through the tops of trees, and even be active upside down without any issue. Sapphee often hung from the ceiling, and it wasn't particularly difficult for her to do so.

Glenn tapped on his own ears. "Cyclops are actually weak here," he said.

"W-we're bad at moving, is that what you're saying? I guess it's true that I'm not great at exercising..." Memé replied.

"It's a little different from that. The function of the semicircular canals is normal. It's just that a cyclops's vision is too good. They have a wide field of vision, and they have good eyesight. However, with only one eye, they are incapable of binocular vision, and if they fix their gaze on something, then nothing else can enter their vision."

With one eye, they were very skilled at intently fixing their gaze on something. But their wide field of vision wasn't good at capturing a lot of things at once. It was hard to say that their kinetic vision was particularly excellent either.

"For example, if a cyclops stares at a windmill, or is in a space similar to a carriage that simply moves up and down, because of their extremely good vision, their eyes and semicircular canals stop being able to work together properly. Just standing up will feel like the room is spinning around them, or conversely, they'll feel like they're standing still when moving..."

"Oh..." Memé said, her eyes widening to tell Glenn that she had remembered something.

"The cyclops are a race that can get carriage-sick even without riding in a horse carriage."

The link between the semicircular canals and one's vision was extremely important, but cyclops had specialized vision. With their lack of binocular vision being their key weakness, it was easy for the connection between their eye and semicircular canals to break down.

"Depending on the circumstances, there are some cyclops who start to feel like they're having a hallucination. Their consciousness grows vague and hazy... It's a phenomenon that happens due to how good their vision can be."

"Yeah..." Memé replied.

"You seem to remember something."

If Glenn was dealing with a human, they wouldn't collapse just from nausea. However, there were times, such as after nearly drowning, a human would lose function in their semicircular canals and lose the ability to tell up from down because of the water getting into their ears. For cyclops, even a simple case of nausea—when severe enough—was sufficient for them to lose their sense of equilibrium and collapse.

"What in the world happened?" Glenn asked. "Unless you had been gazing at something massive rotating around for a long time... something like a water wheel or windmill... I wouldn't think you'd become nauseous."

"Th-that's, um, probably because I had been making the needles," replied Memé.

"I see, so that was what did it." Glenn had been able to guess that much. What he was curious about was exactly how she had been making them and what connection that had to a cyclops experiencing carriage sickness.

"Th-this will work out perfectly. I'd like Dr. Glenn to take a look at them anyway... And Miss Arahnia, too."

"...Show *me?*" Arahnia said, cocking her head to the side. But Glenn also felt that since Arahnia would be using the needles in the operation, it would be a good idea for her to look them over.

A mint fragrance floated in from the other side of the curtain.

Knowledgeable when it came to medicine, Sapphee was also well versed in preparing medicinal herbs and plants. Glenn assumed the herbs she was currently using were those she had harvested from the Aluloona Plantation—a place Sapphee was on very good terms with. It was a pleasant fragrance, and mint was effective at calming the mind.

"Well, I'm a useless cyclops anyway, and honestly I can't do anything well, but...this time, *this time*, I really did try my best."

Memé's face no longer looked pale or flushed. Glenn imagined it was because her symptoms had been relieved, thanks in part to the minty smell.

It appeared there was a glimmer of hope in sight for Memé's needle production. Reflected in her large eye was a confidence in her own work—the confidence of a craftswoman.

✕ ✕ ✕ ✕ ✕

Rumble, rumble. The colossal machine groaned as it spun around and around.

It was so massive that it was difficult to figure out what the machine was, but it seemed to be some giant hexagonal contraption that spun horizontally. The power it possessed was the pride of the workshop and came from currents flowing in from the large water wheel. Glenn couldn't even imagine how many centaurs worth of power the machine could demonstrate.

Around and around it went.

It was situated in the prototyping room where Memé had collapsed. Even looking at it, however, Glenn had no idea what was what.

Having brought the now completely healthy Memé back to the Kuklo Workshop, Glenn was once again visiting himself, this time with Arahnia in toe.

Memé constantly apologized to the cyclops they met as they passed. She bowed her head a great number of times in apology to the boss as well. She was more regretful that she had caused trouble for the workshop than about having collapsed. Her loyalty was admirable, but her overzealous apologies had the opposite effect and made those she spoke to unsure of how to react to them. The boss looked like he had been forcing a smile as she bowed to him.

But that was neither here nor there.

"A spinning wheel..." Arahnia muttered as she looked at the machine.

At her words, Glenn realized the horizontal rotation of the machine *did* appear similar to a spinning wheel used to wind thread. The wheel looked just a bit bigger than Memé. The fact that the craftsmen were able to operate such a machine reflected just how skilled the cyclops of Kuklo Workshop were.

Yet, it wasn't winding thread. With the power of the water mill, the machine thinly stretched and stretched the raw materials it used to make one thing—steel.

It made threads of steel.

"A-at first I tried to temper iron to make the needles..." Memé explained. She faced the ground and mumbled her words, so it took some effort to hear what she was saying. "B-but they were too brittle to use on a dragon's body... I changed the material and tried all sorts of different things, but a sturdier needle would be as expensive as the materials I was using to strengthen it, and it would take a lot of time to manufacture, so I couldn't mass-produce them..."

"That makes sense," Glenn replied. Memé's problem was balancing both the quality and the quantity.

"That's when I used this machine!" Memé proclaimed, proudly puffing out her chest. Her large, healthy bosom sprung up and down. Although she had gotten changed, she was wearing nothing below her undershirt. Despite how easily she got embarrassed, she was careless with these other details.

"This machine...what exactly does it do?"

"By rotating, it stretches out materials. This time I stretched out steel and made wire. That's right—not a needle, but a wire!"

"Ooh..." Glenn said unconsciously, in admiration. It was attacking the problem from a different angle.

"By stretching out wire like this, cutting it short and using it in place of a needle, it can be mass produced, and it's made with quality steel so it should hold up to practical use. As far as the strength of the materials, I'm sure they'll only hold out ten or so uses when stitching up a dragon's blood vessels, but by manufacturing them this way, I can make sure there's enough made that there isn't any problem with them being disposable! This way, I'm positive it'll prove useful for the dragon operation, though I'm sure nothing someone like me would make is going to be used anyway, but I thought that if I could do at least this much then maybe Dr. Glenn would even use them for me, even if you were reluctant about it, so I—"

"M-Memé, you're too close," Glenn said, cutting her off.

"Ah!"

Glenn was happy to have things explained to him, but somewhere along the line Memé's face had gotten right in point-blank range of his. Memé stepped back in a panic and cast her eyes to the ground. The way she leaned in as soon as she started talking about her work was very much the nature of a craftswoman.

Glenn had to agree that she did have a point—this was way more efficient than forging them one at a time.

As far as strength was concerned, he expected that as long as Memé was responsible for the needles, they would be fine. After all, even he hadn't gotten the idea to use wire for the surgery— that was how Memé's creative power had manifested itself.

Giving a meaningful cackle, Memé took out several of the needles. Glenn figured they were prototypes. Memé handed the wire to him and Arahnia. He thought to test it by trying to bend the needle, but it was harder than he expected. With his slender arms, the needle wouldn't bend even when he tried putting more power into it.

"They're surprisingly...durable," he concluded.

"R-right?"

Glenn thought that since Memé had referred to it as a wire, it would easily bend, but that didn't appear to be the case. He could imagine it bending if he used all of his strength, but that showed just how sturdy the needle was. It appeared that Memé had perfectly followed the conditions laid out in the order form after all.

"Hmm. Well, this seems fine to me, does it not?" Arahnia said, staring fixedly at the needles. All of a sudden there was a thread attached to the back of the needle. Even without an eye to pass through, the silk of the arachne was adhesive and stuck to the needle. "Having no eye not only seems to simplify manufacturing, but this could pass through smaller spaces. And my silk fastens on just fine. Dr. Glenn, with this, could it be possible to skip piercing through the dragonscale and slip it between them instead?"

"It's a possibility. For how durable lizardfolk scales are, they do have gaps in between them. If dragonscales are similar, then..." Glenn pondered. Scales *appeared* to uniformly cover the entire body, but there were a surprising number of gaps. Lamia and lizardfolk had spaces in between their scales, so it was possible that dragonscales might be the same.

"We've got some hope in our sights now, don't we?" Arahnia said. "How truly spectacular little miss Memé is. It looks like we have a future woman workshop boss in our midst."

"P-please don't compliment me—I know you just have ulterior motives. You're planning on demanding something from me later, aren't you?!" Memé said, looking down at the ground and growing more and more embarrassed. "I-I still need to make the finishing touches, but with this, your surgical needles are finished. All that's left is for you to inspect them, Dr. Glenn."

"Okay. We'll need Dr. Cthulhy to look over them, too, but...I think this is good, Memé," Glenn replied.

Memé once again mumbled something in a voice too quiet for Glenn to hear properly, but for now her first assignment had been finished. She had done it all without incident—well, Glenn couldn't exactly say that, but whatever the case may be, she had completed the job.

"You're just adorable, Memé. Truly precious," said Arahnia.

"Yes...but I don't want you fainting any more, okay?" Glenn remarked.

"Why, Dr. Glenn is here for her, are you not?" Arahnia replied.

"I can't be everywhere at once... It's best you avoid collapsing again."

Glenn stared up at the machine, groaning as it rotated. Memé had collapsed from looking at this machine. In order to observe the wire-making process, she had sat unmoving in this prototyping room, watching the hexagonal machine spin around. Judging from the large amount of gastric juices in Memé's vomit, she had not eaten anything at all while she had been monitoring it.

Memé's eye, spinning around in circles—Glenn felt like he could perfectly imagine it all.

"U-um, w-well, Dr. Glenn..." Memé began.

"What is it?"

"Th-th-thank you...for entrusting th-this job to me..." For Memé, these words were a rare occurrence—truly rare words that lacked any sense of self-deprecation or servility. She always hid her true feelings by putting herself down. Seeing her true self behind her timidity wasn't difficult, but it was very rare to hear it straight from Memé's mouth.

"You even helped me when I collapsed... Um, I'll do my best not to collapse again," she continued.

"That's right, it's important that you rest properly, okay?"

"I, um, understand, and, well, one other thing." Memé hesitated, but still tried to say something to Glenn. "B-but don't get the wrong idea! Don't think that I'm a good worker just because of this! I'm still just a totally useless newbie, got it? Don't even *think* about trying to ask me to do any more work!"

Glenn wondered if it was just his imagination that Memé sounded like she actually wanted him to give her work again.

"I'll have to consult with the boss about that. But I really think it's incredible that you were able to pull this off so well at your age."

"Hehehehehe," giggled Memé.

"Also, you need to lift your head up properly and look in front of you. Tripping and bumping into things is bad enough, but it would be really serious if you got hit by a cart or something like that, you know."

Memé gave a startled gulp.

She had even fainted this time, so Glenn assumed that she had learned the risks her body faced. He thought that saying she might get hit by a cart was a little too frightening a threat to make, but nevertheless, there were many centaurs pulling carts and carriages in Lindworm. Such an accident wasn't an impossibility.

"Th-that's a little too much..." Memé protested.

"Still, it's dangerous," Glenn insisted.

"Hnnng, d-do I *really* have to?"

"There are already a lot of accidents involving cyclops to begin with."

With one eye, cyclops had no sense of distance. While most had no trouble walking through a town they were unfamiliar with, going around with their head down like Memé only increased the risk of injury.

Finally giving up, Memé brushed up her bangs and raised her head. Her single eye aimed straight at Glenn's face.

"There we go—see? Your face looks great," Glenn replied.

"Ah, um, eep!" Memé repeatedly opened her mouth to start talking, then immediately closed it. It appeared that she really was unused to looking directly at a person's face. Her cheeks turned red.

"You're a cyclops," Glenn said, "so it isn't strange for you to have only one eye, okay?"

"But I... My eyebrow."

"Your eyebrow?"

"I-it's weird right?"

Now that Memé mentioned it, Glenn noticed that her eyebrow leaned to the left a little.

Just like their eye, cyclops had only one eyebrow. However, there was individual variance in where the eyebrow sat on their face. Memé's eyebrow leaned noticeably to the left. But the lean itself didn't indicate any issues with her overall health.

"Don't worry about it. It's just some individuality. Not just your eyebrow, but your pupils and iris are totally healthy. You should have more confidence in yourself."

Being sick had a completely different meaning to it from being "weird," but Glenn feigned ignorance of this variety in meaning.

With her face still raised, Memé gave a blushing smile. Whether it was because of the shape of their massive iris, or because of the light reflected in their eye, Glenn didn't know, but when a cyclops smiled it seemed like their eye was sparkling. It wasn't a just a figurative feeling—their eye did indeed hold a mysterious, beautiful tint to them.

Then—

Memé's face quickly grew even redder, and she let her bangs fall back in front of her face.

"Y-y-you pervert doctor! M-making eyes at me, th-this is sexual harassment!" Memé cried.

"H-huh?"

"I'll, I'll sue you! Got it?!" Memé ran away, her face beet red.

While he knew it had come from embarrassment, Glenn could only stand dumbstruck by the brutal parting words that Memé had left as she escaped.

"...I guess my treatment was a little too drastic."

"I do wonder," Arahnia said. "Even if it was too much, it goes without saying that that girl's submissive attitude is quite the serious condition."

Glenn wondered how long it would be before Memé made her name known as a craftswoman. At the very least, it would be difficult until she fixed her personality, so he imagined it was still a while off for her. He imagined the next time they met she'd have some kind of self-deprecating comment for him. Either that or she really *would* accuse him of sexual harassment.

But there was just one thing Glenn thought about it all.

Her eye really was beautiful. It resembled a shiny decorative ornament—like the kind of work that Memé Redon would some-day make with her skilled and dexterous fingers.

Glenn wished with all his heart for that day to come.

CASE 03:
The Arachne with Bad Habits

THIS IS MY MEDICAL RECORD. A record that I, Saphentite, will never show anybody. For example, even if my beloved Dr. Glenn were to see this, then, well...

That would be quite a problem.

At any rate, this is somewhat like my personal diary. The clinic operations are all left in public record. Why then, you ask, am I leaving these personal records separately? That would be because, while I don't want them to be seen by Dr. Glenn, I have a variety of things that I want to write down.

It's as simple as that.

I do know that Glenn isn't the type of person to take a peek at another person's secrets, but...

Just in case, what would I do if he saw this? Poison him? Even I think that is a bit excessive, so if he *does* peek at my diary, I'll have to settle for seducing him. Seduction is a kind of poisoning of the mind, after all. Having inherited all the assassination techniques of my family, the Neikes, I am ever prepared to seduce the person closest to my heart, if necessary.

Of course, even I feel embarrassed at the thought of seducing him, so it will be a last resort at best.

✖ ✖ ✖ ✖ ✖

Dr. Glenn has become remarkably busy as of late.

It's only to be expected.

This spring, the Litbeit Clinic began making preparations for Miss Skadi's big surgery. Thanks to the efforts of Miss Memé from the Kuklo Workshop, we were able to meet our delivery deadline for the large quantity of surgical tools we ordered. But this also means there are fewer reasons to put off Miss Skadi's surgery. The more our preparations continue forward, the more real the operation becomes. There is no backing out now.

Dr. Glenn's work includes Arahnia's special training and meeting with Dr. Cthulhy. On top of all that, he needs to convince Miss Skadi, but it doesn't seem like things are going very well on that front. Because of how thin he's stretched himself, I am left more and more in charge of the essential clinic business.

Taking care of the clinic while he's gone is, in a word, lonely.

I don't mean to complain about my work, but we're supposed to manage this clinic together, yet I don't spend any time with him.

Though it's not like I've even had time to feel lonely. I have to soothe and humor Arahnia—who whines whenever I say anything to her—and prepare the reagents for the anesthetic using the Aluloona herbs I ordered, all while examining every patient that visits the clinic every day. Even with the fairies, I don't have enough hands to do everything. I find myself wondering—if I were multi-legged like Arahnia, would I be able to work a little more?

No—it won't change anything to ask for the impossible. All I can do is somehow endure this with the fairies' help. These thoughts had been on my mind when—

"Are you tired?"

One of the fairies touched my finger, looking as if they were worried about me.

The fairies are about big enough to fit in the palm of my hand. With their big heads, they look somewhat childlike, and have androgynous features. It's difficult to distinguish whether they are men or women, and I can't quite tell them apart individually. Similar to social insects like ants or bees, they don't have much individual personality, and they are known as a race of monster that prosper by living together in colonies.

"It's okay," I replied to the fairy at the time. I squished their head as I spoke, and it seemed like that tickled them.

The helper fairies and I don't have any sort of mutual under-standing. We are simply employer and employee, connected by one singular condition—a plate of milk for their payment. Yet this one fairy actually showed personal concern for me.

I still had a number of different anesthetics that I wanted to test out, so I couldn't afford to relax and take it easy. As a pharma-cologist, it is my job to puzzle over the medicine I make.

But more than my medicine, what had me troubled and puzzled were the habits of my close friend Arahnia. It was truly such a waste of my brain power.

Why was I troubled? Because her habits were one more thing that I couldn't consult with Dr. Glenn about. I didn't want to hide things from him, but women do have their own secrets.

"Huuh?"

This happened around the time the fairies were comforting me during my busiest days. Dr. Glenn spoke up, distressed, as he peered at the clinic's shelves.

"Hey, Sapphee, do you know what happened to the antiseptic solution I left here?" he asked me.

"No idea—could the fairies have put it away for you?" I replied.

When Dr. Glenn left medicine bottles lying around, the fairies were often sensible enough to clean up and put them away for him. This was the least of the work that the hardworking helper fairies did in the clinic.

"No, I was sure that I put it properly away in here..." he continued.

Dr. Glenn thought long and hard about where it could be. I surveyed the small clinic. Now then, wherever could it have gone?

If it was in the clinic, then I knew I'd get my hand—or rather, my tail—on it. Casting my gaze around, I immediately found the medical bottle in question. It was on the shelf right behind where Dr. Glenn was standing.

"Here it is, Doctor," I said.

"Huh? It was *there*? Whoops—my mistake—but I really didn't remember leaving it there at all..." he said.

"Please be a little more attentive, Doctor."

I coiled my tail around the medicine bottle and carried it to Dr. Glenn. Sometimes I feel like my long tail is quite a nuisance, but I always end up coming to the conclusion it is convenient compared to other two-legged or four-legged species.

"Didn't you mention recently that you lost your stethoscope, too?" I asked.

"P-probably... In the end I found it in another spot when I went looking for it," Dr. Glenn replied.

"You should at least understand where you place your tools. This is *your* clinic, after all, Doctor."

At my words, Dr. Glenn scratched his head with a distressed look upon his face.

He is totally unreliable.

Well, that's only natural—even I am apt to forget the fact that Dr. Glenn is still seventeen years old. The other day he was so happy at Miss Memé's remarkable personal growth, like he was actually her guardian and not her doctor, but from my perspective both Dr. Glenn and Miss Memé looked as though they were the same age.

Since he is managing his own clinic at such a young age, it would be stranger, if anything, if he *were* reliable. He is still Cthulhy's junior pupil, and it doesn't seem like these chances to scold him for his mistakes will be going away any time soon.

Although this makes me a little happy, in its own way.

"Sapphee, you haven't asked the fairies to do anything weird, have you?" Dr. Glenn asked me.

"...Huh? What do you mean?"

"It's just, well, I was just thinking maybe my tools are going missing because the fairies are putting stuff away in the wrong places...or something like that."

"You're overthinking things. Neither myself nor the fairies have done anything of the sort."

Well, well, well. I had thought he was unreliable, but it appeared that unbeknownst to me, Dr. Glenn had matured somewhat. They say that men can mature greatly when you stop watching over them for a while, but it seemed he had improved his abilities of perception somewhere along the way. "More importantly Dr. Glenn, I believe it's time for you to head out, isn't it?" I reminded him.

"Wait—already?" he replied.

"You're heading all the way to the Council Hall, right?"

Dr. Glenn started preparing to go out in a panic. Recently, it seemed like his head was always filled with thoughts about his discussion with Miss Skadi.

I hadn't seen it directly, but a second heart had grown on Skadi's chest. Miss Cthulhy, and Dr. Glenn and I all barely had time to sleep as we prepared for the surgery to excise the tumor. The tools had been all gathered, and our outside assistant Arahnia's surgical skills were getting better and better by the day, without any problems whatsoever. All that was left was, well, convincing Miss Skadi herself.

However.

This seemed to be what was puzzling Dr. Glenn the most. I don't know exactly what conversations the two of them have been sharing, but it seems like she isn't being very receptive to his persuasion.

"Dr. Glenn, what about this?" I asked. I grabbed something that was left on top of the desk. It was an accessory made from a golden drake's scales.

"Oh... Well..."

Dragons themselves are rare, but dragonscales aren't that uncommon at all. I've heard that dragons frequently drop one or two scales at a time, and that if you search the forests or mountains you can pick them up easily. There are scale decorations on my own clothes as well, and it is not uncommon, even among monsters, to wear scale accessories.

It is believed that the scales of a dragon give the wearer divine protection, and they are used as talismans to protect the wearer from evil. Lying on top of the desk was a present of golden dragonscale that I had given to Glenn, indeed partly as a protective charm.

Of course, part of my goal was to give us matching charms to wear.

"So you're not going to wear it?" I asked him, cruelly giving my voice a reproachful tone—implying that I was disappointed he was refusing my present.

Dr. Glenn didn't hide his panic. Seeing him panic over something like this—he was just so pure and adorable. I knew I had to make sure he didn't get corrupted by any of the strange bugs hanging about.

"I-I thought today I'd leave it here," he replied.

"And why is that?" I was positive this charm had been attached to his doctor's bag. It was already with him when he left the clinic. So if that was the case, I wondered—why did he take it off today?

It couldn't be—was he meeting with another woman?

Did wearing the charm I gave him make him feel guilty?

There was a woman he thought so tenderly about—other than me?

"Tch," I said under my breath. The fires of jealousy seemed close to burning over inside of me, but I immediately calmed them. Thinking about it logically, I managed to figure out why in an instant.

It was absolutely nothing to be angry about. Yes, yes, of course it wasn't.

"Oh—you're being considerate of Miss Skadi's feelings?" I asked.

"Y-yeah. Miss Skadi's a dragon, and I kinda thought that maybe she'd...not like dragonscale stuff."

"I think you're reading into it too much, but... No, it might be best to treat her with that level of courtesy."

I was sure that she wouldn't have any problems with dragonscale goods. For example, even I wouldn't think anything of someone using my molted skin to make a good luck charm. I've actually heard of some businesses decorating their building with lamia skins. Nevertheless, that didn't necessarily mean that Miss Skadi felt the same way.

I did think that consideration was necessary. Dr. Glenn's

shortcomings weren't going to be fixed overnight, of course, but he should pay attention to the things he's able to notice.

"I understand. In that case, I'll put the charm away for now," I replied.

"S-sorry Sapphee. I'm heading out now."

"Okay, have a good trip—you better not fool around while you're out."

"As if I have time for that."

Dr. Glenn even gave a serious reply to my joke—although I'm sure he really didn't have the time to spare.

I was left alone in the clinic.

Lately, the clinic had been receiving fewer patients, perhaps because of the beautiful spring weather. This was a windfall for Dr. Glenn and me, as we had a mountain of problems to deal with—I was able to spend time adjusting and tuning the anesthetics I wanted to try, so I found the freedom was a boon.

But I wasn't actually alone. Running in between my legs (though since I don't have legs, maybe I should say "close to the underside of my snake tail," instead?) were the fairies. Even I didn't know how many of them there were total, but I knew that there were a considerable number working at the clinic. Whether it was organizing the medical equipment or cleaning the clinic itself, they devoted themselves diligently to any work they found that needed doing.

In addition to the fairies, there was one more person.

"Arahnia. Your break should be just about over by now," I said to Arahnia, who was occupying one of the clinic's beds.

"Hnn... Now just a little longer won't hurt, right?"

"Nope. Time to get up."

Arahnia moved her jointed legs and squirmed up out of the bed. Perhaps it was due to the unfamiliar work that Dr. Glenn and I were asking of her, but she seemed particularly sleepy as of late.

Climbing out from under the covers, Arahnia's face looked pale. I could see her exhaustion. It wasn't uncommon for the fashion-crazed designer to be subject to such overwork. I wondered if she was reluctant to use makeup, if only just to hide her tired complexion.

Well, makeup was strictly prohibited in the clinic either way.

"Hey, Sapphee, have you ever seen blood vessels or nerve bundles in your dreams before? I saw them in mine last night... Teehee, it was my *first time*," Arahnia said, seductively.

"I did back when I was at the academy," I replied.

"I'd expect nothing less from a professional," Arahnia said, sluggishly beginning to work.

Lately, Arahnia hadn't just been focusing on her suturing practice, but also helping me out with the clinic chores. Even with the fairies here, the clinic didn't have enough people helping out. Having a clever woman like Arahnia assisting me often proved useful in some way or another.

I had warned Dr. Glenn that Arahnia had some ulterior motive she was keeping to herself. Although my doubts hadn't been completely dispelled, in reality, the fact that she was as utterly exhausted as she was made me think she didn't have enough energy for any secret schemes. Nevertheless, it was important to keep oneself in good shape. I thought she might need a breather soon.

"This surgery—I wonder if it will happen," Arahnia said. It was rare for her to express such a sentiment.

"Are you worried?" I replied.

"But of course. Why, to think, if after I've tried so hard, we end up not being able to do it..."

"I'm sure Dr. Glenn will convince her somehow. It'll be fine." Those were the words I replied with. But they were just words. In fact, I was worried. I was *very* worried! It didn't show on my face, but inside my mind, I was rife with anxiety.

After all, Dr. Glenn was still young, still unreliable! And the person he was speaking to was a dragon who not only had been alive for an unknowable number of years, but possessed wisdom and intelligence that helped turn Lindworm into the rich and plentiful city it was today. That's who he was going to convince? Could Glenn really do it?! My tiny little Glenn?!

The gap in their life experience was too big. It was probably impossible for *any* human to ever have as much experience as a dragon, no matter how long a life they led. That was the type of person Miss Skadi seemed to be.

If I was being perfectly honest, I wanted to do everything for him.

Dr. Glenn was only incredible when it came to medical knowledge and techniques. He was totally useless when it came to anything outside of that. When it came to the practical side of daily life, he couldn't do anything—cooking, cleaning, laundry, none of it. If it was in my power, then I wanted to do everything he couldn't do for him. Of course, that wouldn't be good for Dr. Glenn himself, so I had to maintain some level of self-control.

"You really do love the Doctor, don't you, Sapphee?" Arahnia asked.

"Yes, I do." I nodded. It took courage for me to proclaim my love in front of Arahnia, but I tried to answer as calmly as possible.

Arahnia has a bad habit. It was an extremely irritating habit. She always wanted to claim the people or things that others held dear and precious for herself. Previously, she had tried to get her hands on Dr. Glenn. To be perfectly frank, her hobby was stealing away and sleeping with her friends' lovers.

Not only that, she would insist that all of it was done for the sake of her art.

She was beyond help.

Thanks to this personality of hers, even when she made friends, she would steal her friends' lovers and sour the friendship. Repeating this over and over again, Arahnia finally lost her popularity.

Fortunately, it appears that she hasn't been entirely ostracized among her own race—this habit of plunder and thievery is more or less common among the arachne. There are truly some awful species of monsters out there in the world.

Even if she is understood by other arachne, the other monster races aren't so understanding. It's incredible that I've even been able to become friends with such a woman, if I do say so myself. Arahnia is a strange woman for sure, but I might be a very eccentric person myself.

"I'm fine if you fool around with him, but you can't ever get serious, Arahnia," I said.

"You're saying I *can* fool around?" she replied.

"As long as it doesn't become serious, I'll allow him to have any number of mistresses he wants."

It was a lie. An outrageous lie.

I had thought that maybe I'd be fine as long as his mistress was Arahnia... But thinking about it again, I really did hate it. It may be odd for me to say this about myself, but I do think I'm very possessive of Dr. Glenn, so while I might try not to be excessively overbearing toward him, I still can't help detesting an idea if I truly hate it.

However, as long as Dr. Glenn didn't become serious about anyone besides me, I ended up thinking that I'd be fine with him fooling around with someone else. My possessiveness came from my desire to always be Dr. Glenn's number one, which made me feel that so long as he kept things casual, I'd be okay with letting him flirt, and see as many other women as he liked.

Am I contradicting myself? I probably am, aren't I?

"...Well, that's a little boring, I'd say," replied Arahnia.

Huh? I thought she would say that even being lovers would be fine so long as she got to enjoy herself, but her response came as quite a surprise.

Did Arahnia want to be his number one, too?

I realized that while I thought we were close friends, it might actually be impossible to figure Arahnia out after all. She was an arachne, a race of all women. Women were annoying creatures no matter what race of monster they were—this annoyance was probably all the more worse among a race of all women.

Even for other women, it was impossible to understand a woman's heart. As if a man could ever understand it.

"Arahnia," I said, addressing her. Possibly because of her exhaustion, she seemed somewhat absentminded.

"Yes?"

"Tonight, do you want to go out for a drink?"

✗ ✗ ✗ ✗ ✗

The Giant Squid's Inn.

It was a large bar that was found a little ways past the Central Plaza and its fountain, en route to the Merrow Waterways. The owner was a kindhearted kraken madam. Their specialty was their squid-ink pasta. It was Arahnia and I's favorite spot to go drinking together.

I love wine. Arahnia, on the other hand, enjoys a type of alcohol made in the eastern regions of the human territory known as "ginjo." There aren't many bars in Lindworm that carry both. The Great Squid's Inn was one of the rare places where we could drink together despite our different preferences in alcohol.

"Phew..." Arahnia sighed after taking a gulp of ginjo from her cup, which was small enough to fit in the palm of her hand. It was as if she were expelling all her daily exhaustion with the sigh.

"Arahnia, are you really not going to use a glass?" I asked.

"When drinking alcohol from the east, it's proper etiquette to use this choko to drink it. One ends up drinking far too much with a regular glass," Arahnia replied.

"Choko...? Like chocolate?"

"No, no, no," Arahnia answered with a cackle.

I was enjoying a glass of white wine from the Aluloona Plantation. It was a mass-produced vintage of not especially high quality, but it had a very full-bodied flavor that I enjoyed.

I wondered if Miss Aluloona was doing well. The owner of the plantation, she was a woman I often bought medicinal herbs and plants from, but I hadn't met with her recently.

I suddenly thought about her arresting green skin and extending vines. Miss Aluloona had an influential voice in the city council, and was close to Miss Skadi, so I imagined that she was busy at the moment as well. I decided that I should take the time to visit the Plantation soon.

"Now then," Arahnia began as she poured more alcohol into her choko cup. "It's been a while since I've gone drinking with you, Sapphee, but...before we begin the festivities, may I ask you something?"

"What could that be?"

"Why is *she* here?" Arahnia said, pointing her finger at the third woman sitting at our table. The woman she pointed to disregarded Arahnia's remark, using a fork and knife to continue digging into the humongous salad in front of her. For a drink, she appeared to have some kind of carrot juice.

The picture-perfect vegetarian.

"I was invited too," replied Tisalia the centaur nonchalantly. "Sapphee, the vegetables at this restaurant are very delicious."

"I'm glad to hear you like it."

"Why, of course I would love it! Oh, waiter, could I get another serving?" Her bowl completely empty, Tisalia got the attention of a passing waiter.

She ate far too fast. She was eating so much good food every day—was that still not enough? What was truly maddening was that despite all she ate, none of it went to her stomach and all just went to her breasts instead. I wonder if becoming an arena fighter would give me that ideal body.

"You know this is a bar, don't you? What's with that red juice of yours?" chirped Arahnia.

"I simply don't drink," Tisalia replied.

"I called her here, Arahnia. I haven't gotten a chance to see her in a while," I replied.

Tisalia Scythia. She was the daughter of the head of Scythia Transportation, which was responsible for the transportation network in Lindworm. To me, she was my natural enemy for Dr. Glenn's affections. On the other hand, I couldn't help having a soft spot for her straightforward personality.

She was an attractive woman—which was precisely why she was also capable of stealing Dr. Glenn away from me, and therefore someone I needed to be cautious around. I had to meet with her every once in a while and check up on her inclinations toward Dr. Glenn.

Seeing her wasn't solely about deepening our relationship as I had my own self-interests in mind as well.

"Yes, well, I did have some things I had to speak to you alone about, Sapphee..." said Arahnia.

"It's fine, isn't it? It's just us girls today, so feel free to confide in me everything you can't talk about in the clinic," Tisalia replied.

"Well... You do have a point. It makes no difference whether Miss Scythia is here or not," Arahnia sighed.

"That's right," I replied. Part of Arahnia's objections might have come from the idea that having a non-drinker with us might stifle the fun of our drinking party.

Our drinking get-togethers were always quiet and leisurely. It wasn't the type of party to get loud and noisy. We liked having a gentle, peaceful chat together, like a steadily pouring rain storm. The addition of a slightly gluttonous centaur wouldn't stop us from having an enjoyable time.

"That reminds me, Sapphee, are the surgery preparations going well?" Tisalia asked.

"Yes. Thank you very much for your cooperation, Tisalia," I replied.

"Oh, please don't mention it, it's just... Considering you ordered anesthetic ingredients..." Tisalia trailed off.

An anesthetic to use on a dragon. This was my task. I guess I could also say it was a test imposed upon me by Dr. Cthulhy.

Heart surgery required whole-body anesthesia, but in all of my studies, I didn't know of a single anesthetic that worked on a dragon. While the lamia were known as the pharmacologists of the monster world, performing surgery on a dragon was something completely beyond anyone's imagination.

"Did you figure out a solution in the end?" said Tisalia, finishing her thought.

"Yes. I still need to experiment, but...I've found an ingredient that will work on dragons," I said, pointing my finger at the ginjo that Arahnia was enjoying. Arahnia stared back blankly, the look on her face suggesting that she didn't know what we were talking about.

"Why—what is it?" Arahnia asked.

"I'm saying that alcohol you're holding seems like it will work," I replied. I had seen the story while I was reading an old document. "There was an eight-headed dragon that appeared in a country to the east. Apparently the dragon demanded sacrifices and ate the people of the country, but it got drunk off that alcohol you're holding and fell asleep, and a hero used the opening to cut off its heads. It said the hero cut them all off one at a time."

"I see. Everyone seems to have their own fairy tales about killing dragons, don't they?" Tisalia chimed in.

"I got a hint from this story. Basically, this eight-headed dragon wouldn't die unless all of its heads were cut off, so it hit me—assuming that the dragon had been asleep because of the alcohol, hadn't it been alive while its heads were getting cut off one by one?"

Arahnia was listening attentively. I continued.

"In other words, wouldn't the alcohol be able to act as an anesthetic? I was thinking that so long as nothing vital is severed in the surgery, the alcohol might be able to calm Miss Skadi's pain during the operation."

I believed that this line of reasoning had put me on the right track. That being said, it was nothing more than a single line of reasoning. That was why I worked with Tisalia to order some alcohol from the country to the east. I still needed to do experiments on whether the alcohol would actually have the desired effect.

With the power of the Scythia Transportation company, ordering some liquor from a country in the eastern part of human territory seemed simple enough. Besides, even the Giant Squid's Inn had stocked up on many bottles of the eastern liquor, and there was already an established trade route, as well.

"Ah... I see. You're as clever as ever, Sapphee," Tisalia replied.

Arahnia had listened attentively to my description of the old story I had found (it had been called yamata-something-or-other) and to the idea that the story had given me.

"There's the story of this snake in the east, called 'uwabami,' that's supposed to like alcohol as well. Although, snakes and dragons might not react the same way..." said Arahnia.

"If it's from the east, then that means there's a chance it's a subspecies of the dragon. I'll have to look it up," I replied. I was fairly certain that Arahnia was somewhat knowledgeable about the eastern edge of the humans' territory. The clothes she wore looked like they were from the eastern countries. I'm told that when she was studying, she even traveled through the human territory on foot. I knew without a doubt from her achievements as a designer that she had experience living there. It was safe to say that if someone in Lindworm happened upon an exotic piece of clothing, it was probably Arahnia's work.

This wasn't good. Dr. Glenn also came from the human territory. If he talked about his hometown, he might hit it off with Arahnia. I needed to stay vigilant. After all, I know a thing or two about the human territory myself.

"Anyway, I still need to prove my theory with an actual experiment. If this goes well, it'll be a big step toward producing an anesthetic," I continued.

"I hope the surgery can move forward without any delays..." Tisalia replied. She also seemed to be concerned for Miss Skadi. Everyone was worried for the dragon. It was plain to see just how much prestige she had gathered for herself.

"Yes. However, there's still one problem," I replied.

"What problem?" Tisalia asked.

"That," I said, pointing toward Arahnia once more. She didn't seem to be paying attention at all, and hummed a tune as she enjoyed her alcohol. She was ordering a refill, meaning she had drunk all of the ginjo that had been in her small earthenware bottle.

"Gulp, gulp, gulp... Aaah!" Arahnia licked her lips and continued to savor the flavor of the alcohol.

"Arahnia's not actually a doctor, but I think she is doing very well. Even still, it will be her first experience doing actual surgery. She's been practicing on Miss Kunai's dead flesh, but I wonder what her reaction will be upon seeing real blood vessels, nerves, and organs... I remembered what I thought at the time, that the insides of a living organism can be quite disgusting to look at," I continued.

Tisalia watched Arahnia enjoying her alcohol as if she were looking at some sort of rare beast. For a non-drinker like Tisalia, the sight of a heavy drinker like Arahnia must have been bizarre. As someone who also enjoyed alcohol, it was a gaze that I had often seen cast my way.

"Hehehe, Sapphee?" said Arahnia.

"Yes, Arahnia?" I replied.

"Are you drinking?"

"For the most part," I replied. It seemed I had also gotten a little tipsy. The wine was superb, as usual.

It would be nice if I could drink with Dr. Glenn, but he doesn't seem to enjoy alcohol very much. Besides, it might be better that way, since it would be a problem for a doctor to love alcohol.

"Sapphee, you really are adorable." Her words slurring as she spoke, Arahnia gave me a sidelong glance.

Well, she was clearly drunk. She had probably lost some her tolerance as a result of our recent alcohol ban. And she had been particularly exhausted, so I wondered if that made the alcohol affect her more.

"You've had a little too much to drink, Arahnia," I said.

"Why, I've had practically nothing!" she replied.

I ordered her a glass of water. The only snack we had ordered was a simple egg dish, and Arahnia hadn't even eaten that. She was always a light eater, but having nothing but alcohol in her body was concerning, whatever the circumstances.

Tisalia gave a curious look at the red-faced, giggling drunk.

"Is she always like this?" she asked.

"No, normally she's more...docile," I replied. Even when she had had too much to drink, she had almost never looked this intoxicated before. Perhaps because she was hot, she took off the ornaments she had around her neck. I had a feeling that if she wasn't stopped, she'd be stripping off all her clothes entirely.

Every movement as she took off her ornaments was suggestive—erotic. I'm sure there are many men who would fall madly in love from seeing it. But even though she had stolen the hearts of countless people's lovers before, she had yet to try and settle on a partner herself. Once she grew tired of one of the lovers she had stolen, she would quickly kick them to the curb. She had less interest in the person or thing she was taking away than the act of snatching them away itself.

She was quite the ill-natured arachne.

"Miss Arahnia, do you remember our quarrel in the harpy village?" Tisalia asked.

"Hmm? Oh, that, I definitely remember that," Arahnia replied.

"Back then, you asked me if my love for Dr. Glenn was real or not, didn't you?"

"I did, didn't I?" Cackling as she spoke, Arahnia didn't show any signs of regret for her actions.

The incident at the harpy village hadn't been a mere quarrel. If I hadn't gone and stopped them, either Tisalia or Arahnia would have gotten seriously hurt. Of course, it had been entirely Arahnia's fault for making a move on Dr. Glenn to begin with.

I wondered just what would happen if she tried to lay her hand on my sweetheart—and yes, Dr. Glenn is my sweetheart—or the lover of another woman. I *knew* that Arahnia was aware of what would happen. And yet, despite that, she went out of her way to provoke people.

"Well, then... Miss Arahnia, do you know what real love is?"

I almost gave a triumphant clap at Tisalia's question. Instead, I used my tail to clap quietly against the floor.

Arahnia smiled in satisfaction, as if she was scheming something. It was a very suspicious smile—but I understood. Tisalia had touched on a sensitive subject with Arahnia, and Arahnia was just trying to gloss over it with a smile.

"I wonder..." Arahnia began, slurping down a sip of her drink. "Love, lust, fancy, hatred—you see, I just *love* the diplomacy of it all. But is there any *real* emotion in any of that, or is it all just lies? Everyone might just be lying. Everyone's feelings might be true. Is there any way you can verify if your love is true or not?"

I sensed some sort of sensation on my pinky. Without my realizing it, a thin strand of white had wrapped itself around my finger. Looking over, I spied a similar piece of white silk on Tisalia's pinky as well. The glittering white spider silk had been wound around Arahnia's finger, too.

"A red thread connecting two pinkies is proof of two lovers' destiny. Now it may not have any color, but I can connect anyone with my silk any time I want. Not just between a man, but between other women as well—look, just like this," Arahnia continued.

Connecting the three of us with her threads of silk, Arahnia was overjoyed. At least on the surface, she seemed to be in high spirits.

"Us three—our pinkies are tied together, so we're friends," Arahnia continued.

Really? It would be simple for Tisalia to use her dinner knife and cut right through the thread. Was Arahnia trying to say that this thin web had tied the three of us together? I had no idea what she was so happy about or why she was grinning so much. It felt as if she was trying to confirm that our friendship would be everlasting.

"Yes... That's right, Arahnia," I replied, for the time being. I knew very well that Arahnia couldn't satisfy herself with relationships that could be severed whenever she wanted.

You may ask how I know that.

Of course I do. After all, she's my best friend.

The commotion in Lindworm grew louder day by day.

The city newspaper had apparently written a new article on Miss Skadi's illness. This time, they even mentioned how the Central Hospital would work with the Litbeit Clinic to operate on her.

Well, the Central Hospital, Kuklo Workshop, and Loose Silk Sewing were all major institutions that had many different people coming and going from them. If one went around collecting all the available information, it was probably an easy guess that we were preparing for surgery. But it didn't seem like Dr. Cthulhy was strictly enforcing a gag order, either.

We medical professionals weren't about to get involved with the commotion. It was clear what needed to be done, so all that was left was for us to push forward toward our goal. Fortunately, it appeared that the paper had done its research properly this time and hadn't spread irresponsible rumors around the city.

It wasn't that which was causing a stir in my heart.

"Yes, that's it right there. Be thorough. Like you're gently pinching it. This area's important, so be careful... Yes, that's it. You've gotten much better," said Dr. Glenn.

"Oh, come now, it's only because you're such a good teacher, Doctor," Arahnia replied.

"This time, why don't you try doing it faster?"

"Okay, I'll try."

They were close. They had been too close to each other for a while now. But there wasn't anything I could do about it. Dr. Glenn was looking over a body with a surgical sponge and having Arahnia practice her suturing. Arahnia had an instrument in each of her four arms, and Dr. Glenn stood next to her with his face close to hers, watching how she used her hands.

This practice was necessary for the surgery, so I just had to deal with it, but nevertheless, they were, well, quite close to one another. It was irritating.

"Here...and here, Miss Arahnia."

"Understood, I'll just squeeze here and... Okay, Doctor, how is that?"

"Good—very good."

Hold on a second. What exactly were they talking about?

Listening to the words out of context made it sound like bedroom talk—no, no, no what was I even thinking? This was all because Arahnia's very existence was indecent. Enough that even innocent surgery practice ended up sounding obscene. Yes, that's right, this was all Arahnia's fault.

"Doctor, you are so fantastic. Why, it feels like I'm taking more of a fancy to you with each passing minute."

"Ah ha haha..." Dr. Glenn's smile twitched as he laughed. It was only natural he'd be unsure how to handle Arahnia's confession, considering he had already been attacked by her before.

"Dr. Glenn," I said forcing myself into the conversation, unable to bear listening any longer. "About this medical record."

"Huh? Oh, um, yes?" replied Dr. Glenn.

"The pages are all out of order. Please make sure to arrange them properly."

"Understood... But still, that's strange, isn't it...?"

Oh no—I ended up scolding him.

While it was upsetting that Arahnia was so close to Dr. Glenn, if I acted too harshly he'd just end up hating me. I knew that, and yet, I still acted this way.

"It's fine. I'll just fix it. You'll be going to the workshop and the Central Hospital today, right?" I said.

"...I'm sorry, Sapphee. Oh, and I'll be stopping by the Council Hall today, too," he replied.

"In that case, I'll prepare a late dinner."

I was right—it seemed he was having a difficult time convincing Miss Skadi. That was why his trips out of the clinic were getting more frequent. Every time I thought he'd stay in the clinic for once, all he did was coach Arahnia instead—if you could even call their subdued whispering to one another coaching.

Was I just being ignored? Was that it?

I couldn't stand this. Nothing but jealousy—I couldn't stand what I was becoming.

"I'll be waiting for you to come back, Doctor," I said.

"Yeah, I'll leave the rest to you, okay?" Dr. Glenn replied.

Even I could feel the sardonic tinge to my words. I was sure Dr. Glenn picked up on the irritation I couldn't hide. But he was so thoughtful that he faced my jealousy with calm composure.

No, that wasn't it. I'm sure it was simply that he didn't have the time or energy to fully contemplate my feelings. Dr. Glenn just wanted to help Miss Skadi and the other monsters of this town.

"Are you fine with that, Sapphee?" Arahnia asked me after I had seen Dr. Glenn off, never breaking her smile.

"With what?"

"You have to say to him, 'Doctor, please pay attention to me.' A man will never understand unless you tell him properly."

"It's fine."

That's right. I was looking after the clinic as always. It was proof that Glenn relied on me. I'd look after it, organizing documents, while Arahnia continued her four-armed suturing practice.

I knew that Arahnia wanted to provoke me. But unfortunately for her, that wasn't going to work.

"This isn't the first time I've looked after the clinic," I continued.

"Hmm? What does *that* mean, exactly?" Arahnia replied.

"We've been separated from each other once before. We parted, and I thought that I would never see him again."

Back then, I had lived at Glenn Litbeit's family home. He was from a major merchant family, and I only lived there because of a ruse involving both my family and Glenn's—a hostage exchange, in a sense. But I was able to meet Glenn through that, so I was grateful to my family, the Neikes, for everything, and didn't bear them a grudge at all for involving me in their plot.

For less than a year, I spent time with the young Glenn. During that period, I was completely taken with him—so much so that I wanted to howl when it came time for me to return to my own home. Lamia don't have tear ducts, but we are still able to express our sorrows with loud cries.

I thought it was a final farewell—that I would live my whole life with the memories of the days I spent with a boy named Glenn, my first love, without ever seeing him again.

"Can you understand what it felt like back at the Academy, when I was reunited with my first love?" I asked.

"I wouldn't know, but I'm sure that was quite the surprise," Arahnia replied.

"Yes, very much so."

I *had* been surprised. The young boy from so many years ago had arrived at the Monster Academy, now a student overflowing with genius. There wasn't any among Dr. Cthulhy's students at the time that could rival his knowledge or his skill.

The once-young boy had now started to become a man. My

knowledge of pharmacology, too, was easily eclipsed by his passionate pursuit of learning. His skills weren't just for show—they were recognized by Dr. Cthulhy, and he was the only one among her students who had been permitted to open their own independent clinic.

Anyone would fall in love with him, wouldn't they?

Or rather, I should say it was practically a given I'd end up falling in love *again,* wasn't it?

Glenn Litbeit is a man I have seriously fallen in love with twice in my lifetime. The first time, I found him adorable, while the second time I found him attractive. That's why it was already too late—my heart is a slave to Dr. Glenn.

I wouldn't be moved, even by Arahnia's little provocations. I absolutely. Would not. Be. Provoked.

"Dr. Glenn really is loved, isn't he?" Arahnia remarked.

"Yes, that's right. So you keep out of it," I replied.

"I'm rather jealous."

As I organized the documents, I wondered. My reunion with Glenn had made me extremely happy. Although we currently slept in different rooms, we were living together in the same clinic. It wouldn't be too much to say that we were already in a de facto marriage. Yes, that was exactly right, and I wouldn't hear any objections that said otherwise.

But...

That personality of his—the one I fell in love with—was exactly why he was so often absent from the clinic. This was most evident at times like now, when he was the most busy. There were many things he had to handle outside the clinic. So long as there were only two people working there, I would have no choice but to look after it while he was gone.

Of course, there were also times we would take trips as part of our clinic work, or go out shopping together, but it was a little lonely right now, as even that was out of reach.

I can only imagine what would happen if these feelings of mine were made clear.

I'm not good at being by myself and not cut out for watching the clinic while Dr. Glenn is gone. Not to mention the fact that when I'm left alone here, all sorts of thoughts come into my mind. Thoughts like the possibility that Dr. Glenn might go somewhere far, far away in order to help someone—far enough that no matter how I may stretch out my tail, I'll never be able to reach him.

Even if I tell myself that there is no way it could happen, in the back of my mind I remember that, when I was younger, I had already experienced parting from him once.

"...Sapphee, you're making a rather frightening face right now," said Arahnia.

"You're the one who said something strange," I replied.

"Really? Well then, I suppose it's my fault then."

The golden dragonscales—Glenn hadn't been carrying the pendent I had given him today, either. It should have been carefully tucked away in his bedroom. So that meant that he was actually meeting with Miss Skadi today. He *did* mention he would be stopping by the Council Hall.

I found myself touching the dragonscale attached to my own

clothes. I felt a little bit of peace of mind when I was touching the charm—probably because it matched the one that Dr. Glenn had.

I had things of my own that I needed to do. I could wait until it was all over before I selfishly asked Glenn to dote on me more.

"Arahnia. Time to get back to work. Let's work hard," I said.

"Snakes sure can be mean and cold, can't they?" she complained.

"I'm just hiding it. If I were *really* that cold, I'd be hibernating."

Women never say what they really mean. Isn't it shameless to expose anything and everything, all the more so if it is to someone you love? The boiling passion in a woman's chest is always desperately pushed beneath the surface.

So I hope that in front of Dr. Glenn, I will always be his reliable senior professional and assistant.

✻ ✖ ✖ ✖ ✻

I have an awful, terrible confession to make.

My...

My mother was a thief.

My beautiful mother was greedy. There was always something she wanted. What made it worse was that she didn't know a single way to curb her own desires.

Her modus operandi was shrewd. She would use her natural beauty to con the men who approached her and control them. Even when she would make her men steal for her, and snatch things from others, she made sure never to get her own hands dirty.

The men that she ensnared wouldn't even balk at committing a crime if it was for her sake.

My mother stated that the one thing she absolutely wouldn't do, whether directly or indirectly, was murder someone. But even that felt suspicious to me. She was a woman who would do whatever was necessary to get what she wanted. If, for example, she had used the chaos of the great war to take someone's life, I wouldn't have been surprised at all.

I had always thought her behavior was wretched—being unable to restrain oneself from wanting something, the inability to endure the fact one couldn't have something. As such, she was a woman who would take advantage of any sort of good will or kindness that was directed toward her, and do anything in order to satisfy her desires.

It was only natural that I detested her.

Nevertheless, my mother's blood runs through me.

My mother thoughtlessly had intimate relationships with many different men, so I don't know who my father is. My mother didn't neglect me at all, but I wouldn't say that she cherished me, either.

She probably just saw me as a by-product of her escapades in seducing men.

How unfortunate—to have such an ugly and indecent woman's blood in my veins.

Not only that, but I am similar. I am very much like my mother. I inherited her inability to restrain herself from the things she wanted.

Possessions, love—I want all of it.

I want to control it all.

My mother acted like a queen, with all those men following her every beck and call, and her blood does indeed flow through me as well.

That's exactly why I'm different from her. I wanted to show that I'm different.

For example, any clothes, jewels, food, or even men—if it was something I could obtain, then I did so relying only on my own power. I made use of nothing but my own talent and my own charm.

Even if what I did was wrong, I didn't want to become someone who uses others for their own purposes, like my mother.

Well, I didn't want to *completely* avoid becoming like my mother.

Even now, I still believe that I am different from her. Yet despite that, an emotion flares up within me from time to time. It's probably because I used to watch my mother's audacious behavior from up close, but sometimes, there are things that I can't help but want. A fierce desire burns within me, and I lose the ability to think about anything else.

I feel a growing desire to pluck up and take away something another holds dear, without at all considering the trouble I would cause for those around me.

Alas, how wretched a thought!

Yet, the more I think about how contemptible my mother was, the more I despise myself for being so much like her.

That's right—a perfect example would be this very moment.

I couldn't contain these feelings, very similar to those of my mother. The thing I wanted most to avoid was acting exactly as she would. In that case, what was I to do? At the end of my inner turmoil, what I reached out for was—

"Don't even think about it."

It was then a voice spoke to me, interrupting my thoughts. I was sure there hadn't been anyone around. In spite of myself, I turned around.

"You didn't even plan a trap. That's pretty careless of you."

Oh, what a lovely voice and a lovely face. Standing there was my close friend, truly far too good for a person like me.

"Isn't it now...Arahnia?"

"Sapphee... How did you know?"

"Oh, what's that? Not even using that hokey dialect of yours? That's *very* unlike you, Arahnia."

Whoops! I had forgotten both my feigned smile and my fake dialect.

I had never shown anyone my natural self before. Lately I had been a little...tired. It was because of all the unfamiliar medical training and studying I had been doing. That was why I wasn't acting like myself, acting careless.

"I don't really care," Sapphee continued. "If you want to swap around the medical vials in the clinic and put them where they don't belong, or mess up the order of some of the medical records, I'll overlook that level of mischief. But *that* is off limits. That's something very special that I gave to Glenn."

I had it gripped in my hand. It was a golden dragonscale charm—something Glenn always carried on him and held dear to his heart.

I had tried to steal it *because* it was something he always kept with him. How unsightly. In the end, I was a thief, just like my mother.

Dr. Glenn's bedroom.

I had crept in knowing that there shouldn't have been anyone inside, but Sapphee had been lying in wait. In retrospect, it should have been obvious to me. Sapphee was well versed in the arts of the assassin. Outwitting a simple thief should have been easy for her.

"Tch!" Throwing the dragonscale charm, I escaped.

I have confidence in my ability to escape. Arachne exoskeletons are as sturdy as they are light. While Dr. Glenn's bedroom was on the second floor, leaping from tall spaces and other physical maneuvering was the specialty of the arachne, and didn't pose a problem.

Fortunately, the window of the bedroom was quite wide. I could slip through. I wrapped my silk around the handle and pulled. It was unlocked, and I was able to open it in a split second.

I would escape.

Tomorrow, I would leave town.

It was a fitting fate for someone like me, unable to curb my thieving nature. But through it all, I still believed that I was different from my mother. My mother would probably have held the golden dragonscale charm in her hand even as she was making her escape. I, however, had cast it aside as I left, either because I wanted to return it to Sapphee, or because it wasn't really the charm that I had wanted. Which was it, I wonder?

I probably don't even know myself.

But as for what I was really after—was that even something that could be stolen? Was it really something that a cowardly, greedy, black-hearted person like me could get their hands on?

"Hnh!"

My eight legs absorbed the impact of landing on the ground.

I wouldn't be able to carry through with the work that Dr. Glenn had asked of me, and it would cause trouble for Loose Silk Sewing, but it was hard to believe that either of them would even ask for the help of a thief like me. Lindworm was a pleasant city to live in, and I had grown attached to it, but I had brought this on myself. This was the end of my time here.

Or at least, I had thought it was the end, when—

"I've been waiting for you."

I had escaped from the clinic's second floor—or so I had thought—but there was a large figure standing outside to greet me. I was dumbstruck.

It hadn't been just one person lying in wait for me.

There was a massive figure standing in the road.

Miss Tisalia had already drawn her spear and made her intention clear—she wasn't going to let me go a single step further. I couldn't win against a powerful woman like this head on. While I was confident in my nimbleness and speed, I had no knowledge of the martial arts.

"Now then, you're going to have to explain yourself, Miss Arahnia. *In detail*, understand?" said Tisalia.

"Tch." Could I escape? Perhaps I could use my agility to slip right past her.

It seemed difficult—my opponent didn't seem to have any holes in her defense and had blocked off the path of my escape with her spear.

Maybe I could use my silk to jump up and escape?

In forests or inside buildings, this option was effective. However, Lindworm was a well-developed cityscape and there weren't many superfluous things to grab hold of around the town. I couldn't see any convenient starting point I could use to attach my silk. My vision in the dark wasn't that strong to begin with, either.

In that case, I had to go back. My segmented legs immediately cut backwards—but I knew it was impossible.

A figure fell with a thud from the second floor. Coiling her long lower body, the assassin blocked my retreat.

"...Give it up, Arahnia," Sapphee declared, with a look of reproach in her eyes. I had tried to steal something of importance to Dr. Glenn, so I couldn't expect anything else.

I sighed, giving up. It appeared that I had once again managed to lose a friend.

The arachne were supposed to be skilled at ensnaring others, yet in the end I was the one who ended up being captured. All I could do was shrug my shoulders in defeat.

It seemed that this bad habit my mother passed down to

me would never be something I, Arahnia Taranterra Arachnida, could cure.

× × ✖ × ×

It was already late at night, but the Great Squid's Inn was still open.

Tisalia and I brought Arahnia with us to our regular pub. I was completely at my wit's end. I couldn't believe Arahnia. I had realized her intentions long ago and only wished she hadn't waited until the middle of the night to make her move.

Arahnia looked on in amazement.

"Um... Aren't the two of you going to hand me over to the patrolmen?" she asked. Her dialect had returned. This sounded much more like the Arahnia I knew, whether or not it was an artifice. Even if it was just a quirk she had stuck to herself to try and hide her own personality, using the dialect of the eastern countries suited Arahnia much better.

"Why?" I asked.

"What do you mean...?" Arahnia replied.

"You haven't taken anything. Isn't that right?" Tisalia said next to me, nodding her head. Arahnia's face turned more and more perplexed.

"You've been tasked with a nigh-impossible job, Arahnia," I said. "I know that the stress of it was what caused your bad habits to come out. You just started wanting to mess around with other people's things, right?"

"Augh... It looks like I've been found out..." Arahnia replied.

"Dr. Glenn thought they were all his mistakes, but the medical vials moving around, the documents being rifled through and messed around with... All of that started after you arrived. So it was logical to think it was all your doing, wasn't it?"

I opened up my hand. Hopping up and down in my palm was a fairy, wearing a small cap. The helper fairy, always quick to appear when called for, crooked its head sideways as if to ask what was going on.

"You know, I'm pretty friendly with the fairies," I continued.

"Oh yes, that's true, isn't it... These little ones are always helping out with the chores around the clinic," Arahnia said, letting out some silk and winding it around her finger. Sensing the presence of something entertaining, the fairy made a flying leap from my palm onto the silk. Grabbing it, it swung side to side like a pendulum.

I had thought the fairies were a race of monster that didn't particularly enjoy doing things for their own amusement, but it seemed that even if the impulse was weak, they still had a desire to be entertained.

"Weee! A swing!" The fairy shouted in joy.

"I'm honored you're enjoying it so much," Arahnia replied.

Just then, the server brought over our orders. I hadn't hesitated to order some wine. Arahnia had ordered her favorite ginjo but wouldn't even touch it.

"That's why I thought with how tired and irritated you were, Arahnia, that you would try to do something eventually. I spoke about it with Tisalia, as well," I said.

"That's right. I lie in wait near the clinic every night. It also served as a nice evening walk for me," Tisalia said, puffing out her unnecessarily large chest in pride.

"I see. So, then, Miss Tisalia joining us for drinks the other night... It was all a part of this, then?" Arahnia asked.

"That's right. I got to keep an eye on you and see how you were doing, all at the same time," Tisalia replied. It appeared that even Tisalia could clearly see Arahnia's state of exhaustion. She had said so to me after our get-together.

Arahnia seems like she's up to something. Be careful, Sapphee.

"I was of the same opinion. After all, you aren't a woman that can restrain herself," I said. My words prompted a sour expression on Arahnia's face.

"Leave it to you, Sapphee," she replied, as if she was giving up, and as if she was ridiculing herself with her words. She limply rocked the silk that was suspended from her finger. The fairy squealed and looked to be enjoying itself. "Leave it to the clinic pharmacologist. You're right—I'm at the mercy of an inescapable ailment known as kleptomania. If I want something, I can't control myself, whether the something belongs to me or not. It doesn't take me long to start desiring my friends' lovers. The flirting in the clinic, for example..."

"To try and capture Dr. Glenn's attention...? Miss Arahnia, you still haven't given up on him, have you?" Tisalia replied, her ears jolting to attention. This behavior suggested Arahnia's words had put Tisalia on edge.

Arahnia had attempted to rape Dr. Glenn at the harpy village.

I didn't think Arahnia would give up at such a small setback, myself. There was no way she had abandoned her plans—the emotions held within her were much more complicated than that.

"You had some sort of ulterior motive when you accepted the work at the clinic in the first place, didn't you, Arahnia?" I asked.

"Quite. Well, I would never say my motives were 'ulterior' or anything of the sort... I was being honest when I said I wanted to wear matching outfits and work together with you. It's just that I wanted to know more about Dr. Glenn on top of that...or perhaps I wanted to get closer to him? I wonder," she replied.

As I put my glass of wine to my lips, Arahnia at long last also began to drink. It appeared that she had something difficult to say. If that was the case, I thought, borrowing a little liquid courage wasn't a bad idea—Arahnia wasn't very good with alcohol to begin with. Why not loosen her lips with some liquor?

"Up at the harpy village, I tried to steal the doctor," Arahnia began.

"Yes, that's right," I replied.

"That's a perfect example of it—my awful habit. Stealing the doctor who was so precious to you, Sapphee... At the time, I boasted that it was all for the sake of my art and designs, but... while that wasn't entirely a lie, what I was *really* doing was testing you, Sapphee. I thought—could you still be my friend? Someone who would try to steal the man you love from you, a terrible person like me," said Arahnia.

What an unbelievably cowardly arachne. Without trying to test me, she couldn't even believe in our friendship.

Previously at the Giant Squid's Inn, Arahnia had coiled her silk around our fingers and had declared the three of us friends. Yet, the one who believed the least in our friendship was none other than Arahnia herself.

This woman couldn't form relationships with others, unlike the silk that she had spun herself that night.

"Even when you came to talk about the surgery, honestly, I was astonished. I couldn't even imagine what you were thinking, after I had done all those things to both of you," Arahnia continued.

"There wasn't any other person for the job," I said.

"Putting your feelings aside and taking the best course of action for the situation at hand... That is much easier said than done. Dr. Glenn really is able to be calm about these decisions, isn't he?"

"Dr. Glenn praised you, too, Arahnia," I replied.

It wasn't a lie. Her growth in such a short time was remarkable. Dr. Glenn and I had been coaching her, but her improvement was the result of Arahnia's own work ethic. She had been so serious about her work, so why all of this nonsense?

"I can't help but find it strange," remarked Arahnia looking off into the distance. She was looking at someone who wasn't there. I'm sure she was thinking of the same person who always occupied my own thoughts. "Every day, that man would carefully teach me as though all the indecent things I had done were forgotten. No matter how much I teased him, tricked him, he didn't seem to be hurt or offended at all... For Sapphee's beloved doctor to be *this much* of a softhearted, good-natured person—I couldn't believe it."

"He is, isn't he?" I replied.

"As I thought about all of this, I began to want to know more about what was going on inside him... I started to want to pick on him. To test him," Arahnia continued.

"That's true. You are that sort of person, aren't you?" I replied.

"It's awful. That man truly is unflappable."

I wondered just how good-hearted Dr. Glenn could be.

Setting up a harmless prank, Arahnia wanted to see his reaction. If the prank had made him angry, that would have been that—she would have understood the type of person he was. But Dr. Glenn not only failed to even notice the pranks, but thought they were his own mistakes instead. He didn't even consider the possibility that it had all been Arahnia's doing.

"Well, normally," Tisalia chimed in with a look of exasperation, "that would be the end of it. Can't you just be satisfied by knowing he's incapable of distrusting others? Why do you have to reach out for more and more?"

"I wonder. I guess it's my own cowardice, after all. No, I think it might be because I don't trust anyone to begin with. You two are different, of course. But both humans and monsters, if you peel back a single layer, they're all just masses of greed and desire, and anyone who doesn't appear to be that way makes me suspicious. It's impossible to tell just what black thoughts and deeds someone is hiding inside them, no matter how good-hearted they may look," Arahnia replied.

"There you go again, acting like the bad guy. I've had more than enough of your cheap sense of evil," Tisalia snapped. I couldn't stop myself from laughing at her reply. Her words got to the heart of the matter.

No matter how hard Arahnia tried to pretend to be an evil woman, a thief, or some kind of villainous mastermind, I knew the true extent of her malicious motives. She was just pretending to be a trifling scoundrel—transparent even to someone as simple and straightforward as Tisalia.

"Either way, I still think that going for the dragonscale charm was going too far," Tisalia added.

"That's off limits, Arahnia. If you stole that, Dr. Glenn would try to get it back—I'll give you that. But you won't get the reaction that you're hoping for. He would take it back, and that'd be the end of it. You won't get strung up like a criminal or anything like that. Dr. Glenn is so busy he doesn't even have the time for it," I said.

Arahnia hung her head silently. She was reflecting on her actions. No, that wasn't it—she should have known from the start that what she was doing was a crime. She was a woman capable of differentiating between what she should and shouldn't do.

So why did she do it, despite knowing that?

The answer was simple—she truly wanted to put it to the test. Would Dr. Glenn still refuse to turn her away, even after she stole the most precious thing he owned? Would he hate her? After she had crossed the line with her pranks and done something to be hated for, would the kindhearted Dr. Glenn truly hate Arahnia?

She wanted to test just how far Dr. Glenn's good nature went.

It was a bad habit.

She couldn't feel confident her relationships wouldn't collapse until she had completely stretched them to the breaking point. An arachne, more cowardly than anyone else, and because of it, unable to make any friends.

Although I wasn't one to be laughing at another's cowardice.

"Lately, I've even felt strange to myself," Arahnia said, putting her head in her hands. "I accepted the job because I thought I'd try to get close to Dr. Glenn and embarrass him a little. But even though that doctor has such a hard time handling me, he doesn't try to avoid me at all..."

"He's not the type to do that, you know," I remarked.

"When he's closely watching me and teaching me how to suture, his face will get red when I tease him a little, yet he doesn't even try to lay a hand on me... He's so careful with his work, and gentle... What's the *idea?!* Does he think that I'm a terrible woman? Aaaargh, honestly, I have absolutely no clue what that man is thinking!"

Was Arahnia's face red from her ginjo? Or was it, perhaps, some other reason?

"Arahnia, why don't I give you an exam?" I asked.

Her eyes widened in surprise at my abrupt change of subject. Normally, Dr. Glenn would be the one to give exams, but—I was sure it would be fine. I could handle being his replacement without a problem.

"E-exam?" Arahnia replied.

"Recently, have you been thinking about Dr. Glenn when you fall asleep?"

"I already told you, didn't I? That strange man is all I've been able to think about."

"Does your chest tighten when you do?"

"Now that you mention it, it does sometimes..."

"Does your head begin to hurt, and does your face get hot?"

"I haven't had any headaches, but...I suppose, lately...I have felt some heat come to my face."

"Do you think about wanting to tie Dr. Glenn down?"

"Always."

Oh boy, I thought. I exchanged glances with Tisalia. It was something so easy to understand, yet Arahnia was in total confusion. She hadn't realized it herself. I had talked with her under the assumption she knew why she was consumed by thoughts of Dr. Glenn, but Arahnia was, generally speaking, slow on the uptake.

"Arahnia, you're definitely sick," I continued.

"You mean my habit of stealing things, don't you? I know that, but—" she began.

"No, separate from that. Arahnia, you've stolen away men from other women and slept with them before, right? And you still don't get it? Really?"

"Hm...? I have absolutely no idea what you could be talking about, but seducing men is part of my habit of stealing things, isn't it?"

"Yes, and I'd assume that would entail sharing intimate feelings with another person, correct?"

"Hm? This conversation is becoming more and more confusing. You see, I'm skilled at seduction, but I have no experience with what comes after. I'm just satisfied taking a man from another. I discard them as soon as I've taken my prize."

My goodness, I thought, that was no doubt quite a cruel ending for the targets of her seduction.

This time I let out a good, loud laugh. I had reached my limit and couldn't hold it back any longer. Tisalia joined me, and with her laughing too, I couldn't stop myself—thanks in part to the wine I was drinking.

"Pft, hahahaha." It was truly too funny for me to handle.

"Hey, what the heck is *with* you two?! Why are you laughing?! Do you have something to say?!" Arahnia exclaimed.

"Arahnia, it seems you've been distressed about all this for a while, but for us, this is something we've already had quite a lot of experience with..." Sapphee replied.

She was testing Dr. Glenn? She couldn't stop a bad habit, one that was bred into her?

These excuses were laughable. True, Arahnia could be a slightly troublesome woman, but that and the reason she was so interested in Dr. Glenn were completely different. As long as she spouted these inconsequential anecdotes of hers and failed to realize her own true feelings, try as she might to make herself seem rich with experience, she was just the same as any other innocent young virgin.

I had finally figured it out.

Arahnia's worst habit of all wasn't the stealing or her desire for the things of others. It was that she didn't understand her own true feelings at all, despite speaking with a pretense of wickedness and villainy.

"I'll tell you all about it. You see, Arahnia..." I begin.

I was glad that I was one or two steps ahead of Arahnia when it came to matters of the heart. Tisalia also seemed triumphant that she could get back at Arahnia for what previously happened between the two of them.

Together, the two of us carefully explained it all to Arahnia—that the truth of what she was currently feeling was something Tisalia and I were very familiar with.

It was lovesickness.

Arahnia was surprised at first, her six eyes growing wide, then at long last her face turned red, and she finally tried to hide her blush by finishing the rest of her drink all in one gulp.

It was definitely an unhealthy way for her to finish her drink. However, she probably didn't have any other way of dealing with the fact that she was in love—perhaps for the first time in her life.

✖ ✖ ✖ ✖ ✖

What exactly did these three young maidens discuss on that day in the Giant Squid's Inn?

That is something I can't possibly write here.

All I will say is that it might have been a little bit more vulgar and a little bit craftier than a gentleman of the world might expect. Of course, either way, it was simply a drinking party. It wasn't a particularly significant conversation.

What I *can* write is that our dinner party was very fun—and the party continued without any mention of Arahnia's attempted theft. Arahnia hid her face and told us that she had a good pair of friends. She had most likely been crying, but she was too proud to show even her closest friends her tears.

After that, Arahnia's pranks in the clinic came to an abrupt end. She would probably never want another's property again. The reason was simple. It was because now she realized she didn't want the things of others—what she *really* wanted was something all to herself.

✗ ✗ ✗ ✗ ✗

Just when I thought everything had come to a peaceful conclusion—

"...What are you doing, Arahnia?"

"S-Sapphee?! W-well, you see, hmm, this is just, well... How should I explain it...?" Arahnia was unusually panicked upon realizing that I had entered the room.

But it was probably natural she would be flustered. After all, both of us were standing in Dr. Glenn's bedroom. While I was confident she wasn't thinking about trying to steal one of Dr. Glenn's belongings again, it was nevertheless troubling to have her barging into the doctor's room on a whim—troubling for myself in particular.

"Well, let's see... Promise not to laugh at me, okay?" Arahnia said, continuing her explanation as she withstood my ice-cold glare.

"Okay."

"At first, you see, I tied myself up in my own silk, you know, to act like I was stuck, and call out to Dr. Glenn, 'Ahh, I've been caught, please help poor little me!' That's what I was thinking anyway..."

"Yes?"

"...But I ended up *really* getting caught instead," Arahnia confessed, a defeated tone in her voice as she stood covered in silk.

Both her four upper arms and her six lower legs had all been intricately entangled in a way that made me wonder how in the world she could have even ended up in such a state. It appeared she had made a large amount of her prey-capturing silk, and the sticky slime clung firmly to her arms and legs.

It was absurd to believe that an arachne so at home with handling silk could be so unskilled in its use. However, it then dawned on me that while she had used her silk to capture prey before, she had probably never had any experience tying herself up.

I guessed her secret plan had been to show Dr. Glenn what she looked like all tied up, have him save her, and—if everything went well—charm him with her wiles. The fact that I happened to find her before he did meant that her plan was doomed.

Arahnia moved her long, segmented legs and tried to wriggle free, but it seemed futile. Her silk was such that the more she struggled the more she ended up entangling herself.

"I'll go and call Dr. Glenn," I said.

"Aaaah! W-wait hold on! This is too embarrassing—I can't let the doctor see me like this!"

"All the more reason to call for him, right?"

"Demon! There's a demon in the clinic!" Arahnia shrieked.

"Who are you calling a demon? I'm a snake."

She was honestly annoying to deal with. While she had previously behaved calm and composed after awakening to her love for Dr. Glenn, as if she could see through everything, she had begun showing off more innocent and maidenly forms of expression. Meanwhile, I was worried to death at the appearance of another rival for Dr. Glenn's love.

As her friend, I should have been happy that Arahnia was now able to honestly face her own feelings. But that was an entirely different matter.

As long as she had become a rival, she was the same as Tisalia in my eyes. I couldn't let her take Dr. Glenn away from me. This time, it wasn't just for Arahnia's own amusement or a practical joke—she had become a serious rival for his affections.

"All right, then, what do you want me to do?" I asked.

"...Will you help me out of here somehow?" Arahnia replied.

"All right, all right," I answered, slithering into the room. My decision to help her had been an unwise one.

"Huh?!"

I'm sure this goes without saying, but I am a lamia. I'm different from the humans and monsters that wobble along on two or four legs. The long tail of our lower body lies flat against the floor and is far more stable.

Therefore, "tripping," or any similar sort of blunders, are completely irrelevant to us lamia.

However, there are some times when I forgot how overly long

my body truly is. And the inside of Dr. Glenn's bedroom was already covered in spider silk thanks to Arahnia's schemes.

In other words, I didn't fall down—I simply hadn't paid attention to the silk, got my tail stuck in it, and my body ended up losing its balance. As simple as that.

"...Now I've done it," I said, having fallen prey to Arahnia's silk and tumbled forward into her chest.

"Sapphee... Now, I may not be one to talk, but you're pretty clumsy yourself, aren't you...?" Arahnia said.

"This is all your fault in the—No, saying that won't make any difference."

Grabbing Arahnia's breasts, I tried to get myself free. A soft, rice-cake-like sensation spread across my palm. Her bountiful chest was unbelievably aggravating. I wasn't able to prop myself up at all.

Nevertheless, it was pointless after all. Arahnia's silk extended across her whole body, and it almost seemed to have a mind of its own as it entangled me as well. The slime had even gotten stuck to my face, but when I tried wiping away the unpleasant sensation, my hand ended up getting stuck, too.

The spider silk—strong enough to capture the arachne who created it—was not to be underestimated.

Arachne could make proper use of both prey-capturing silk and non-prey-capturing silk by controlling the amount of their sticky secretions. On the other hand, when this white slime was used incorrectly, it could lead to the miserable state of affairs that I had found myself in.

"Ahn...! W-wait, Sapphee, where are you touching?!" said Arahnia.

"I'm not touching them because I want to—Hey! Where are *you* touching?!" I replied.

"What am I supposed to do—it's too sticky for me to move!"

Covered in silk, the two of us briefly squirmed before we finally realized it was useless and became still.

I knew for a fact that the old Arahnia would never have made this kind of blunder. For better or worse, by relaxing a little, her naturally careless disposition had come to the surface. Either way, her carelessness had ended up getting me wrapped up in the damage as well.

"Hey, Sapphee," Arahnia began.

"What?" I replied.

"...Forgive me, please. For always causing you trouble."

"It's fine."

Seeing this moment of tenderness, I suddenly wanted to act a bit nicer toward her. When I thought about how she only ever showed me this side of herself, I felt a little sense of pride and superiority.

"After all, we're friends," I continued.

"Sapphee..." she replied.

"That being said, we have to do something about our situation."

I tried using my long lower body to grab on somewhere, but Arahnia's silk had a rigidity to it that made it hard to move anything well. My tail could usually grab on to things, but with the slime getting in the way of friction, it had lost a lot of its usefulness.

"It would be awful if Dr. Glenn saw us and had some strange misunderstanding," I remarked.

"Oh yes, about that," Arahnia replied.

"What?"

"From the beginning, I'd planned to lie in wait around the time I assumed he'd be back. In other words—"

By the time I had realized it, it was too late. Sensing that someone had entered the room, I turned around, and there stood Dr. Glenn.

His face—I couldn't really bear to look at it, but I was sure he was shocked.

"D-Doctor..." I stuttered.

"Um, uh, well..." Arahnia began.

Arahnia's four arms were tied down, and she couldn't move her body. I had my face buried in her chest, covered in slimy silk. Our clothing had become disheveled from our struggles.

Troublingly, my tail was intricately twisted around Arahnia's eight legs, in what I was sure was an indescribably titillating scene to behold.

"Well, you see, I thought that I'd head over to the Council Hall, but... I would have never thought the two of you would, uh, be in my room like this..." Dr. Glenn began.

"S-Sensei! Um!" I called out.

"P-please, take your time?" Dr. Glenn said, leaving the room as if to escape.

"Take our time?! No, you've got it all wrong!"

"Dr. Glenn! Wait! Please help us!" I yelled after him.

"It seems he's already gone," Arahnia replied.

"Nooooooo! Drat!"

In the end, we borrowed the help of the fairies and managed to tear ourselves out of the silk. It fell away easily with some hot water. While it only involved boiling water, it ended up taking the fairies a significant amount of time.

During the wait, Arahnia and I remained as we were, tightly embracing one another. My head began to hurt when I thought about how to explain the circumstances behind the incident to Dr. Glenn.

Falling into your own trap.

Those were the words that came to my mind.

One could say Arahnia had always been tying herself down. The ties binding her couldn't be unraveled in a short period of time. But if it was her awakening to her love for Dr. Glenn that made her return to acting like a normal young lady, then I thought it was absolutely wonderful.

That being said, my assistance as a medical professional ended here.

If she was going to try her best to attract Glenn, then I couldn't relax my guard, either. After all... I, too, love Dr. Glenn. I felt like my tail was on the verge of rattling in warning. Arahnia wasn't the only coward.

"Hey, Arahnia, did you notice?" I asked as I wiped down my body with the towel the fairies had provided us.

"Notice what?" she replied.

"Dr. Glenn was wearing his dragonscale charm."

"...Wait, did he find out? About my crime?"

"I wonder..."

I always thought of him like a slow-witted younger brother, but perhaps he had noticed that Arahnia had tried to steal the charm.

I brushed off this thought as being absurd, but then I considered the fact that Dr. Glenn *was* very smart. If he had actually figured it out, then that meant that he was still allowing Arahnia to work in the clinic as normal, knowing all about the pranks she had been playing. Should that be true, then it truly meant there was no limit to how kindhearted and good-natured he was.

"On the other hand, maybe he finally convinced Miss Skadi...?" I pondered.

"Now, if that's the case, then the time's finally come, hasn't it?"

Whatever the truth was, it meant that Dr. Glenn had likely also seen through my attempts to hinder Arahnia's schemes, which I had kept hidden from him.

Men truly did mature before one knew it.

Nevertheless, while that may be true, I wouldn't take my eyes off him.

I'm on the lookout, so don't think I'll let you flirt with other women, Glenn.

✖ ✖ ✖ ✖ ✖

That night, Dr. Glenn returned to the clinic and happily announced that the date of the surgery had been set. He truly looked like a child in his triumph at being able to save Miss Skadi.

At long last, all the plans made for the big operation were heading toward their final conclusion.

CASE 04:

The Dragon with a Heart Condition

THE OPERATING ROOM in Lindworm Central Hospital had been built to be quite large. Even with the bulky frames of a scylla and arachne and the long body of a lamia in it, there was still space left over. In the middle of the room, surrounded by beings both monster and human, was the operating table on which lay a single young girl.

She wore a simple surgical gown without a single decoration or adornment. There wasn't any sign of nervousness or anxiety on the patient, Skadi Dragenfelt's, face.

"Now, then, Miss Skadi, we'll start with this," Sapphee said, and handed her an inhaler made of rubber and glass. It was another item born of the advanced technology of the Kuklo Workshop. "The anesthesia will gradually make you sleep, but please just allow yourself to relax. When you wake up again, the surgery will have finished."

"............" The small dragon gave a nod of her head.

The anesthetic had been specially made by Sapphee. Glenn had heard that the main ingredient was an eastern variety of liquor. The results of her experiments had determined that alcohol had an anesthetic and analgesic effect on dragons. He had also heard a story of a fire-breathing red dragon that fell into a deep sleep under the influence of mead. Although they were said to be the strongest beings alive, they seemed to have quite a surprising weakness.

Sapphee's skill was truly marvelous, to be able to use this weakness and produce a practical anesthetic in such a short time. Glenn was sure that if she hadn't been there, Skadi's surgery would have been impossible.

No, he thought, that wasn't quite right. It wasn't just Sapphee. The same went for Cthulhy, Arahnia, and the two who weren't present for the surgery, Memé and Kunai, as well. And there were countless other people who had striven to help the cause, without whom the surgery would have truly been impossible. That alone showed how much everyone wanted to help Skadi. Of course, Glenn himself felt the same way.

"One... Two... Three... Yes, just like that—take deep breaths..." Sapphee said, speaking to Skadi. She appeared to be counting and confirming the depth of the anesthetic.

With each breath she took, Skadi's eyes began to sleepily close. Her breathing became shallow. As the concoction affected the dragon's central nervous system, the minimum amount of life-supporting functions inside her body would be maintained. Together with the anesthetic Sapphee had made, the technique seemed like something Glenn would have written a paper about back at the Academy.

But now Sapphee's skills were being used to actually save a life.

"I've administered the anesthetic, Dr. Cthulhy," said Sapphee.

"Thank you," Cthulhy said, nodding.

Anesthesia was normally used to ease a patient's pain, but this time the aim was to sedate both the patient's body and mind so she wouldn't move no matter what was done during the surgery. Since the patient was a dragon, if she acted violently during the surgery, no one there would be able to stop her.

With her mouth covered by a cloth mask, Cthulhy used only her eyes to tell Glenn to steel himself. Taking deep breaths, Glenn mentally reviewed the surgical plan and his role in the operation.

It's okay, he thought. He could do it.

"...It's time to begin."

At Cthulhy's command, the operation to excise the dragon's second heart had begun.

✳ ✖ ✖ ✖ ✳

The surgery was proceeding smoothly.

Making the incision in Skadi's chest, first up was exposing the diseased area—the fake heart. Clinging to the top of her ribs, the fist-sized heart beat steadily. The inside of it flickered with blue light, as if it were burning.

Excising the fake heart was Cthulhy's role. First came separating it from its roots—the fake blood vessels that extended from a number of different areas. Cthulhy immediately determined the best position to make the incision and began severing the tumor and blood vessels. There wasn't a hint of hesitation or disorder in the movements of the single most skilled physician on the continent.

Glenn used an instrument to grab the severed blood vessels and connect them to where they originally should have been. This was to minimize the blood loss incurred from severing them.

It was a fight against time. They couldn't waste any of it. It was Cthulhy's view that with Skadi's physical strength as it was, she wouldn't be able to endure a long surgery. They had to curb the blood loss and finish the operation in the shortest time possible.

Thus far, they had yet to experience any real problems with excising of the tumor or suturing the blood vessels.

Glenn wasn't working alone. Arahnia utilized her four arms to connect the blood vessels as well. While she wasn't a proper medical professional, her handling of a needle and thread was indeed wonderful. The practice had been effective, and even though she was now faced with her first real surgery, there was calmness to her technique.

Glenn took a peek at Arahnia's face. She wore a transparent mask made of organdy cloth, and her straight, taut mouth was visible through the material. She seemed to be a little nervous, but she remained focused on her work.

"Dragons are strange organisms," Cthulhy said as they progressed through the surgery.

There wasn't a single acknowledgment of her words. Glenn

and Arahnia were focused on their hands and didn't have any energy to spare on conversation. Glenn was sure that Cthulhy herself hadn't been expecting any answer. It was simply that she couldn't calm herself down unless she said something.

"Dragons can greatly alter their appearance depending on their location. Wyverns, wyrms, naga, orochi, mizuchi... In human territory, they were all revered as gods or subjugated as monsters. The first generation of dragons all possessed unique biology that allowed them to alter their appearance according to where they ended up living. Whether they continued to possess extreme intellect, or lost their reason and became nothing more than true monsters, was a product of a way of life that they individually chose. However, if you trace them all back to their source, there aren't actually many different races of dragon," Cthulhy continued, speaking almost as if she were giving a lecture back at the Academy.

Glenn then realized that this was something she was used to talking about. That was why it unconsciously spilled out of her mouth—she wanted to pay close attention. She couldn't let the operation fail.

"One way of classifying dragons is by the type of breath they have. Namely, water dragons, fire dragons, poison dragons, and those dragons that cannot use any sort of breath attacks. Four kinds in total. Skadi is representative of the fire dragons, and by combining the gas made inside her, the air from her lungs, and the spark created from mashing her teeth together, she can ignite the gas. From there, she can let loose a blaze of fire."

If anything, listening to Cthulhy's lectures calmed Glenn's nerves as well. While he had become independent from Cthulhy as a doctor, it felt for a moment like he was a student again.

"For both fire breath and poison breath, the essence of both comes from the combustible, noxious gas that is generated inside them. This is why, in order to protect the inside of their bodies from the noxious gas, the various dragon races protect their organs—whether it be with pyrite, vivianite, et cetera. Even though she's changed into a human form, Skadi still has iron content left over in her organs."

It appeared Glenn's guess had been correct and the glowing blue area of Skadi's body had been created with a type of mineral. However, the real question was the fake heart that Glenn and the others were in the middle of removing. If he assumed it had been formed from her somatic cells swelling up inside her, then it wouldn't be completely out of the question for the vivianite in her tissue to mix with the tumor and cause it to glow blue.

That being said, Glenn wondered if a normal tumor would be so precise in shaping itself into the form of a heart. Furthermore, he pondered whether a normal tumor would then send its roots out into the host's blood vessels and behave like it was a real heart.

The tumor mimicked both the heart's color and shape. The more Glenn thought about it, he couldn't describe the way the tumor was acting as anything but mimicry. It was absurd—he knew there shouldn't be any way for a tumor to have a will of its own.

"...I've cut away all of its outspread roots. How are you doing, Glenn?" Cthulhy asked.

"We've finished the suturing on our end as well," Glenn replied.

Next to him, Arahnia sighed heavily through her mask. Although she was incredibly skilled, Glenn felt sure that, since she had never participated in an abdominal operation before, she must be under a considerable amount of mental anxiety.

"Okay, I'm going to begin on the tumor itself," Cthulhy declared. Now they just had to remove the tumor that was stuck to the top of Skadi's rib cage. It didn't require as much delicacy as the work of suturing the innumerable amount of blood vessels. It was quite an easy process.

"Dr. Cthulhy."

"What is it, Sapphee?" answered Cthulhy.

"Her blood pressure and pulse are rising," Sapphee replied. In addition to overseeing the anesthetic, Sapphee had also taken on the job of watching Skadi's vitals during the surgery. By watching Skadi's blood pressure and pulse, she constantly verified that there were no abnormalities during the surgery. With her pulse and blood pressure rising, Glenn considered the possibility that their increase signaled some irregularity in Skadi's original heart, when—

"Glenn, look," Cthulhy said. She was pointing exactly at Skadi's chest, past the ribs that had been cut open and exposed, to the other side of those bones.

It was glowing.

Glenn wondered what was shining—the fake heart was blocking his view, so he couldn't really see. While he looked inside, some sort of steam-like gas rose up from beyond her rib cage.

"What the...?!" Glenn said in surprise.

"When fire dragons find themselves in danger, they raise their body temperature. In doing so, the flammable material inside their fuel sacs grows hot and spontaneously combusts, filling the insides of their esophagus, lungs, and stomach with flame. With this, they then start shooting out an endless stream of flame and violently struggle in anger. It's said the scales on the outside of their bodies become like a burning frying pan. It's the peak of a fire dragon's rage, used to make sure they can deal with any foreign threat," explained Cthulhy.

"But I thought she was supposed to be anesthetized..." Glenn replied.

"It's an involuntary reaction. It's fundamentally the same as a human's body temperature increasing when faced with a cold. Seriously, dragon biology is just as foolish as ever. Step back a little, all of you."

Before Cthulhy had said anything, Glenn and the others had already put some space between themselves and Skadi.

They couldn't verify whether or not there was any flame, but Glenn imagined the fuel inside Skadi's body was on the brink of igniting. The fact that she was fine even if the inside of her body was on fire illustrated to him just how tenacious the organs of a dragon were.

"Her body temperature's rising, but the fuel still hasn't ignited. Glenn, we're going to proceed with the operation immediately," Cthulhy declared.

"W-while she's like this?!" Glenn replied.

"A doctor shouldn't lose their nerve!" Cthulhy's harsh rebuke startled Glenn. "If her body temperature keeps climbing and gets to the point where the fuel ignites, Skadi's organs will light up in an instant! She may be a dragon, but not only is she in a weakened state to begin with, she's in the middle of surgery with her body cut open—Skadi won't be able to endure such temperatures! We have to finish the surgery before she ignites! Hurry up!"

There came a crackling sound. The smell of live flesh being scorched filled up the operating room.

"Hng!"

"D-Doctor!"

Cthulhy was holding the scalpel and forceps against the fake heart. However, Skadi's body had already become hot enough to pose a danger to other living organisms. The heat passed through the metallic surgical tools and burned Cthulhy's tentacles. Arahnia let out an involuntary groan of nausea at the sound and smell of burning flesh.

Cthulhy didn't take any notice of her own burning tentacles.

"Glenn, cut it off," she said.

Glenn steeled himself.

"My tentacles are holding it down. If it's severed in an instant, then you won't be burned at all. Hurry. Please..."

Cthulhy had already used her eight tentacles to anchor the fake heart. All that was left was to quickly sever it from Skadi's body. Glenn knew the more time he took to sever it, the worse Cthulhy's burns would become.

Cthulhy hated fire to begin with. Glenn couldn't imagine the pain her tentacles were suffering from the heat.

The final job had fallen into Glenn's hands.

"...I'll do it," he replied.

Glenn could feel Sapphee's gaze on him. It was an anxious one. Just by taking one step closer, he could feel the heat from Skadi's burning body. The heat was so intense that he doubted the inside of her body hadn't already been ignited. It was only natural that Sapphee would be worried.

"It's okay. You can do it."

Glenn didn't know who it was who said this. Whether it was Sapphee, Cthulhy, Arahnia, or even himself, he didn't know. Perhaps the words had come from Skadi.

He took up the scalpel and quickly brought it up against the fake heart.

It was hot. Nevertheless, Glenn would finish in a flash.

The fake heart pulsated. He couldn't say why, but it seemed as if it were groaning in pain. He asked himself if it was Skadi that was groaning—or were the groans his own? He assured himself that he was calm. In the hand holding his scalpel was all the skill and technique he had accumulated, concentrated together into a central point.

As he was hit by the heat, Skadi crossed his mind for some reason—specifically, the memory of the moment when Skadi finally decided she would undergo the surgery.

It was half a month ago.

Glenn was troubled. Naturally, he worried about Skadi.

He had tried again and again to convince her, but she refused to give him so much as a nod of her head. He had gotten the co-operation of the Kuklo Workshop. With the plan for the surgery firmly established, all he needed was to convince Skadi. But her feelings on the matter had nothing to do with the completion of the preparations. If Glenn couldn't draw out Skadi's will to live, then it would all be for nothing.

Even Cthulhy had left it up to him to convince her.

"...So you actually came."

That day, Glenn hadn't been called to the Council Hall like usual. This time, he came to the tall spire that stood next to the Council Hall. It seemed to have been used as a part of a church back when the city had been a fortress town, but now that a mul-titude of monster races had come to Lindworm, the beliefs of the residents had become multitudinous as well. As such, it was forbidden to erect designated religious institutions in the central plaza, and the church spire's role changed to only ringing its bell to announce the time.

Glenn had heard that sometimes Illy would take a break dur-ing her deliveries on the roof of the spire.

"Do you not get tired of this, day in and day out?" Skadi asked, at the top of the spire.

She had deliberately called Glenn out to the place where one could get a sweeping view of all of Lindworm. It was a spot usu-ally thronged with tourists, but at the moment there was no one else around. Glenn imagined that Skadi had had the area cleared out for their discussion.

The story of her disease had spread across the whole town via the city newspaper, but Glenn assumed it was a delicate topic of conversation for her—one she didn't really want others to hear about. She didn't even bring Kunai with her when she spoke with Glenn about the surgery, and always met with him alone.

"I'm not tired at all," Glenn replied.

"Because it's your job?"

"No... Because I still have yet to accomplish my goal."

"I see. A reasonable response."

Glenn had become accustomed to conversations with Skadi.

At first, he had thought her voice seemed fragile as glass, almost impossible to pick up, but once he got used to catching her words, he could hear her even outside. Of course, that being said, he still needed to draw extremely close to do so—practically huddling up against Skadi's shoulder.

"Golden dragonscales, huh?"

Skadi's conversations lacked any chain of reasoning. This time, she shifted her attention to the scale charm that was attached to Glenn's medicine bag.

"This? I got it as a gift from Sapphee when we graduated from the Academy," Glenn replied.

"You haven't worn it up until now. Were you trying to be sensitive?"

"Y-yeah, pretty much..."

"In that case, why wear it today?"

"It's kind of a long story..."

Glenn didn't know everything about the disturbances Arahnia

had been causing. But he thought that since Sapphee hadn't said anything to him about it, it meant he didn't need to know the details of the matter. Nevertheless, ever since Arahnia had started coming and going from the clinic, Glenn had seen signs that she had been eying his personal belongings. Thus, he decided to keep the one precious thing he would be distraught to lose close to him at all times.

"Scale-made goods aren't enough to offend me. You can even use my fallen scales, if you so desire," said Skadi.

"I-I see..."

Skadi's tail swayed back and forth. It was so thick and long that it was hard to believe it belonged to someone so tiny. Glenn thought it might be twice as long as she was tall. It seemed possible for her to stand upright with just her tail, without any support from her lower body. Skadi seemed to be in relatively good health today, as it stood straight up on end.

Skadi took off her veil and tried to look out at Lindworm. With her height, however, she wasn't able to peek over the spire's safety fence. Glenn thought it natural, considering it had been built to prevent children from falling in the first place.

"Kunai, pick me up... Oh."

Glenn assumed it must have been her usual custom. Skadi turned around and gave an order, but her bodyguard wasn't with her. Instead, she was waiting at the base of the spire. Realizing her mistake, Skadi awkwardly looked downward. Glenn could see her cheeks were a little red.

"D-do you want me, to um, pick you up?" Glenn said, smiling

as much as possible with his arms outstretched, all the while thinking how odd of a question it was to ask the centuries-old dragon that represented the city council.

Skadi wavered slightly until she finally replied—"Please."

"O-okay."

Skadi grabbed on and held herself close to Glenn. He wondered if he'd actually be able to lift her up, but Skadi lowered her own tail and laid it on the floor. Just the extra support of her tail made lifting her easy for Glenn. Her body was delicate and light to begin with. He wondered if it was due to her heart condition.

Skadi's head could now clear the height of the fence, and she was able at last to survey Lindworm. For a dragon that should have been able to fly through the skies, Glenn imagined this was terribly inconvenient for her.

He wondered what she must have felt as she was held in the arms of a human.

Touching her lower back, the sensation was a mixture of human-like skin and hard scale. Her scales were displayed prominently from the sides of her torso to her back. They were hard and sharp, but when Glenn touched them gently, the rough, gritty sensation was rather addicting.

Against his stomach, he could feel Skadi's small wings. Despite the claws and scales growing on them, the sensation wasn't particularly painful, perhaps due to the robe Skadi was wearing. The feeling of the wings' membrane in particular was soft, like a high-quality blanket.

Glenn had realized this before, but he once again confirmed

that Skadi wasn't wearing a single piece of underwear and was completely naked underneath her robe.

Dragonscales were hard and their tips resembled sharp blades. If she wore clothes not suited to her body, then her scales were likely to rip them to shreds. They were unlike the velvety, smooth scales of a lamia. Glenn figured she must wear such loose clothing because her scales could easily rip it apart.

The veil that hid her face was so no one would know she was sick, and she wore her robe to avoid the inconvenience of her scales. Glenn felt like he was unraveling the profound meaning behind Skadi's choice in clothing.

"Can I talk about something with you?" she asked.

"Talk about what...?" Glenn replied.

"About the reason I won't undergo surgery."

Glenn gulped. It was something he absolutely needed to hear about.

Still in Glenn's arms, Skadi extended her thin hands past the tower fence. Between her arms, the picturesque scenery of Lindworm was framed before them.

"What do you think?" she asked.

"What do you mean...?"

Being held in Glenn's arms meant that Skadi's face was very close to his. Glenn was practically close enough to brush up against her cheek, so he could clearly hear her voice.

"Below this spire, there is the central plaza and the fountain. These four main avenues extend in four directions from the plaza. If you go a little further, you have the Central Hospital. If you head northwest, there's the Waterways. Beginning with the Kuklo Workshop in the southern section, there's the artisan's district. In the northeast, the arena."

"I-indeed," Glenn replied.

"If you take the western road, there's the harpy village in the Vivre Mountains. On the southern foot of the mountains, there are the fields of the Aluloona Plantation. If you look to the east, there's the Vivre River. On the northern bank there's the grave-yard city where the undead live. Everyone is welcome here without discrimination, whether human or monster. That's the kind of city Lindworm is."

"That's right... I think it's one of the best places to live on the whole continent," Glenn replied. He didn't embellish his words at all and spoke his truest feelings to Skadi.

Whether human or monster, discrimination based on one's birth or upbringing could be found everywhere. But that wasn't the case in Lindworm. Here it was completely natural even for neighbors to be of different races.

A city where humans and monsters living together was the norm.

"That's because that's how I wanted it to be," Skadi continued.

"I think it's a wonderful thing."

"I hated the war," Skadi muttered.

Glenn naturally didn't think there was anyone that wished for war. Nevertheless, whether it was because of religious differences, the self-serving whims of politicians, or plain greed, there were times when war became desirable.

It seemed that Skadi generally despised wars and the many lives that were lost because of them—whether they were the lives of monsters or of humans.

"I'm a dragon," Skadi continued.

"Yes, I know," replied Glenn.

"I couldn't help but find it strange. Why did humans and monsters fight? When I had my wings, I was always watching the conflicts between humans and monsters from far up in the heavens. Looking down from the sky, I couldn't help but think of territorial quarreling and racial barriers as trivial and insignificant. And yet, both sides spilled each other's blood and killed each other. In the more than a thousand years I have lived, it has always been that way."

"I see."

"I couldn't understand by simply looking down from the heavens, so I even went down into the sea to visit Cthulhy. That woman was always doing research about monster evolution, so she was extremely interested in my own development as a dragon. With my lack of understanding about war, the two of us had common interests. We both wanted to talk with one another."

Glenn assumed that this was how the two of them had developed their close relationship. It had all happened long before he had been born, but Glenn found it wonderful that a friendship that had grown from such a small beginning was still so strong.

"Cthulhy taught me many things. There are actually two kinds of war. War brought on by greed, and war brought on by the urgency of self-preservation. I also learned that civilization moved forward when there were no wars to fight. I despised battle. But those feelings were exactly why, after witnessing countless wars, I thought about how I could end them once and for all."

A pacifist dragon. Glenn would describe her as compassionate—almost too compassionate. He gathered that it was precisely because of the raw power she possessed, and her status as a dragon, that she had no need to fight with anyone.

"At times, I would stand between two armies as they were about to clash and attempt to mediate their disputes. Back then, I had the appearance of a colossal winged dragon, so both armies would simply retreat... However, as I kept intervening in the affairs of humans, it began happening, you see."

"You gradually changed into your current form... Is that what you're talking about?" Glenn asked.

"That's the kind of being we dragons are. Our forms change according to the environment we live in. As I grew closer to humans, I became more similar to them in form as well," Skadi replied.

It was natural for organisms to adapt to suit the environment they inhabited. However, it was inconceivable for it to happen not through generational change, but all in a single organism's lifetime. Glenn truly believed that dragons possessed possibly the most astonishing biology of any organism he knew of.

"When my wings grew smaller, I would have been able to maintain my dragon form if I had then fled from the temperament of humans and returned to the heavens. But...I still wanted to live on the surface of our world, mingling with human and monster. I wanted to spend more time watching over everyone."

Skadi had sought both humanity and monsterkind. That was why, even though she was a monster, she had changed into a form resembling a human. Glenn had heard there were some dragons that could freely change their appearance between that of a dragon and that of a human, but judging by the way Skadi spoke, she could no longer return to her original draconic form.

She had gone that far just to witness conflict and discord. Glenn wondered why she had done so, when she herself said that she despised such conflicts.

"I saw the entire war between humans and monsters from its start one hundred years ago," Skadi continued.

"............"

"As far as I know, it was the most foolish war of all. The trigger was a trivial dispute, yet so much blood was spilled in the conflict. The continent was corrupted by all the spilled blood and leftover corpses. Having already lost my draconic form, I wasn't able to mediate the conflict," Skadi said, looking at her own hand.

It was covered in scales, but it had five fingers—just like a human. Glenn wondered just how unreliable the slender arms of her half-dragon body must have appeared to Skadi.

"I hadn't imagined it would continue for a hundred years. There wasn't anyone who could end it. I tried to do what I could, but in the end, what created the opportunity to end the war was the work of your father, Dr. Glenn. A mercantile executive."

"...That was just a coincidence," Glenn replied. He was surprised she knew so much. But when he thought about it, it was natural for her to have known. She was the town representative, and a dragon that had lived for a thousand years.

"It might just be coincidence. But one's achievements should be spoken of in hindsight. As far as the actual results of his work are concerned, your father's achievement has been a great one. Then...with the war over, I was able to do my job."

"Job...?" Glenn asked.

"Creating a city without the slightest hint of war or conflict," Skadi replied.

A war-hating dragon, a pacifist dragon. Glenn imagined it was natural for her to think this way. She was kind. Too kind, so that even though she had lost her original draconic form, she still worried about disputes between humans and monsters.

"There could never be another war like the previous one. That's why I remade this town on the border between the two territories. To allow both monsters and humans to live here together, and gave it the name of a dragon. To give it the divine protection of the dragons."

Still in Glenn's arms, Skadi shifted her focus to the golden dragonscale affixed to Glenn's medicine bag. It was a talisman. So long as Glenn wore it, it was said to give the divine protection of the dragons to the wearer.

"By remodeling a fortress city that stood along the trading routes, I made it possible for merchants to come through the city. I called on the centaurs and developed the city's transportation system. I made the Waterways to make the city habitable for aquatic monsters. I explained my plan to build the city to Dionne and the harpy village elder. Employing Kunai as my bodyguard, I used her advice to make it possible for the undead to live here. With the Arena and Waterways driving the tourism business, many humans came and visited as well... I'm very happy."

It was all the result of policies Skadi had proposed with the co-operation of the city's residents. Tisalia. Lulala. Kay and Lorna. Illy. Arahnia. Cthulhy. Memé. Skadi. And Sapphee. Glenn thought deeply about the monsters he had come into contact with. Each resident of the city had contributed to the development Skadi spoke of. They had all lived their lives in realization of Skadi's goal.

"Dr. Glenn. I truly want to thank you."

"...Huh?"

"Cthulhy is here, and she brought you with her as well. As a city's population grows, doctors become necessary. Nevertheless, the monster races have a wide variety in biology. There aren't many doctors who are well versed in them all. I thought that I was putting a heavy burden on Cthulhy, but... Dr. Glenn. You're here, too. Thanks to you, the burden she bears has grown smaller, and the people of the city are readily able to visit the doctor."

"Oh, no, well I'm just... I'm just doing what I need to do."

"As is the case with us all. Myself included. We're all trying to fulfill our own missions. But among all of us, your achievements have been major contributions to the city," Skadi said. She was returning to her idea that achievements should be spoken of in hindsight.

Glenn thought that, by that logic, Skadi herself should be given credit for her achievements. She was the one who made

Lindworm into the city it was today, making a place for many humans and monsters to live. She had even indirectly given Glenn the opportunity to have a practice of his own by inviting Cthulhy to the town in the first place.

It was all the more reason to consider her someone the people of the city couldn't lose.

"This body is in decay. But I'm fine with that," Skadi continued.

Glenn didn't hear much defeat in her voice. If that was the case, he wondered, why she was thinking this way?

"My body is that of a dragon. Even if my form is changed, this body is sacred. Bury my remains in the earth. Endless blood was spilled in the last war, but I'm sure burying the body of a dragon will be of some help toward expelling the corruption that has seeped into the continent. Having a dragon's corpse close to the earth is quite the valuable commodity, isn't it? Dragons usually die in places high up, where no other being can reach, after all."

Glenn was speechless. What the hell kind of logic was that?

There was technically nothing incorrect in Skadi's words. She had exerted herself for the sake of the city. As a result, the city had seen immense development. That much Glenn could agree with. He could also comprehend the idea that this was all Skadi's personal mission.

Nevertheless, Skadi was saying that since she had fulfilled her mission, she should die. She had finished everything she needed to do. After everything, she had been unfortunately stricken by disease. So she believed that she should simply fade out peacefully. Was this her line of reason?

If he was going to borrow Kunai's words, then was this truly her "destiny?"

"That's..." Glenn begin.

"Hm?"

"That's not true at all," Glenn said, seized with anger. Still holding Skadi, his arms inadvertently filled with strength. Without realizing it, he was now tightly embracing her. "Isn't that wrong? If you were the one to make the city what it is, doesn't that mean it's your mission to watch over its future, too?"

"Watch over it?"

"Miss Kunai has been constantly concerned about your health. Dr. Cthulhy has been racking her brains nonstop in order to treat your condition. Sapphee's prepared your anesthetic, and Memé and the other cyclops of the Kuklo Workshop have forged the necessary tools. Even the city paper that Illy delivers has articles expressing their concerns for your health. I've heard Lulala is singing in the plaza every night—praying for your recovery."

"Are you saying I should live because of how much everyone thinks of me?"

"That's not it. I'm not trying to push it on you, it's just..."

Glenn hadn't worked out what he wanted to say. The small, yet massive life that still hung in his arms stayed silent and listened to his words. He knew he must seem diminutive and powerless to Skadi, but nevertheless, he had something that he needed to say to her—a thought that he needed to get through to her.

"The people here... The people here in Lindworm, they're good people. Good monsters."

"Indeed. That is so," Skadi replied.

"You were the one who made such a city, Miss Skadi." *That's why,* he thought. "Don't you want to see more of this city's future? To see where a city filled with such charming people will go?"

A human's life was short. A dragon's was long.

Glenn was positive that Skadi would be able to stay at the city's side and watch over the manifold happenings in Lindworm. Just like the draconic figure that had once watched over the fate of the war.

"Your destiny still hasn't ended," Glenn said.

"............."

"There's nothing I can do to change one's lifespan. I will agree that your body's become weaker now that you have the form of a human, and there isn't anything I can do about that, either. But, at the very least... This fake heart you have is an illness that I can treat. We've determined that it can be treated. And if that's so, then that means you haven't come to the end of your life."

Even Glenn didn't understand the true value of a life.

Contrary to expectations, she could continue to live on even after death. There were even stories from the far western edge of the world of dragons that moved after becoming nothing more than bone. In a city where the undead strode through the streets, the value of one's life wasn't something Glenn could easily determine by himself.

"If you're interested in making sure this city stays on its path, then please, allow us to assist you to see that goal through, Miss Skadi," Glenn pleaded.

"Hmm, is that so?" Skadi said, letting out a small laugh. "Hmm. I wonder if it *is* okay for me to live a bit longer."

Skadi began to want to continue living. Before continuing, Skadi looked someone far off in the distance. She was a dragon who had witnessed war, and who had built a city where monster and human could live together. Glenn wondered, where exactly was she looking? How long would she be able to watch over the future of the city?

"Nevertheless, Dr. Glenn," Skadi began.

"Y-yes."

"You had no difficulty telling me to see the city into the future, but... Living for a long period of time just to watch over something is surprisingly boring. It's not as if there will only be fun and interesting times ahead. Sometimes such boredom can claim a life far more easily than war or disease."

"I-I see..." Glenn imagined this was a real concern for creatures that had such long lives.

"What is there to stave off the boredom?" Skadi asked.

"W-well I think it'd be best to live freely... Miss Dionne and Dr. Cthulhy both seem to do whatever they want to do, however they want to do it. Wouldn't it be best to live a leisurely life similar to those two?"

"It wasn't my intention to line myself up with them, but... For a while now, I've spent all my time on managing the city, you see, and it's been so long I've forgotten what one would do to enjoy oneself."

"I see, I see... What about eating delicious food? Or sweet things?"

"A new candy shop went up in the Waterways, didn't it? What else?"

"Indulging in fashion, maybe... It might be a bit expensive, but what about collecting jewels or something similar?"

"Oh. I see. Jewels, is it? Precious metals are a good idea. The shinier, the better," Skadi said, nodding repeatedly. It was said that dragons loved treasure, and it didn't seem that Skadi was any exception.

"What else? What is there besides that?"

"R-right, let's see now..."

Skadi's tone of voice had the dignity befitting the city council representative, but her demeanor suited her outward appearance. Glenn couldn't help but think that she resembled a child, pestering her parents for more and more of what she wanted.

"M-maybe love?"

Confectionery. Clothes. Jewels. Love. Glenn desperately gave Skadi examples that he thought a woman would like, picked out of his meager experience with the opposite sex. However, when he gave it a second thought, he was sure that they were all things such a long-lived dragon would have experienced before. He doubted these things would suddenly make Skadi's boredom bearable.

"I see... Let me give it some thought... Also, you can put me down now," Skadi said, flapping her legs about.

"Oh, r-right, right," Glenn replied, flustered. He tried to set her down, but Skadi used her own strength to hop out and escape from Glenn's arms.

Glenn thought that maybe the hug had been unpleasant for Skadi, but that didn't seem to be the case after all—Skadi once again faced him and gave a deep bow of her head. The horns on her head that reached up into the sky moved with her, and pointed themselves toward Glenn as though they were singling him out.

"I'll leave the rest up to you, Dr. Glenn," she said.

"Yes, I understand," Glenn replied.

She had begun to want to live. Even with her body's transformation into something half-dragon, half-human, she still held the energy in her to live.

"Somehow, please. I'm begging you."

As soon as she said this, it appeared. Skadi's smiling face looked like a blend of her hopes and anxieties, a complete change from the dreary expression she had worn up until that moment. It looked so innocent, it made it hard to believe that she had lived for such a long, long time.

✕ ✖ ✖ ✖ ✕

The memory flashed through his mind like a kaleidoscope.

Glenn couldn't forget the smile Skadi had worn when she decided to keep on living.

He asked himself why he had remembered it in the middle of her surgery. The operation was still not over. As a final finishing stroke, Glenn sank his scalpel into Skadi's second heart.

He was positive he'd be successful. With this confidence in his heart, Glenn began the final excision.

The night of this major operation would soon welcome its end.

× × ✖ × ×

Memé Redon was at a loss.

Walking quickly along the side of the canal, she kept wondering how things had ended up this way.

That night, the town of Lindworm lay sleepless. It was the day of the beloved Skadi Dragenfelt's operation. Everyone in the town was too concerned with the results of the surgery to even think about sleep. It was a matter of great importance to the city, and everyone fluctuated between hope and despair at the rumors that flowed through Lindworm, as though it were a personal affair for them all.

Memé's large eye was also wide awake, and sleep was entirely out of the question.

She wondered what the results of the surgery would be.

More precisely, she wondered if the tools that she and the other craftsmen had made would fulfill their roles properly.

She had confidence that the surgical needles that she had made would be useful, but Memé had completely painted over that confidence with her pitch-black anxieties. No matter how many times she tried to erase them, her abject thoughts that nothing she had made could ever be good enough began to overflow within her. Normally, during times like this, she would cower under the covers of her bed and eventually find sleep as she tortured herself with her self-deprecating thoughts.

But just for tonight, she wondered why she was walking toward the central plaza.

"Come on, come on, hurry up!"

"Ah, uh, w-wait!" Memé replied. She thought she was walking quickly, but the young girl running—or rather, swimming—next to her didn't slow down for Memé at all. The girl would sometimes poke her head out of the water and urge Memé on.

That girl was Lulala Heine. She was a songstress who used the fountain in the central plaza as a stage for her performances.

"Jeez, Memé! I even told you that you *absolutely* had to come! It didn't seem like you would in the end! You may not think so, but I'm really busy, you know! You gotta keep your promises! Why the heck do you think I've been singing every night?!" Lulala shouted.

"Um, no, it's j-just, there's a lot of people, at the, um, central plaza," Memé replied.

"Yeah, and that's why I'm singing there!" Lulala shot back. The cheerful Lulala didn't seem to pick up on Memé's distress from her shyness or her fear of areas where large groups gathered. Memé imagined that for someone with Lulala's personality, her worries must have seemed trivial.

Memé had recently grown friendly with Lulala. It would be more accurate to say that Lulala started conversations with everyone she met, and Memé had been no exception. Memé tried to avoid approaching the bright young girl as much as possible, but Lulala always found Memé and loudly called out to her.

Today had been the same way.

Memé had heard that tonight, Lulala was going to sing all night in the central plaza. To pray for Skadi's surgery to be a success, she was going to sing a song in an ancient language, loud enough to reach the Central Hospital.

A song wouldn't change the outcome of the surgery. All that would determine the outcome was the skill of the doctors performing the surgery and the precision of the tools they used. That was how the craftswoman Memé thought of it.

While that might have been her opinion on the matter, she did know that there were people who cheered up at hearing Lulala's song. Even Memé thought that if she listened to Lulala's prayer song, it might calm her self-loathing.

However, Memé would never have imagined that Lulala would come directly to her lodging to get her.

"I-I was in the middle of changing..." said Memé.

"You were, weren't you—you gave me such a shock when you came out in your underwear! More importantly, your boobs sure are big, Memé... I wonder if someday mine will be, too... Wait, just forget that for now!" Lulala replied.

"I thought for a moment that there was a seal outside my house or something."

When a merfolk came up on land, the way they moved by crawling closely resembled a seal or sea lion. They weren't able to walk due to the way their body was constructed, so there wasn't anything merfolk could do to avoid the comparison.

Incidentally, Memé had never seen a sea lion before, but there were quite a number of seals in Lindworm—rather, there were quite a number of sealskin-clad monsters called selkies—but that wasn't important.

"Anyway, it's not my fault! You're the one who didn't come even though you promised you would!"

Lulala's blunt words stripped Memé of any means of rebuttal. Memé could only challenge Lulala by saying that she would have liked Lulala to have told her if she was going to come to her house, but she was so shy around other people she couldn't even manage this basic level of conversation.

"I-I was planning to go, but..." Memé stuttered.

"'But?' But what?!" Lulala replied.

"...I-It's a pain."

"You always get like that, don't you, Memé?!" Lulala said, bursting into laughter.

Memé said it was a pain because for someone as scared of strangers as she was, stepping into the traffic of the central plaza meant being forced to consider those around her and to make sure she didn't startle anyone. What was truly a pain for her to deal with was how she overthought everything out of fear of strangers.

She didn't intend to imply that getting together with Lulala was bothersome. But Lulala loudly laughed off Memé's hesitation and indecision. Memé thought that someone like Lulala, as bright as the sun was in the southern countries, didn't have the troubles Memé did. Memé was both jealous of her and wished she could be the same way.

For Memé's large eye, the sun-like radiance of Lulala was glaringly bright.

"Well, I guess I can be pretty annoying, can't I?" said Lulala.

"N-no, that's not..." Memé replied, completely taken aback. Lulala was cheerful and candid in her relationships with others, but there were times when she could be almost cruel in how readily she spoke her mind. Memé had yet to get a handle on the young girl's personality.

"Oh, Lulala, they're waiting—shoot." Memé began. They were drawing close to the central plaza. There were visitors gathered at the entrance. Standing among them was a harpy with red wings.

It was Illy, an employee of Scythia Transportation. Memé had heard she had been caught up in some of the recent incidents that had made waves through the city, like the slave trader disturbance and the commotion with the giant god, but Memé didn't know much about it all. She just knew her as the young girl working to deliver the mail. However...

"Oh, h-hello..." Memé begin.

"Eeeeeeeeeeeeeek!"

As soon as Illy saw Memé, she let out a shriek and ran away.

"Ah, uhm, ahh..."

It was the same as always—Illy spread her wings and soared off into the sky. She fled with such speed that she looked like a waterfowl taking off from a lake.

The reason for her escape was simple. Much like birds hate eye patterns, harpies hated the giant eyes of the cyclops. This had less to do with Memé and Illy's relationship than their racial compatibility. Either way, it meant that every time Illy laid eyes on Memé, she quickly ran away from her.

"Aww, Illy left. Sheesh—there's nothing for her to be afraid of," sighed Lulala.

"Y-you're, um, friends w-with Illy too?" Memé replied.

"Well, we're close to the same age."

The three of them—Memé, Illy, and Lulala—were all similar in age. Being friends with someone just because they were close in age was the kind of straightforwardness that was inconceivable to the self-deprecating Memé. Making just a single friend took her an excessive amount of time.

"H-hey, um, Lulala?" said Memé.

"Hmm?" answered Lulala.

"I-I'm gonna go back after all..."

"Huh?! Why?! You've come all the way here! Look, see, the plaza is right there! It's not scary!"

"W-well, look at me, I'm so cowardly, and I'm not cute, and arriving with the star of the plaza might mean some bad rumors get spread about you, too, Lulala, and Illy hates me too, and I know even you're just thinking that I'm just some indecisive, gloomy, self-hating, annoying, useless cyclops, aren't you?! If that's the case..."

"Yup! That's all totally how it is!"

"Y-you're not gonna deny it?! Y-you're supposed to cheer me up!"

"I don't want to—it's tiresome."

Lulala's unflinching declaration left Memé in shock. With her plucky, energetic voice, Lulala completely acknowledged all the bad parts of Memé's personality.

"And? So what?" Lulala continued.

"Huh...?"

"Do not coming to hear me sing in the plaza and your personality flaws have anything to do with each other?" Lulala asked, turning around in the water and rocking herself back and forth as she swam on her back through the night waters of the canal. Memé was impressed that Lulala could make it look so effortless.

"Um, but, I—"

"There's no 'buts' about it! I'm going to sing, so everyone awake is here to listen! And we're going to pray—pray that Skadi's illness is healed for good! C'mon, lift your head up! Stop staring at the ground!"

Memé couldn't tell if Lulala was trying to scold her or just saying whatever came into her head.

As she talked with Lulala, Memé finally found her way into the middle of the plaza, right in front of the fountain. Lulala swam into the fountain and lay down on the marble stage within as if there weren't anywhere else she belonged. Memé suddenly raised her head.

It was bright. So bright that you wouldn't think it was nighttime. Lamps made out of the Waterways' special merrow glass lit up the area. Memé could tell at first glance that all the lamps had been carefully crafted by the artisans of the Waterways. She wondered if they had gone out of their way to bring them all the way from the canals to the plaza.

She wondered why. But the answer was simple. Everyone knew it would be a sleepless night, and had decided instead to fully embrace their sleeplessness. They gathered in the central plaza and lit the lamps. Memé knew that the lamp oil wasn't cheap. It just went to show just how awake everyone in the city was that night.

All to hear Lulala's song of prayer.

"Okay everyone, sorry to keep you waiting!" Lulala called out to the crowd gathered in the plaza, who then applauded her appearance.

Even the sidewalk café facing the plaza was open and seemed to have a fair number of customers. Memé had thought Illy had run away, but there she stood on the roof of the café. It seemed she had just fled to try and get away from Memé and was still excited to hear Lulala's song.

Memé stealthily disappeared into the crowd. Lulala wouldn't be able to see her from where she was, but Memé found a position where she could still see Lulala. Hiding in a place where she wouldn't stand out, even in a crowd of people, was one of Memé's specialties.

"Tonight I'm going to sing straight on until morning, okay?" said the plaza's songstress with a wink, prompting more applause from the audience.

Everyone had turned up, drawn in by Lulala's charm.

The crowd was entirely focused on Lulala, and not a single one of them paid any attention to Memé or her one eye. It was a city of monsters anyway, so having a cyclops present wasn't a problem to begin with. If anything, the one who was most conscious of her one eye was the abject Memé herself.

"———————————♪"

Lulala began to sing.

Because of the light the bright, sunny young mermaid generated, no one was interested in Memé at all. Memé herself thought that dark and gloomy places suited her best. But standing in the shadows cast by places of light was enough to make her feel at home.

Memé lamented that it was going to be a long night.

"———————♪" The song, sung in an ancient tongue, was gentle on the ears.

Memé found an open space next to one of the nearby lamps and planted herself on the ground with her arms wrapped around her legs. She figured she wouldn't be able to talk to the singing Lulala for a while, but that was a boon for someone like Memé, who had such a rough time conversing with other people.

I don't want to. I can't do it. No way—Memé had said all of these things without end, but in reality, she was happy. She couldn't help but be happy. She was delighted that Lulala had gone out of her way to come and get her.

"He, hehehe..."

She had made friends with someone who was good at singing—this small, trivial fact made a convulsing, eerie smile appear on Memé's face. She told herself it was easy enough that even *she* could do it if she wanted.

Nevertheless, she couldn't help laughing—she was just too happy.

"Hehehe..." Memé giggled to herself with a smile spreading across her face. She was completely ignorant of the human couple sitting next to her as they put space between themselves and Memé.

✕ ✕ ✖ ✕ ✕

It was dead.

Kunai Zenow believed that it had finally died off completely.

Her right arm—a piece of her body she had been with for many years. It had been made by connecting the muscle from four different men. Tonight, at long last, she had stopped being able to hear their voices. It was rare for her to stop hearing the voices all at once.

The parts had come from a soldier, a bloodthirsty murderer, a noble from a military family, and a cargo worker. All of them had been men of valor, each boasting an equal amount of strength, and had supported Kunai's impressive fighting prowess for a long time.

Kunai Zenow was a flesh golem. There were times when she could hear the regrets and thoughts of the corpses that had been used to construct her, almost like voices in her head. Recently, these voices had grown much quieter. Previously they had tormented her by echoing in her head around the clock. But ever since she started having Dr. Glenn suture her together, the voices had become mere whispers, like lightly falling rain.

In her right arm, they had gone silent.

Something similar had happened before. Parting with their regrets, the souls within her body parts vanished. With it, the corpses that made up her body never uttered another word.

Drinking coffee at the sidewalk café in the plaza, Kunai moved her right arm back and forth. It moved. She could still move it with her own willpower, down to the tips of her fingers. That didn't change, even if the flesh of her arm was now dead.

However, as was her way of doing things, Kunai had decided to bury the now-silent dead flesh and search for a new body.

The signs had long been there.

Lately, she had stopped hearing the murderer's voice whisper about slaughter and killing. Kunai assumed that the murderer, along with all the other souls inside her patchwork right arm, had returned to heaven.

"I guess I worked it too hard..."

In order to give Arahnia practice, a needle and thread had been run through Kunai's right arm over and over again. Maybe the souls in her arm had gotten tired of it. She felt a twinge of regret for making them stay with her as a single part of her body.

It was said that the undead had forgotten death, but even their kind experienced what it was like to die. Zombies' bodies rotted. Skeletons' bones eventually disintegrated. Whether they were living or not, there would eventually come a time when they would perish.

Kunai knew that someday, the time would come when she no longer could maintain her own existence, no matter what occult magic was used on her. Her body was born from a loathsome and abominable experiment, but no fault lay with the patchwork of corpses used to make her.

There was promise in Kunai's search for a new right arm. She was sure that the manager of the graveyard district in the northern side of the city had fresh, good-quality corpses stored under his purview. Kunai figured that she simply needed to bring Dr. Glenn along with her and make a call on the manager soon.

"Excuse me."

"Hm...?" Kunai replied.

"Do you mind—"

"—If we sit here?"

"Sure," Kunai nodded without looking at who she had spoken to.

The open air café was quite crowded. Kunai figured everyone had been drawn in by Lulala's singing voice. Despite being the middle of the night, the plaza was packed with people.

Lulala was singing in the fountain, and Memé sat enraptured by her song. Illy sat on top of the café in which Kunai was sitting. With the merrow glass lamps illuminating the central plaza, the commotion resembled that of the harvest festival.

"Hmph. Well look who it is..." said Kunai.

"Why, Miss Kunai— "

"—Did you let us sit here without even knowing who was asking?"

The two centaur ladies-in-waiting giggled as they took their places at the table. The café tables were built to match human height, so the tall centaurs were able to sit at them just by folding their legs under themselves, not needing any chairs.

Kunai remembered their names—Kay and Lorna. They were the attendants to the daughter of Scythia Transportion. She assumed that they had asked to share her table because she was someone they were familiar with. Kunai thought it unlikely that the two had anything in particular to speak with her about.

"It's been quite some time since we've talked, hasn't it?" one of them said.

"When we had just become arena fighters, you were kind enough to give the two of us some lessons."

"Did I?" replied Kunai.

"Well..."

"We wouldn't expect you to remember tiny details like that, Miss Kunai."

"...I'm ashamed." Even now, having retired from the arena as a fighter, Kunai would use the pretext of training the fighters there to go back and visit. If she was being honest, there were a large number of centaur fighters in the arena, and it was too much for her to remember them all. There were times when she would fight close to a hundred of the fighters back to back. She had grasped that Kay and Lorna were both fighters, but any memories of helping them train or giving them lessons had been lost in the depths of her memories.

"Is your mistress not here with you tonight?" Kunai asked, inquiring about Tisalia.

The one equipped with a sword shook her head—Kunai wasn't able to tell which one of them was Kay and which one was Lorna. She could only tell them apart by knowing that one wielded a sword, and one carried a bow.

"Our mistress doesn't stay up late."

"She's made it her motto to lead a well-regulated life."

"Hmm. That's a healthy motto to have," Kunai replied. For someone like Kunai, who didn't sleep, it didn't concern her at all. Why then, she wondered, were Tisalia's two attendants here with her?

"Shouldn't you be guarding her?" she asked.

"Well now, that's quite the thing to say, isn't it?"

"What about yourself, Miss Kunai—why aren't you at Miss Skadi's side?"

"Hmph..." Kunai replied.

"The two of us are faithful servants to our mistress. However..."

"We'll still have our nightly chats while she is resting, you know." Kay and Lorna looked at each other and gave a nod of agreement.

They looked a lot like each other, Kunai thought. She judged from their bearings that the one with the sword was the more martially skilled of the two. Nevertheless, the other one seemed to move as if she was compensating for the gaps in her partner's defense. Kunai was confident that she wouldn't have any trouble going up against them one-on-one, but figured that fighting them both at the same time would prove troublesome. It was clear proof that the two centaurs had been training with each other from a young age. It was in Kunai's nature to unconsciously size up and contemplate the martial prowess of those around her.

"What do you talk about together?" she asked.

"Things we can't say in front of our mistress."

"Like our complaints, for example."

"Complaints?" Kunai replied.

"Yes, of course. There's always something, isn't there?"

"We're women, after all. Naturally, we have a complaint or two we've kept to ourselves." They again turned to one another and gave a nod of agreement.

"Honestly, our mistress can be such a handful—she's only ever gone out to dinner with the doctor once."

"Yes, that's right, and it was the same just recently, too. She was so unsure of herself regarding whether she should go give him a pick-me-up, since he has been working so hard."

"We egged her on until she finally went to meet with the doctor, but—"

"—She is such an inexperienced young maiden about everything that just watching it can be so irritating."

Kunai gathered that the doctor they were speaking about was Glenn Litbeit.

It was a widely known fact that the young daughter of the Scythia Transportation company was in love with Glenn—although Kunai thought it was something anyone could figure out just by seeing the two interact. Kay and Lorna had said they had complaints, but it seemed they were really just impatient about their mistress's lack of initiative when it came to Glenn.

"Indeed, Dr. Glenn should come and visit the mansion," one said.

"Oh, and have an audience with the Master? That might be a good idea."

"The question is whether he would come obediently or not."

"Indeed, what if we tied him up first?"

"Yes, why, that just might be unavoidable."

"We could, of course, take the opportunity to have a little fun ourselves—"

"I'll have you two end your scheming there," Kunai said, interrupting in spite of herself, unable to let the two centaurs' conversation continue any further.

The lamia pharmacologist, the well-bred centaur arena fighter, the songstress mermaid—it seemed to Kunai that there were many people in love with the young doctor. She imagined there might be more she simply didn't know about. She knew a man popular with two different women was bound to be popular with even three or four others.

It appeared to Kunai that the two centaur bodyguards in front of her were considerably taken with Glenn as well.

"It's just a joke, Miss Kunai."

"That's right, look, you've relaxed a little bit, haven't you?"

The two of them giggled. As they sat there enjoying their herbal tea, they nibbled on the nut cookies they had with them. Kunai was wondering exactly when the two had even laid out these cookies, when the bow-wielding centaur reached out and offered her one.

"What are you playing at?" Kunai asked.

"'Playing at'? Why, nothing at all!"

"It's just sort of a sleepless night tonight, that's all."

"I'm sure you yourself, Miss Kunai, have one or two complaints about your own master."

"You do, don't you? Let's talk about them. It's that kind of night."

"I don't have any complaints at all," Kunai said, biting freely into the offered cookie, which prompted Kay and Lorna to giggle at her again.

Kunai thought the two centaur ladies were quick to start laughing. Women were gossipy creatures, but she felt that if they could laugh so cheerfully, they could be forgiven for it.

The flesh that had been used for Kunai's stomach came from the corpse of a well-trained female knight, but the knight seemed to have suffered terribly during her life and would always start complaining about the unfairness she had been dealt. Kunai was told the knight had been put to death for a crime she didn't commit. It was unbearable for Kunai to always be forced to listen to the knight's story.

What was annoying was that this stomach of hers was close with her chest, which had come from a young virgin. When something happened, her stomach and chest would join together, and the voices inside her would tell Kunai all about what they had wanted to do in their lifetimes. Kunai found that doing womanly and feminine activities worked best to silence her chest and stomach.

One example was what she was doing now—the conversation among the three women had satisfied both her heart and stomach, silencing them.

That was to say nothing of the romantic lamplight or the beautiful singing voice of the mermaid songstress—currently singing a song of prayer for the safe conclusion of the night's operation.

Kunai couldn't imagine a more maidenly, romantic night.

"Oh, come on now, Miss Kunai—"

"I'm sure even Miss Skadi isn't perfect."

"You're right, she isn't perfect." Kunai said, thinking about her master and the surgery she was undergoing at that moment. "Despite how the Lady Draconess appears, she's very spoiled, quick to cry, often relies on me to help her, and even though she gets lonely easily and likes to talk to other people, she always tries to act tough and never wants to show her true self to others— she's got an extremely annoying temperament."

"See, you do have some complaints."

"Not only that, but more than us by the sounds of it..."

"However, none of that is really anything I'm dissatisfied with," Kunai declared calmly. That was right, she thought. She didn't have any complaints about Skadi. All she had was her own wishes for her master. "I simply want to reduce the amount of miscellaneous noise that troubles her and have her be able to enjoy herself more... That's all I ever think about."

Kunai thought back over the days that had gone by since she had become Skadi's bodyguard.

Skadi was always using her own time for someone else's sake. She had devoted her life to making the happiness of both humans and monsters a reality. That was wonderful in itself, not to mention her ambitious resolve to prevent war. That was precisely why Kunai felt the way she did.

Lindworm had become a place of calm and peaceful scenery, much like the plaza was at that moment. It was a city without any quarrels between either human or monster, a city where its residents could pray for the well-being of someone else.

Kunai thought Skadi had done enough and could now use her time for herself instead.

"In that case, you're just like us," one of the centaurs said.

"We're always praying for our mistress's happiness, after all."

"...Really?" Kunai replied.

"Yes—"

"—Of course."

The coffee was delicious. Kunai didn't need to eat, but she was able to enjoy the flavors of food and drink. She was especially fond of coffee. It felt like when she drank some, it permeated the dead flesh that made up her body.

"In fact, let's pray now," one said.

"Yes, that's a good idea." The two attendants locked their hands together and closed their eyes.

Kunai found it strange that the two of them had looked like a pair of conniving women up until that moment, but now seemed almost to resemble a pair of demure nuns.

She made a fist and put it up against her forehead. Praying didn't suit her, she thought. Who should a corpse be praying to—God?

No, she thought, it was different. Just this once, she felt that if she prayed along with Lulala's singing voice, it would reach its destination. There was only one person to whom she would be praying.

"Dr. Glenn... I'm counting on you."

Kunai, who hated doctors, pleaded with the one and only doctor she trusted.

The night in Lindworm wore on. A long night. A sleepless night.

The announcement that the operation was finished ran through the city, right at the moment Lindworm's bright moon finally descended and the dawn had begun to break.

EPILOGUE:
Lindworm's Major Operation

AN AUDIENCE HAD GATHERED at the Waterways. The scene closely resembled the recent commemoration ceremony— a large crowd gathered around the bridge over the largest canal, and a platform had been set up on top of the main bridge.

Also just like the previous ceremony, Skadi stood atop the platform.

Standing at her side was Kunai Zenow. Unlike before, however, she was standing a step back from her master, and only watching over her. Her position signaled she had no intentions of speaking for her master.

"...Forgive me for worrying you all."

A hushed sound of awe reverberated through the audience. Skadi had spoken straight from her own mouth.

"Because of my condition, I have long been unable to directly reach you with my voice, and for that I ask that you forgive me."

Her voice wasn't loud at all. Nevertheless, with her clear way of speaking, she was able to sufficiently carry her words to the people in the audience.

Skadi had taken off her veil and her face was exposed. No matter how one looked at her, she had the appearance of a little girl, but no one in attendance found it comical. Even if she were a child, everyone knew just how great her achievements were in contributing to the development of the city.

"Thanks to the outstanding doctors from the Central Hospital and the Litbeit Clinic, my tumor has been safely removed. I still require regular treatment, but I will shortly be returning to my council duties. I'd like to thank all of the people who were involved in my operation."

Her voice came through. Skadi found it comforting that she could reach everyone with her own words again.

"From here on out, I'd like to devote myself to the official business of this city, without any fear or anxiety for my own health. I'd like to ask you all—and thank you all—for your support."

Applause and whistling echoed across the area. The citizens of Lindworm were fond of festivals in the first place. They raised both hands in delight at things worth rejoicing over. This seemed to be the influence of the city's relatively recent construction and their status as a tourist and merchant destination.

It occurred to Skadi that she had probably been viewing the world through a veil without even knowing it—despite the fact that when she had her dragon form, she had been able to freely lord over the continent from the heavens above. Looking through a veil, one can't truly see what one wants to see. She wondered if she had even been aware of what kind of city Lindworm was becoming as she built it.

If everyone was so happy just because her surgery had been completed successfully and without incident, then maybe—she thought—it might be all right for her to try a little bit harder to enjoy the city for what it was.

"Since I ruined the original ceremony, we will be holding it again today. I ask you to eat and drink to your hearts' contents, and enjoy your time with each other here in the Merrow Waterways," Skadi declared.

Underneath the bridge, Lulala had already finished her preparations. She had been singing throughout the entire night of the surgery. Skadi hoped that Lulala wouldn't harm her throat or her gills again, but she had heard that Lulala would only be singing one song today, so she gathered that it would be fine.

As Skadi came down from the top of the platform, Kunai bowed her head.

"Your address was magnificent, my Lady Draconess."

"Please—it was just a simple speech."

"Just hearing you speak with your own words was more than enough. Although I must admit it's a little sad to think that I will no longer be able to act as your interpreter."

"I'm feeling well—thanks to Cthulhy and the others."

The truth was that, during her address at the previous ceremony, Skadi had planned to announce her retirement. She was going to hand over her position as council representative and retire from public life. As for who would replace her—she still considered Aluloona to be the best fit.

Then with everything taken care of, she would wait for her death. The fake heart would slowly kill her.

But there was no need for that anymore.

Skadi had decided that she would watch over the city a little bit longer from her position as the council representative. After all, she thought, she had been looking at it through a veil until now—there might still be a lot that she had yet to see.

She considered that it might be a good idea to lighten her load with the city council a little and stroll through the city. She also thought it would be nice to make plenty of time to speak with her old friends, Cthulhy, Aluloona, and Dionne.

"...Did Dr. Glenn and the others receive their invitations?" Skadi asked.

"Yes, of course, I sent it to them all. However, it seems they aren't able to come today after all."

"So they're at the Central Hospital?"

"Yes."

"I see..."

Skadi didn't see the forms of the doctors that had performed the surgery in the crowd. She had known that they wouldn't be able to come today, but the fact still made her feel lonely.

Skadi was a pacifist dragon. After all this time, she suddenly asked herself what made her love peace so much. Was it just because she hated war? Then, it finally hit her. Considering the close to one-thousand-year-long life she had led, the realization might have been far too slow in coming. Well, she thought, no matter how long one's life was, there were always blind spots that one would fail to notice.

In the end, she loved life. She loved all living things. Discriminating between neither human nor monster, she loved connecting with other people. In simpler terms—she just didn't like to be alone.

Now that she realized it, it was quite a mundane conclusion for her to come to.

"All right then, let's go," said Skadi.

"To the Central Hospital...? Is it okay for you to leave the ceremony?"

"I'm not going to hold back anymore. I'm going to do what I want to do. I'm not going to care about my position or anything else... That's okay, right?"

Skadi was sure Kunai would tell her to properly carry out her responsibilities. She waited for Kunai to become angry with her, but a gentle smile came to Kunai's face. Skadi had always watched over the city of Lindworm, but this stubbornly serious bodyguard of hers had, in turn, always watched over Skadi. That was, in its own way, a difficult task.

"If the Lady Draconess wishes so, then I see it to be correct," answered Kunai.

"Thank you."

Skadi had decided to continue living. However, her life was a little too long, and she was sure it would be a long, long time before it came to an end. As such, she needed to enjoy her spare time as much as she possible could.

She had done what she had needed to do. Now it came time for her to do what she *wanted* to do.

"You can feel free to do what you want, too, Kunai."

"Understood," Kunai responded, giving a respectful nod of her head. Yet, she didn't stray a single step from her position behind Skadi.

Skadi figured that no matter what she told her bodyguard, Kunai didn't have any intentions of separating herself from Skadi's side. Skadi thought that in a certain way, Kunai was more stubborn than she was.

It seemed like Kunai would stiffen up if she kept standing at attention, so Skadi quickly urged her forward.

What Skadi wanted to do, for now, was see Glenn and Cthulhy as soon as possible. She had to let them know what would happen if this lonely dragon was forced to get serious.

✖ ✖ ✖ ✖ ✖

"You're quite the crybaby, aren't you, Glenn?" Cthulhy said, sounding almost like a mother. "There isn't anything worth crying about, you know."

They were in the director's office at the Lindworm Central Hospital. Glenn's eyes glistened with tears, and Sapphee had drawn herself close to him. Staring at the two of them with a rather gentle expression was Cthulhy.

Inside the office there was a massive octopus pot.

It was a completely ordinary octopus pot, save for its size, which appeared able to fit two adult humans within. It was half-submerged in water that had been drawn up to the office all the way from the canals, and was constructed so there was water in the pot itself as well. Peeking out of the pot were Cthulhy's head and tentacles.

Cthulhy's glasses were off, and her high ponytail had been undone. The boneless lower half of Cthulhy's body was tightly, neatly stuffed inside the pot. Extending a tentacle, she wiped away Glenn's tears.

"But... Dr. Cthulhy," began Glenn.

"Why are you crying? The surgery was a huge success. As doctors, we were able to save Skadi's life. It's fine, isn't it?" replied Cthulhy.

"It's not fine. You've been seriously injured."

It happened during the surgery.

Cthulhy used her own tentacles to brace the fake heart. It was a job that had to be done, but the metallic surgical tools had conducted the dragon's body heat and had inflicted severe burns on Cthulhy's tentacles. Even while she suffered these burns, Cthulhy continued her work and got through Skadi's surgery, but the festering wounds on her tentacles were too horrible a sight to bear.

After Skadi's surgery, Glenn cut off all of Cthulhy's tentacles. In some cases, burn wounds carried with them a risk of infection. At the time, removing the festering areas of her tentacles had been the best course of action.

"They'll all grow back, so it doesn't really matter, right?" said Cthulhy.

"It will take three weeks for them to fully grow back. Until then, please make sure to stay in bed and get lots of rest. Doctor's orders," Glenn replied.

"Blub, blub, blub!" Soaking in her octopus pot, Cthulhy made light of Glenn's concerns.

"Are you listening to me, Dr. Cthulhy?"

"More *importantly,* Glenn, did you end up eating my tentacles after you cut them off?"

"I did not."

"How mean..."

Glenn truly wished his mentor would give him a break from her insistence that he taste her arm meat—especially considering her current situation.

"See, get a good look here. They're already growing back." Saying this, Cthulhy's tentacles extended and coiled themselves around Glenn's arms and torso. The ends of them had been cleanly severed, but just as Cthulhy had said, small tentacles had begun to grow out from the surface of the cut section, like the sprouts of a plant.

Cthulhy's tentacles extended toward Sapphee without hesitation. Sapphee seemed calm even as the tentacle coiled around her chest. On a closer look, however, Glenn noticed a small twitch in her temple and realized she was irritated.

"If you two get burned, it can take a long time to heal. A scylla's regenerative ability can heal these wounds much, much faster than you both can. Someone had to do it, you know," Cthulhy continued.

"I know..."

Cthulhy had inflicted the burns on herself in order to successfully see the surgery through. Sapphee and Glenn both understood her sacrifice and silently put up with affectionate physical contact from her tentacles.

"If you're so worried about me, Glenn, why don't you come into my pot here and act as my body pillow?" asked Cthulhy.

"There's no way I'd allow you to do that, Dr. Cthulhy," replied Sapphee.

"I'm sure if he did I'd heal much faster."

"That has nothing to do with it!"

"Glenn, since you'll be coming into the water, let's make sure to take those clothes off. It's fine, I don't have any on either. I think I'll be able to calm down and go to sleep if I have something to hug with my tentacles. Now then, Glenn, come on over."

Sapphee clenched her fists tightly at her mentor's endless teasing banter.

"Dr. Cthulhy, cut it out already!"

"Sapphee, calm down, okay? Dr. Cthulhy is just bored because she can't do anything but sleep." Glenn said.

He imagined what it would be like to be stuck fast to Cthulhy inside the octopus pot, with her eight tentacles wrapped around him. Inside the water, he'd be entwined with the secretions and suckers of her tentacles. With the suction power of her tentacle suckers, their bodies would be locked together in ways that no other experience could compare to. Adding to the excitement and arousal was the fact that Cthulhy was always completely naked while inside her octopus pot.

Glenn wondered what it would feel like to be caught and held by her, feeling her hair, tentacles, mucous, and other parts of her body. It had a charm to it that was slightly different in nature from the feeling of being squeezed by Sapphee.

However, there was a possibility that in her half-sleeping state, she would strangle Glenn or shove him under the water. Glenn wanted to politely decline her offer and avoid putting his life in any danger. The inside of the pot would be too cramped for someone with a bone-filled body like Glenn in the first place.

"Excuse me, Dr. Cthulhy," Sapphee said, speaking up.

"What is it, Sapphee?"

"By any chance, do you still have feelings for Dr. Glenn...?"

"That's a good question, isn't it?" Cthulhy replied. Her tentacles stopped fawning over Glenn and slithered back into the octopus pot. Instead, she lifted her upper body a little out of the pot. The way her bare breasts flickered in and out of sight was tempting for Glenn to look at. Her unbound hair formed a delicate barrier that protected them from view.

"To me, both you and Glenn are like my children. No matter how much time may pass," Cthulhy continued.

"And what about your preference for young boys?" Sapphee shot back.

"That's different from what I'm talking about. You're like my own children, so I can't help myself from wanting to fawn over you and pamper you. And it makes me want to be strict with you, too. But I wonder if that's what love is... There are times where even I don't know myself. I suppose it's because I've lived so long,"

Cthulhy said, giggling. "I've lost the ability to differentiate between what's love and what's just my affection."

"...Wait just a moment. So basically, you're saying you haven't given up?!" Sapphee cried.

"That's what I mean—I just don't know."

Glenn rubbed the marks that Cthulhy's suckers had left and gave a wry grin.

Cthulhy would be recuperating for a while. To make sure her tentacles grew back, she needed to get a lot of bed rest and not overexert herself. This meant that the business in the Central Hospital would fall behind.

Of course, since it was a major hospital, Glenn imagined it wouldn't cease all its functions just because of Cthulhy taking a break, but he thought that maybe this meant a certain percentage of the patients in the Central Hospital would be transferred over to him. He imagined it would make it hard for the three of them to talk to each other like this if that happened.

"Do the absolute best work you can, Glenn. This time I may have actually gone past the limits of my own endurance." Cthulhy said, with a big yawn, looking sleepy as she lay in her octopus pot. "You too, Sapphee."

"Right now I'm doing my best to protect Dr. Glenn from your dirty tricks!" Sapphee replied.

"Oh, yes, that's right, I also went ahead and wrote a thank you letter to Miss Arahnia. I made sure to tell her she could feel free to use Glenn whenever she wanted. She told me her silk-flow wasn't good, so she might be stopping by the clinic soon for an exam."

"Stop! Adding! To our work! And my anxiety!" Sapphee cried. Her tail rattled back and forth. Whenever she talked with Cthulhy, Sapphee always got worked up by her mentor's provocation. Conversely, when Cthulhy spoke with Sapphee, she would often chuckle to herself, as if she were playing with her own daughter.

"How noisy. Cthulhy, may I come in?" a voice echoed in a bell-like tone. Glenn thought it was clearer than it had been when he last heard it.

"Skadi? What's brought you all the way here?" Cthulhy asked.

"I came to check up on you," replied Skadi.

"Shouldn't you be the one being checked up on?"

"Of course. Still, my primary doctor had her tentacles cut off in her efforts to save me, so I don't think it's that strange of me to come and visit. Here, I brought dragon dumplings."

"Put them on the desk."

Dragon dumplings were the first thing that came to mind when one thought about souvenirs from Lindworm. Glenn was sure Cthulhy enjoyed them as well.

Skadi still hadn't completely recovered, but she looked to be in good health. Despite the fact that she had had a whole fake heart removed from her, she was making a speedy recovery due to her unique draconic vitality. Glenn imagined it wouldn't be long before she stopped needing follow-up care.

Kunai waited in the doorway to the director's office. She stood at attention without saying a word. It appeared to Glenn that she intended to focus silently on her bodyguard role.

"Thank you, too, Dr. Glenn, for your hard work," Skadi continued.

"Huh? Oh, yes, thank you," Glenn replied.

"Now then, Cthulhy, I'll be borrowing your pupil," explained Skadi, with a blank expression on her face.

"...Huh?" Cthulhy and Sapphee's reply came at the same time. Before Glenn had any time to ask her to repeat herself, Skadi gently wrapped herself around Glenn's leg.

"I want to see the street stalls at the ceremony. Come with me," demanded Skadi.

"H-hold on just a second, Miss Skadi. I was planning on heading over to the Waterways later, but you want me to accompany you?" Glenn asked.

"I guess it's what one would call a date?" Skadi gave an adorable tilt of her head, but Glenn was at a loss at her question. Still hugging his leg, she glanced upwards at him. Glenn didn't know why, but her eyes were wet. He wondered, did dragons even have tear glands?

"Can't you come with me...big brother?"

"B-big brother?!" Glenn never could have imagined there would be a day when a transcendental being like a dragon would refer to him as "big brother."

He glanced over to Kunai, a pleading look for help. Glenn was sure the capable bodyguard would come flying in between the two of them and denounce him for his insolence in trying to seduce the Lady Draconess.

Yet, Kunai's eyes also widened as though what was unfolding

in front of her was beyond her comprehension. Her face looked as if she hadn't a clue what was going on.

"So anyway, I'm going to be borrowing big brother, here. It's okay, right, Miss Sapphee?" Skadi continued.

"Y-you can't have him!" Sapphee replied.

"Only for a little while."

"Absolutely not! Dr. Glenn promised me that we'd go around the stalls together, so I'm very sorry, but he has no time to spend with you, Miss Skadi!"

"Well, this is awkward..." Skadi said, not looking the slightest bit troubled by the situation.

Skadi clung to Glenn's leg without letting go, repeatedly tugging and pleading with him to go with her. When Glenn considered their difference in size, he thought that it was probably inevitable that they'd get mistaken for brother and sister. The more he thought about it, he realized it would be a major scandal if the city representative was caught calling him her "big brother." There was no doubt in his mind that it would end up in the papers for starters—and in the worst way possible.

"M-my Lady Draconess, please wait just one minute! Why have you become so attached to *him*?! If you need a hug, you have me right here!" Kunai had finally come out of her daze—but Glenn couldn't help thinking that Kunai was a little strange herself.

"After all, he cured me didn't he?" Skadi replied.

"Th-that is indeed true, but still!"

"Look," Skadi said, unfastening the button to her robe. Without any hesitation, Skadi bared her chest in front of everyone. Glenn had thought that Skadi didn't wear anything under her robes, yet—

Before he could finish his thought, the naked white body of a young girl stood in front of him.

On her chest was a clear scar left over from opening her up for the surgery. The straight-lined scar from where she had been cut open was forcibly stitched together with wire. If her wound closed, then it would become necessary to remove the wire, but Glenn was sure that there would still be an obvious scar. Glenn and Cthulhy would need for Skadi to come in for several regular check-ups.

Glenn didn't have any problems with all of that. He wondered whether she had actually needed to expose herself. Her robe had covered her entire body, and when she opened it up, everything from her shoulders to her stomach was revealed with it.

"Lady Draconess! How improper!" Kunai cried.

"Did it excite you, Dr. Glenn?" Skadi asked.

"Does looking at a young child's body like this make you happy, Dr. Glenn? Is that it?!" said Kunai.

"Not in the slightest!" Glenn replied. He didn't know why, but for some reason Kunai was lashing out at him. Despite how calm and composed Kunai always was, she truly acted strange whenever Skadi was involved.

"Anyway, please put your clothes on," said Glenn.

"Dr. Glenn. You do it," Skadi replied.

"Why me?!"

It seemed like she would draw closer to him if he made any more complaints, so Glenn gulped back his objections and fixed Skadi's clothes. She didn't resist him at all.

Glenn wondered where exactly her dignity as the city council representative had gone.

"Glenn," Cthulhy said, exasperated. "What sort of persuasion did you use to convince her?"

"E-everything I said was totally normal!" Glenn cried.

"What do you mean by 'normal?'" asked Cthulhy.

"Well I mean, you know... I just told her to try living more freely. I just told her that if her responsibilities and sense of duty were putting such heavy pressure on her... that maybe she should try using her free time to do what she wanted. That's all."

"Aaaaahhh... I figured it was something like that," Cthulhy replied, a long drawn out sigh echoing from the octopus pot. "Listen, Glenn, let me tell you something."

"W-what?"

"Even under normal circumstances, dragons all live self-indulgent lives. Skadi is no exception. She got into her pain-in-the-ass position as the city representative just because she wanted to. Anyway, I'm sure you told her something unnecessary, probably something about how since her life is so long she should try her hand at love in her spare time, right?"

Cthulhy's guess was right on the mark. Of course, Glenn's choice of words had been different, but he couldn't deny that that was the general substance of what he'd said.

"If that's true, then that's how it's going to be. Dragons are a greedy bunch. If they get you in their sights... it's no laughing matter, you know," Cthulhy continued.

Glenn thought that he was in deep trouble.

He wondered if he had indeed done something serious, and if he had gone too far, saying something unnecessary. However, he hadn't had any other words he could have used to persuade Skadi at the time. He had intended to do everything in his power as a doctor to save her. As such, Glenn hadn't a single regret about the words he had ended up using to persuade her.

Nevertheless, his lack of regret had absolutely nothing to do with how to get him out of his current situation.

"Big brother," said Skadi.

"Miss Skadi, for now at least quit it with the big brother stuff... I beg you," Glenn replied.

"Dr. Glenn! What about our promise?!" cried Sapphee.

"We'll go, don't worry. F-for now, how about the three of us—"

"*No!*"

Glenn fell silent at the strong rebuttal that came from both sides of him. He had no idea what he should do, but when he saw the fierce look in Sapphee's eyes, he wasn't confident any of his words would reach her.

"U-um, Lady Draconess, while I *did* tell you to do what you wanted... This is far too, well—how should I put it—bold... and I'm not exactly sure what I should do..." Kunai said, looking unusually flustered. She had a pale complexion to begin with, but now her face appeared downright ashen. Unfortunately, Glenn was just as much at a loss as she was.

"You sure are being pulled in every direction. Nothing's better than being popular, is it?" Cthulhy said, stifling a yawn as if to say it was someone else's problem—although Glenn had to admit it really didn't concern her. He thought it was big talk coming from Cthulhy, considering she had more than enough tentacles to be pulled in any direction she wanted.

"Dr. Cthulhy, please give me your advice," Glenn said.

"I see. Well, in that case I'll give you a good idea," Cthulhy replied, lifting a tentacle from her octopus pot and beckoning Glenn over. "Stand both of them up and come sleep with me. That would earn you full marks."

"Ab-so-lute-ly not!" Sapphee cried. Her tail started to go berserk. Making her escape, Cthulhy squeezed her whole body down into the octopus pot.

Glenn glanced over to Skadi. Skadi was smiling happily, as though she was simply enjoying some mischief. He had heard her say she hated war, but it seemed she had absolutely no qualms about attempting to lure Glenn into breaking his previous promise to Sapphee. Glenn desperately racked his brain for a way to pacify Skadi and go shopping together with Sapphee.

Both Skadi and Sapphee had scales.

The problem Glenn now faced was how he could get through the situation without ruffling either of their scales. It was a problem far greater than any test he had taken in his years at the Academy.

But the one who would grade him, Cthulhy, was happily asleep inside her octopus pot.

✳ ✳ ✖ ✳ ✳

No one knew.

The heart that had been excised from Skadi was soaked in liquid medicine and preserved in the Central Hospital. This mysterious tumor was an important specimen. Cthulhy planned to use the tumor to identify its cause and do research on ways to, if possible, prevent a similar disease from occurring in the future.

But something happened one night.

The tumor began to tremble and quiver.

It changed into a mollusk-like shape and skillfully opened the lid of the jar it was stored in. Using the small opening that it had created, it slipped out of the jar.

With a splat, the *thing* fell to the floor.

There was no longer any trace left of the heart that had haunted Skadi—the transparent blue object jiggled its body back and forth and made its way toward the city of Lindworm.

No one knew.

No one knew that the *thing* had escaped. Or where the *thing* would go.

No one knew anything about it. Yet.

Afterword

HELLO, IT'S ME, Origuchi Yoshino.

A manga adaption is in the works! How fantastic!

People have often left reviews about this series saying, "I bought this by accident and thought it was manga," and "this book would be better as a manga, anyway," but it appears that, one way or another, plans are moving forward on a manga adaptation!

At the time of writing this afterword, I still don't know what's going to end up happening, but I am praying that everything goes smoothly and that it's a huge success.

Now then, for my acknowledgments.

To my editor Hibiu-san. As always, I appreciate all of your support. I feel guilty for having you work on so many things at once, now including the plans for the manga adaption. I hope you'll be able to ride this momentum and find your way to the end of the manga adaption process.

To the illustrator who has continued to work through volumes one, two, and now three—Z-ton-san! Memé is just so, so, cute I just don't know what to do with myself. Speaking of Z-ton-sensei's impressive one-eyed illustrations, their power was even enough to awaken my editor to the cuteness of one-eyed girls. Thank you so very much! And of course I'm at an absolute loss for words for the color illustration of the three girls. Their girls' night chat is just sooooo cute! (My vocabulary needs work.)

And to Shake-O-sensei for your comments! You've been drawing pictures of my work and posting them on Twitter ever since the first volume. Now the long-awaited debut of Memé Redon that you asked for has come. I suggest you all read *Nurse Hitomi's Monster Infirmary*—it's a masterpiece! Look, world—behold the beauty of one-eyed girls!

Thanks to all of the other writers who always hang out with me. Thanks to my family, who are always innocently providing me material for my stories. Thanks to all of the proofreaders who never fail to point out even the smallest of my mistakes. And more than anything, my biggest thanks to all of you for reading my book.

I even snuck some hints at what's coming in the next volume in here, so it'll be rough if volume four never comes out. Especially for me.

What monster girls will appear? Stuff like fairies and alraune! And that amorphous blob thing, too!

—Origuchi Yoshino

About the Author, Yoshino Origuchi

It's been exactly a year since the first volume was released.

I can't hide my surprise that a light novel targeting an extremely niche demographic has made it to its third volume during this publishing recession. Not only that, a North American release is scheduled to be published, and a manga adaption is currently being planned!

Surely this means the age of the monster girl is not far on the horizon. Best wishes to all who are not human.

About the Illustrator, Z-ton

Lately I've been building up muscle in the upper part of my pecs and my shoulders.

This is because monster girls are physically strong by nature, and I need to build up my strength if I want to keep up with them!

Experience these great light novel titles from Seven Seas Entertainment